THE EAST END BECKONS

IAN PARSON

This book is a work of fiction. With the exception of recognized historical figures, the characters in this novel are fictional. Any resemblance to actual persons, living or dead, is purely coincidental.

Copyright © 2015 by Ian Parson

All rights reserved. This book or any portion thereof may not be reproduced or used in any manner whatsoever without the express written permission of the publisher except for the use of brief quotations in a book review.

Printed in the United States of America
Cover Design: Jon Hardy
Cover Photo: Ian Parson
Editor: Lee Porche

Linkville Press
linkvillepress.wix.com/home
linkvillepress@gmail.com

ISBN-13: 978-1512275780
ISBN-10: 1512275786

To Oliver

CHAPTER ONE
1840

It was February the 10th, four days before the feast of St. Valentine. Precisely on the stroke of mid-day an elaborate golden carriage passed through the arch at Buckingham Palace. Heavy rain was falling, yet the crowds were thick from the palace gates to St. James Chapel. Londoners were determined to enjoy the spectacle regardless of the weather.

Queen Victoria in a stunning, trend-setting white dress was to marry her Prince Albert today. After the ceremony they would return to Buckingham Palace for an elaborate, no-expense-spared dinner before finally retiring to Windsor Castle where the newly married couple would enjoy some much needed time alone. The crowds were ecstatic. The cannons in a twenty-one gun salute rang out across London.

* * *

The same day a few hours later, off the coast of Cornwall, the bow of a wooden fishing lugger slammed through the mass of icy foam that made up half the six-foot wave. Cold, salty water assaulted all the senses of the young Cornish boy aboard. He forced his stinging eyes to stay open as they reached the peak of the wave and began to tilt forwards. He held on tight as the bottom of the vessel splat down hard. When it did he braced against the wave that would try and tear him off his feet. He briefly spotted the silhouette of the Cornish coast before them and his heart longed to be with Betsy, cuddled up in front of the fire. Then the boat rolled and the view was gone. Icy water slapped hard across his face and Betsy faded from his thoughts as the deck moved beneath his feet. There was no denying it, though; he had caught a glimpse of land and that was good enough for him. Holding tightly to the rail he cast his gaze down the side of the boat, and through slitted eyes made out the shape of his pa at the helm, bellowing instructions.

"Veer starboard, boy!" the father shouted as another wave crashed onto the bow and saltwater rushed over the decks, grabbing at their ankles as it streamed down the wood.

The boy tightened the sails and the tough little lugger responded instantly.

"'Ow's it lookin'?" his pa yelled.

He scanned the sea, the horizon, and the cliffs.

"All clear!" the boy shouted back.

The way seemed clear; it was now or never, they should continue at top speed. At the helm his pa understood and the boat jerked forward for all she was worth. There would be no naval cutters patrolling these waters on a stormy night such as this. Those fine sleek vessels were far too valuable to risk chasing the likes of them. The tough little lugger skillfully hugged the rocky coast, oblivious to the foul weather. If lady luck held, the crew could raft the goods over the side and—not a moment too soon—get the hell out of here.

It was not the boy's first time on a 'run.' His pa was a free-trader, a smuggler, just like his father before him, and now the boy was following them in the family business. Smuggling was a side-line that had been the family's main source of income for years. Officially they were fishermen, but the catch had dwindled year after year, so that now the rum running was vital if they wanted to eat.

They considered themselves fortunate indeed that they still owned the lugger the boy's grandpa had built, still had the cottage overlooking the beach, and were still masters of their own destiny. The boy's pa was from a long line of proud Cornishmen, so had given his first born son a suitably Cornish name, Joff Owens. Joff was born into footsteps that cast long shadows.

There were four families like theirs in the village, boat owners living in cottages that had been passed down through the generations. They considered themselves fortunate—most of their friends and neighbours were in much less agreeable situations. Yet good fortune brought with it responsibilities. Miners, villagers, workers in the fields, all relied on the benefits, the treats, and bonuses smuggling provided, and it was up to the skippers to ensure all were included.

But of course if all are to benefit then it is only fair that all should be involved in the risks. As the lugger rapidly approached the shore, Joff knew men, women, and children were all waiting, ready to play their part. The statesmen, the fishermen were standing by for the dangerous job of rowing the cargo ashore. The fit young men were hidden on and about the beach ready to load the barrels onto their broad shoulders and get them out of sight as soon as possible. Old ladies and children were spread out along the cliff tops, ready to light the warning fires at the first sign of trouble. Whilst the old men sat in the Sloop Inn, ready, willing, and able to provide alibis to any who might need them, and Betsy would be sitting by her window gazing out over the stormy sea and no doubt praying for his safe return.

* * *

Squire Bradshaw worked his way through the elaborately decorated ballroom before siding up to the Bishop.

"Good evening, Charles. You look splendid in your new robes. Congratulations!"

The Bishop nodded and smiled, "At last, eh?"

The Squire ignored the jibe and, smiling coldly, replied, "Perhaps you would allow me to refill your glass?" He kept on smiling and the Bishop dutifully smiled back.

"That would be most gracious of you."

The churchman offered his glass but only half straightened his arm, forcing the Squire to move a couple of steps closer. When they were almost touching the two men could talk in whispers that would be less likely to get picked up by the elegant crowds milling about them.

"Tell me, Charles," said the Squire, "did you convince the head of his Majesty's Revenue to grace us with his presence this evening?"

"I did, Percival, indeed I did. He agreed most heartily to support our little cause and has already graced us with his presence far longer than we had any right to expect."

"He's here already? I haven't noticed him." The Squire was frowning slightly.

The Bishop leaned in closer and muttered just loud enough to be heard, "Miss Jackson has enticed him into one of the other rooms." He smirked like a naughty schoolboy. "They have been gone for over an hour," he added.

Sir Percival studied the soldier of God before him whilst attempting a smile.

"Very good, Charles," he said, speaking more softly now, making it impossible for any of the revellers around them to pick up his words. "And the sacristy?" He raised his eyebrows as he leaned back and smiled politely, more for the benefit of the crowd than for the Bishop.

The Bishop, for his part, chuckled modestly and cast his eyes downwards, "Oh that." He raised his voice now, allowing their conversation to be overheard. He sounded amused and slightly embarrassed, "That is all taken care of, Sir Percival. But thank you for enquiring after their health. It is most kind of you and I shall certainly be sure to pass on your regards."

The Squire smiled and nodded in satisfaction. *That sly old dog,* he was thinking. He had played it perfectly. The man was wasted in the Church; surely he is a Thespian through and through. But Sir Percival had gotten the message loud and clear. He had asked the Bishop to make sure that the head of the local revenue inspectors would be unable to perform his official duties this evening. It was of the upmost importance that he was not patrolling the cliff tops, especially between the hours of seven and eleven pm.

As a small sub-favour to this request, the Bishop was to leave the holy sanctuary—the sacristy of the local church—unlocked, and not to take too close an interest in any goods he may or may not stumble across were he to visit his church within the next twenty-four hours or so.

He had asked and the Bishop in his own cryptic way had assured him that all was as it should be. The Squire assumed his thin-lipped smile. One potentially major problem had been laid asunder with a minimum of fuss, and his mind cast naturally to the next possible pitfall. He wondered quietly how the Owens family were getting on with their side of the night's work. Unwittingly the smile had slipped from the Squire's carefully cultivated public face. That Owens was getting far too full of himself these days, that whole family were becoming a definite thorn in his side. The Squire knew they caused agitation amongst the locals. Squire Bradshaw considered the townsfolk his own private workforce and he didn't take too kindly to Owens, with his tales of the bloody revolutions in mainland Europe, rocking the boat.

Squire Bradshaw's face started to redden. France had fallen to the bloodthirsty peasant scum. Monarchies throughout the length of Europe were being forced to acknowledge the ragtag illiterates. In Belgium and Spain they had conceded certain rights. That was all bad enough but now the peasants in England were starting to get ideas above their stations. It was all too much and certain people would have to be carefully watched.

The Squire was sure the Owens family were keeping back some barrels, a percentage of his profits, making their own deals with those no good foreigners. He realised that his smile had slipped and he managed to force it back into place despite the thought of those rebellious thieves who seemed hell bent on ruining his little side-line. Now to cap it all, that Lovett fellow was coming to town. Things had gone far enough. After tonight he would have to do something about the Owens family and all who thought like them.

* * *

The boat crested another wave and the boy caught the unmistakable shape of the long, narrow rowing boats with which their cargo would be landed. His pa had handpicked them himself. They were lifelong friends who had been rowing these waters since they were small boys.

"There! There they are!" Joff pointed and then barked loudly, ensuring his voice would carry.

"Cast out the rafts!" he ordered. "Set to, lads!"

They had already tethered the barrels of brandy into groups of twenty. Joff watched as the crew pushed them over the side and they hit the water, disappearing with a splash below the surface. In calm seas the splashes would be visible for miles around, but when the sea was stormy and angry one splash went unobserved amongst all the others. The men didn't waste time watching for the barrels to pop up. They pulled the ropes tight and moved skillfully onto the next bundle. Joff kept his eyes glued to the surface of the water, making sure each barrel resurfaced as it should, making sure none became dislodged from their raft. Every fibre in his body was screaming to keep scanning for revenue men, but now it was more important to watch over the barrels. He needn't have worried. Six rafts of twenty hit the water and all broke the surface as they should. The rowers hooked the lines together and swiftly floated the rafts ashore. Joff watched them go as the adrenaline pounded in his ears. This was the most dangerous part of the whole operation. They had spies all along the cliff top, but those sly revenue men could pop up unannounced at the most inconvenient of times. The crew changed tack and began veering smoothly further and further from the rowers and the incriminating barrels.

The whole operation had only taken a few minutes. By the pale light, the boy could see the crew smiling and grinning in satisfaction and he sensed they felt the job was finished, that now was the time to relax. He made his way down the rail, keeping his eyes peeled as he passed among them.

"Keep a look out lads! We ain't home and dry yet! Get to lookin' busy, them hills 'ave eyes ya know!"

The smug satisfied expressions slipped away as his words took hold. He may be the youngster on board but he was right and they realised it straight away. The gentle reminder was all that was needed and they slipped back into 'work' mode.

"Let's at least try an' appear as though we are just innocent fishermen!" his pa called out, the words heavily laced with sarcasm, and, to a man, they responded in the manner expected of them.

"Let's get back to the Sloop!" Pa hollered, "The first drinks are on me!"

That always put an extra urgency into them and within minutes they had moved smoothly away from the contraband-laden rowers. The boy could barely make them out they were so far behind them now. The rafts were almost within touching distance of the long, sandy beach where half the men and boys of the village were waiting in the shadows. Waiting and ready to haul the barrels inland to wherever they were to be stored.

The lugger's work here was done. They were responsible for landing the cargo but once the rowers and the villagers hauled it up the sand, responsibility for running it inland fell to Jimmy Flynn, Squire Bradshaw's gamekeeper. Joff had no idea where he would be storing them and as the Squire never tired of telling him, he didn't need to know. Once Flynn took over it would be impossible to help themselves to anything. So they had already sunk a few barrels out at sea and marked them with lobster pots.

CHAPTER TWO

The following morning the storm had abated. Calm, blue seas filled the horizon. It was a glorious sunny morning and Joff and his pa were sitting on the little patch of grass at the front of their cottage.

His ma would have been in the kitchen preparing some breakfast if she were still here. He used to hear her singing through the open window. Some things remained the same though. Gramps still sat in his chair fixing fishing nets. Pa was still in his usual seat, the one in the shade, and the boy was sitting cross-legged on the stone wall that marked the boundary between their property and the lane leading down to the village.

"How did 'e do?" Grandpa asked.

They were both smiling at him now.

"Well?" Grandpa wanted to know.

"'E done good!" Pa said and at his praise the boy smiled along with them.

"You'll be alright boy!" Grandpa declared.

He smiled as though he wanted to please them, to be like them, and they bought it. How could he tell them that he didn't want to be a smuggler or even a fisherman? He wanted to be a musician, a piano player. He had known it for as long as he could remember and every day he nearly blurted it out and every day he managed not to, just.

He smiled, struggling to keep his thoughts to himself.

"An' 'ow's Betsy?" Grandpa asked.

With the smile still in place the boy looked across at who sat there beaming back at him.

"She's fine," Joff replied.

"Is she goin' to be your girl then, bear you countless babies?" He was teasing but the boy wasn't in the mood.

"Wave you off to sea wiv a tear in her eye! Unable to eat until you return!"

He glared at the old man.

"Sit on the dock, wiv all the other maids?"

"She won't be doin' none o' that! I won't be goin' to sea!" he blurted out.

"What?" they said in unison.

"I'm gonna play the piano!" he declared.

"Oh you think so do yer?" his pa muttered.

"'E's goin' to play what? What's a pianer?" Grandpa asked.

The boy stared into his father's eyes, "I can't do what you do Pa, things are changin', you know that!"

"Oh that's them new things, like the organ in the church, only smaller, isn't it? You wan' a play one of them? For a livin'?" Grandpa shook his head in disbelief as though he found the very idea simply staggering.

Joff's pa hadn't said a word. How could he? He knew the world his son was growing into was not the same place he had been a young man in. He went on about it constantly, both in public and in private.

"An' if it's different to your day then it's nothin' like 'is day!" Joff said, pointing at his granddad.

Grandpa spoke, in a calming tone, "The boy's right, you know. The railway is coming to Cornwall now, its official; Mr. Brunel is surveying the Tamar River as we speak. Soon 'e will be linking us to Plymouth. 'E's goin' to construct a giant steel bridge in order to bring 'progress' to this golden piece of God's chosen land." He spat on the dirt, adding, "'E's right, son, this ol' world is changin' fast!"

The boy looked at his grandpa with thanks.

"I suppose yous right," Pa muttered.

"Anyway," Joff jumped down from the wall and headed for the lane, "I'll be late for the funeral if I don't go now."

"You got chores to do don't forget," his pa reminded him, "so straight back 'ome afterwards mind!"

"Of course, Pa!" he called over his shoulder.

"'E spends all 'is bleedin' time playing around with that bloody organ," Grandpa noted. "When's 'e goin' to give up that childish nonsense?"

"The vicar asks for 'im, Pa. What am I supposed to do? Say 'no' 'e can't 'elp with God's work?"

Behind him, Joff heard his Grandpa suck his teeth and spit on the ground.

He walked slowly, adrenaline surging through him. He had done it, he had told them. He didn't want to be a revolutionary, wasn't planning on following in their footsteps. Let them get used to the idea. There was no point hanging around. He quickened his pace.

"Not now, Pa!" he heard his father say.

THat's right, now is not the time, Joff thought. He kept walking away.

For as long as he could remember, as soon as he could walk down this path unaided, when he was not doing chores, he was at the church minding the organ bellows. Ma had encouraged it, always insisted he was kept away from the free-trading and brushes with the law, but she had been dead a few years now and things were changing, he was changing, the world was changing.

* * *

Pa and Grandpa watched their boy take the cliff path down towards the giant church that loomed over everything and everyone in the village. The deep blue Atlantic stretched out before them and gulls floated easily through the sky.

"Think 'e'll be back?" Grandpa asked.

The younger man shook his head.

"Nah I don't reckon!" he replied.

"'E needs to be more modest in 'is expectations, that one!" Gramps mused aloud.

"'E isn't like us. I sometimes wonder if 'e's my own flesh an' blood!" came the reply.

The old man smiled, "Stubborn, blatant disregard for the rules? Oh 'e's your boy all right!"

The old man stopped picking at the fishing net that was draped over his lap and looked up at his son. "Is 'e goin' to the meeting tonight?" he asked seriously.

"Yeah 'e's playin'."

The old man sucked his teeth and spat again.

* * *

At the church Joff pushed open the big, heavy door and with his footsteps echoing off the walls made his way towards the organ. Mr. Boscombe wouldn't be here for another twenty minutes and would expect all the valves and pedals cleaned by the time he arrived. The boy had better be ready to pump the bellows as soon as he sat down to play. Until then Joff had the huge, cavernous space to himself. He looked about to ensure the church was empty, that he really was alone. Then he sat down and played. No sound escaped but that didn't stop him. He ran his fingers up and down the keys, gliding across them, knowing if he had sound it would be note perfect. He played his scales for ten minutes, as he did every morning. Then set about preparing for the arrival of Mr. Boscombe, the official organist. The man who had encouraged him, taught him to play.

CHAPTER THREE

That night the Sloop Inn was packed to the rafters. Men from all across the district had come to hear Mr. Lovett, the guest speaker. William Lovett was one of the founding fathers of the People's Chartist Movement and a man born and raised not two miles down the coast. Workers from tin mines throughout Penzance and as far afield as Camborne were in attendance. They had come from far and wide to hear what he had to say.

When Lovett rose to speak a silence descended over the room.

"Men of Cornwall," he began, "men of my home county." A little cheer rose up in the room. "Do you not deserve to maintain the management of your own affairs?"

Murmurs of agreement went up and heads could be seen nodding in consent.

"Gentlemen," he continued, "we are at a crossroads. The world is fast changing and that change is being accelerated by the new-fangled railways. It is now five years since the line from London to Falmouth was proposed and those plans grow firmer every day." He scanned the room to gauge their attention but he needn't have bothered. He had them; every single man was listening intently to what he had to say.

"Last year we presented the very first Chartist petition to the government. Over a million and a quarter signatures, Gentlemen." They cheered at that. "And this year we have men, good men standing on Parish councils throughout the land. The authorities are alarmed at all the upheaval in mainland Europe, Gentlemen. They no longer have the confidence to ignore our grievances and the working man will, at last, get fairly treated." He allowed his gaze to sweep across the room. "As equals!"

Joff's pa and grandpa sat elbow to elbow at their usual table, listening carefully. They were both glad the boy was here. They both kept glancing across to him at the piano.

"'E don't seem to be taking in these wise words, this glimpse into the future!" Gramps declared unhappily.

This was history in the making as far as they were concerned. At last, they thought, the people were going to be free; serfdom would be confined, once and for all, to the pages of the history books. They saw no irony in their own situation, had no intention of giving up their own, rather lucrative, totally illegal side-line. No, they saw 'the enemy' as men like Squire Bradshaw and the mine owners. Those who they felt exploited all under their command before rejecting them in their more senior years as they turned their attention to the coming generation.

The whole room listened carefully as Lovett painted a picture of a future where the railway would be insatiable for ever larger quantities of tin. Where Cornish men and boys would be used—yes *used*—to make the mine owners ever wealthier. He spoke of how London intended to encroach more and more into their daily lives until every single one of them was working not to feed their families but to provide for whatever the bosses considered best.

Finally the speaker stopped and the barman gestured at Joff to begin playing.

He broke into *The Rose of Allendale* with great gusto and the crowd keenly belted out their own version of the chorus.

"I 'ear piano players are much in demand up London," Pa Owens said while watching his 13-year-old son and the confident way he played in front of a room full of tough miners without batting an eyelid.

"We never 'ad pianos when I was 'is age!" the old man mumbled.

"You never 'ad London when you was young neither!" the son replied.

London may as well have been on a different planet when Gramps was growing up for the amount it affected them down here in Penzance. He had grown from boy to man as all around him the laws of London had slowly but surely been imposed on them. He remembered how they had stubbornly ignored each and every one that they didn't already adhere to, but he knew they could no longer continue to do so. Soon there would be customs huts all along the cliff path. Free-trading was a dying art and he could see that without it more and more Cornish men would become dependent on the good grace of the wealthy few. This speaker, Lovett, was making sense and he was glad his son and his grandson were here to see it, even if the boy didn't seem to be paying much attention. At least he was here. *Some of this is bound to rub off on him,* the old man told himself.

The boy had stopped playing and Lovett was back at the rostrum.

"You need to have the chance to elect into office men who would represent your interests," he was saying. "You must unite of your own accord, with a sincere desire for improvement, mutual improvement, everywhere! We have to join the system to beat the system!" he declared, to a smattering of confused applause. The old man didn't like it either. He was happy with improvement for all but instinctively wary of joining a system that was hell-bent on destroying the independence they all held so dear. Yet deep down, he could see the sense in the words. This capitalist juggernaut had grown so powerful it was time to admit defeat and try to make the most of the few positions of strength they still held.

"Our labour; that is the one thing they need us for! We must unite miners' right across the land, from Cornwall to Durham. Only then shall we be truly strong enough to demand the vote for all men!"

Faces gazed upon the speaker before them as though he were mad. Then gradually all around the packed room men were being made aware that they, each and every one, had to play their part. If they were to relinquish the old communal system that had always worked so well and buy into the industrial revolution they would. If they were to work longer hours under electric lighting for the good of Queen and country they would, but they wanted something in return. They hadn't really known what they wanted, just knew the deal seemed very one sided. Well now here was Mr. Lovett and he was spelling out for them what they wanted. They wanted the right to vote, pure and simple. Every man over the age of twenty-one able to partake in a secret ballot and every vote to be counted. That is what they were demanding in return.

"Well, Gentlemen I thank you all for listening and ask that you make certain to sign or leave your mark on the petition coming round before you leave." Mr. Lovett inclined his head towards the boy on the piano stool.

"I believe the boy is here to entertain you whilst the petition is brought around as quickly as possible. It only remains for me to thank you all for coming and to say once again, 'We are all in this together!'"

They cheered and clapped for all they were worth as the man from London with his blond curls and his silk bowtie moved carefully down the wooden steps at the side of the stage. Joff watched him go and wondered what all the fuss was about. He understood he was a big man but had no idea why. He didn't really understand why his pa was so involved. What had politics to do with them?

Joff waited for the applause to die down before he launched into an upbeat version of *Skip to my Lou*. They always loved that one in here. They loved a good sing song.

At the bar Squire Bradshaw's spy accurately read the mood in the room and took mental notes of who amongst the crowd would have to be watched most closely.

He didn't recognise the grievances laid out before him as legitimate and had no real understanding of the hardships these rural families faced each winter, but he could certainly see a need to suppress all such meetings in the future. Votes for all, safer working conditions, pay rises! He had never heard anything so outrageous in his life. He nodded in mock sympathy and sipped from his tankard without raising the slightest suspicion.

Squire Bradshaw listened intently as his spy revealed the gist of Mr. Lovett's speech and he scowled as the enthusiasm with which it was greeted by the gathered masses was revealed to him.

"We have got to do something about these Chartists. The very idea of workers having rights!" the Squire muttered as he strolled across the room to close an open window.

"My family did not build all this to hand it over to the hoi polloi." He turned, and facing the spy, added, "We have to watch this Chartist movement. Make sure it is not allowed to develop into anything unwanted."

"Yes, Sir, I quite understand, Sir."

CHAPTER FOUR

Two weeks later Joff was holding Betsy to him, hidden in their favourite spot, deep in the shadows of the church. Clinging to each other as the sun fell into the sea behind them.

"Do you 'ave to go now?" Betsy asked.

She had her hands locked together around his back and was reluctant to release him.

"You know I do," he said, leaning in to kiss her one more time.

"One day we will be together proper-like, won't we?" She stroked his leg and electricity shot through his thigh.

"In our own little cottage, won't we?" she asked, smiling up at him.

"We will," he replied, meaning it with all his heart. "We will, my love."

He kissed her on the cheek. "Now go sit with your ma, why don't you?"

She didn't answer and her grip around his waist loosened slightly.

"Betsy," he lifted her chin so their eyes met, "You are goin' to sit with your ma, aren't you?"

He was unnerved now. He knew how determined she could get but didn't know how he would cope if anything were to happen to her.

"But all the girls are goin' up to the cliffs an' you will be..." her voice trailed off and she cast her eyes downwards.

"It's not a game, it's dangerous out there," he warned.

She looked up at him, her eyes full of life.

"You be careful yourself!" she spoke quietly but the words were loaded with defiance.

She released him and rose to leave. He watched her walk away, shaking his head with a giant grin spread across his face. He could see she was going to be no pussycat once they were wed but still he wanted to do it, wanted it with all his heart.

* * *

A few hours later, as the moon began to rise, he stood mid-deck holding tightly to the mast, scanning the beach, trying to make out the rowing boats in the surf. He spotted one of them shove its nose into the white foam of the shore breakers and then another long sleek shadow broke the solid line of white foam. They were landing; he pictured the men jumping from the boats in knee-deep water, using the power of the waves to shove their boats further up the beach. He imagined the young boys breaking cover and running down the sand, eager to lend a hand. He remembered himself at the age of nine, skipping through the dunes for the very first time, running to help haul the barrels to safety. He smiled with fondness at the age-old scene.

Then he heard a shot and the smile wiped instantly from his face. He scoured the shore and in the darkness saw a flash of orange light and heard another shot. It had to be the revenue men.

"What shall we do skipper?" someone asked.

"Maintain present course!" his pa shouted.

Joff stayed where he was, holding onto the rope and scanning the beach for more muzzle flashes. He imagined the villagers running in all directions through the dunes. It would be utter pandemonium on that beach right now.

"There's not much we can do from 'ere lads. Best get ashore and 'ead to the pub as planned, eh," his pa hollered.

He prayed Betsy hadn't gone to the cliff but knew she was sorely tempted, with what a social occasion a landing was around here.

They sailed the rest of the way in silence and moored in the harbour as quickly as they could before heading solemnly to the Sloop.

The pub was already packed to the rafters, loud voices being raised as people desperately tried to adjust to the situation. There was the undeniable hint of confusion in the air.

Joff's pa shoved a path through the drinkers and they followed close behind. He had spotted Flynn standing at the bar and sided up to him.

"Jimmy!" he said.

Jimmy Flynn, the Squire's gamekeeper, turned sharply at the sound of his name but scowled when he saw who was addressing him. He scowled often.

When Pa was right beside him and could speak directly into Flynn's ear, he said, "I see you 'ad company on the beach."

Joff scanned the room. People were definitely looking at them, trying to hear their words and quite rightly too. They all knew their roles in the evening's operation and pretty soon they were going to be looking to Joff's pa and Flynn for some answers. They didn't feel as though time was of the essence, especially if the revenue men decided to show up here.

"Come on, Jimmy, what 'appened?" Joff's pa snapped.

He looked around, taking them all in, and he could see they were in no mood for games.

"They was on the beach, 'idin', waitin' for the rowers to land."

He took a swig from his tankard, studying the skipper's face over the top of it as he drank.

"What about the shots?" the skipper wanted to know. Jimmy smacked his lips and shrugged.

Joff could picture the scene; he would have been ordering people around one minute then running to save his own scrawny neck the moment a shot rang out. Shrug he might, he couldn't say much because he hadn't waited around to know what was what.

"Did you see Betsy up there?" he asked as raised voices filled the room around him.

"What, your Betsy?" Jimmy replied, sneering in a manner not appreciated.

"Yeah!" Joff shot angrily back at him.

He shrugged again, "It was dark, people was runnin' all over the place." He shook his head. "No I never saw 'er," he declared and turned his back.

The boy stared at the back of the man's head as a bad feeling gnawed at the inside of his rib cage.

Joff spotted one of Betsy's friends coming through the door and made his way towards her, trying to head her off before she disappeared into the crowd. Perhaps she would know.

"Matilda!" he called across the crowd as she disappeared amongst the sea of people.

He headed around the L-shaped bar and spotted her again. She had stopped to talk to a group gathered in the lee, tucked out of the wind. This time he pushed through the crowd and grabbed at her sleeve.

"Matilda," he said and she turned to face him.

"Oh, Joff, there you are, somethin' terrible's 'appened!"

She looked panic-stricken and he knew, just knew she meant something terrible had happened to Betsy.

"What? What is it?"

"No one knows where Betsy is." She looked as though she was about to burst into tears.

"Wasn't she with you?" he said as calmly as he was able. Inside the bad feeling was churning into a knot that filled his stomach with fear.

"Yeah she was but there was revenue men waiting. 'Idin' behind the rocks they was and when that first rower 'it the shore they come jumpin' out, firin'!" She cast her gaze downwards briefly then, eyes blazing, looked back at him. "We all ran, we 'ad a plan, Joff. We was to meet at the ol' pump 'ouse. Anyways I gets there an' waits an' she never came."

She looked at him less sure of herself now before continuing. "She never came, Joff. All the other girls come an' in the end we 'ad to come down 'ere." She clasped his forearm, crying out, "Nobody's seen 'er, Joff, nobody!"

The bar was rammed tight when the crew had walked in the place. It was even busier now. Folk were coming through the door singly and in small groups and each of them, every man, woman, and child, had come directly from the beach. In they came and immediately fell into conversation with the first person to hand.

"It's alright, Mattie," Joff smiled at her in as reassuring a manner as he could muster, edging his way through the throng towards the door. If that was the most up to date information there was to be had, then that was the place for him.

People came through the door. One minute there would be a procession of them then nobody for long, horrible seconds on end. Then a solitary individual and another long pause, followed by a gaggle of agitated, loud voices. It was disconcerting, not knowing what to expect next.

Nobody had any captures or injuries to report and it seemed they were all making it back to safety in their own good time. Then Liza came in. She caught Joff's eye immediately and started to make a bee line towards him as time slowed down. The chatter all around slowed, people's movements slowed, everything slowed except for Liza. She headed straight towards him, her eyes never leaving his, and the crowd seemed to part before her, making her progress even quicker.

"Betsy!" she whispered, taking his hands, "she's gone off the cliff!"

Silence fell across those around them. He registered a split second of pure silence before unintelligible noise surged up all around. The conversations were jibberish; all he could distinguish was a whooshing noise in his ears. Words mingling together as the awful news spread through the room. They all knew her, they all knew him.

Then the door burst open again and in fell three old timers.

"They've taken the barrels to the coast guard hut!" one of them announced. "We seen 'em with our own eyes!"

Joff turned to face Liza. The whereabouts of the booty had no meaning to him.

"Show me!" he said.

They walked away from the mayhem, towards the darkness, towards the sand, towards the whoosh of the waves hitting the shore. She told him what she knew.

"We was on the cliff. Not really gettin' involved but ready if we was needed, you know." She was looking down as she spoke. "Then we 'eard somebody comin' along the path an' we pushed ourselves back against the cliff edge, into the ferns, you know." She turned to face him, searching his face for reassurance, for a sign that he did not hold her responsible for the words pouring out of her mouth.

"Go on," he managed to say.

"She slipped, Joff, she fell!"

The words poured out so quickly they registered easily and the knot in his stomach grew into a ball.

"Show me!" he managed to whisper.

She turned hurriedly and he followed in a daze, vaguely aware of a light coming up behind. The masses were spilling from the pub behind them and were following. He didn't turn around. He was still trying to make sense of what she had said. He had been told nothing, yet had been told everything.

Liza had taken these paths countless times on darker nights than this. Joff followed her lead as she veered left at the only fork in the road. Left to the beach, right to the cliff, that was the way it had always been. They were heading for the beach. He didn't really need guidance but let her lead whilst the whole village clambered noisily a little way behind.

She got to the bend in the rock's contour where the coast opened up, where it was possible to look directly down on the beach below. He didn't want her to continue but she carried on regardless and he followed. Even in the dim moonlight the bright sand could clearly be seen against the dark tones of the night, and there directly below them were black shapes breaking into the whiteness. A stream of boulders scattered across the sand, and amongst them something that looked as though it could possibly be a granite outcrop from the shelf beneath the sand, just like all the others, but from the unusual broken twisted shape and from the expression on Liza's face he knew that was no rock.

The flame from a revenue man's torch danced in the slight breeze near it and the barrel of his rifle glinted under the flame. He was standing over the shape on the beach, further proof it was no rock.

"It's her, isn't it!" Joff stated.

Liza nodded, casting her eyes to the ground.

He wanted to go to the beach and cradle Betsy's head one last time before she went cold forever. He moved towards her on auto-pilot, the revenue man growing nearer with each passing step, Betsy continuing to lie still, with her back to him. She looked broken. "That's close enough!" the revenue man declared, raising his rifle.

"Betsy!" Joff wailed, flinging himself at her and the guard stood over them as the boy wailed at his feet, pointing his gun but not really knowing what to do next.

"What you pointin' that thing at 'im for?" demanded an angry voice from the growing crowd.

Joff didn't hear the reply. The chatter faded into the background as the sound of rushing blood filled his ears. He cradled Betsy's head away from the wet sand as they bickered above him.

"I'm just doin' my duty. I don't want no trouble," the revenue man stated. His voice trembled, he was heavily outnumbered, and he had no means of communicating with any of his colleagues.

"Did you do this to 'er?" a woman's voice asked.

"No, no she was 'ere already!" He was clearly frightened now.

"Is that right, well stop pointin' that rifle at 'im then!"

"Yeah, do what you're told!"

The crowd were growing ugly. One of their own was no more and they were turning from a state of shock to a state of outrage. Unfortunately for the solitary customs official, his three colleagues were busily transporting the confiscated rum to their brand new hut. He was alone and pathetically so. He lowered his weapon as instructed; a single shot musket wouldn't be much use against nearly a hundred people at these close quarters anyway.

"Now get away from 'er!"

They were ordering him around now; this wasn't how it was supposed to be. He was the representative of the King. He stood for law and order. He was officially in charge. These damn Cornish, though, had very little respect for the authority of London, or its representatives. He stepped away as he was told.

"An' where's our rum?" an angry male voice wanted to know.

The revenue man had an overwhelming desire to join his colleagues in the solid stone hut way up on the cliff.

"I should leave you to your grief," he muttered, stepping briskly away, towards the path that would take him up the cliff, away from this lot!

There was a little mumbling but they let him through.

The exchange took place over Joff's head; he remained oblivious to it all. Finally he turned and addressed the crowd.

"Get a cart," he said quietly. "Let's take 'er 'ome."

Somebody fetched a cart and they took Betsy's body back home. Joff stayed with her, trying to hold back the tears.

By now the crowd had developed into an angry mob. After dropping Betsy's body home, they took the cart up to the customs hut and laid siege to the four frightened men inside until they released the brandy.

Four days later, Joff was the organist at Betsy's funeral.

He played with all his heart and as the notes soared towards heaven the knot in his stomach threatened to bring forth tears that if allowed to start would never stop.

As the weeks passed Pa and Grandpa indulged his preference for music. They knew that Betsy and he had planned to marry and raise a family of their own.

Knew he had taken her passing really hard and were giving him time to get over his loss.

Slowly the Joff they knew began to return, but he was different, quieter. He listened now as they discussed the topics of the day. He started to see that he needed a path in life, something that didn't rely on the local Squire's benevolence. Saw how his neighbours were forced to treat the Squire as though he was one step removed from God himself. Joff would not accept such a life. Nearly everyone around here worked in the Squire's mines and on his farms. They lived in his rooms and on his land. They were indebted to him in ways the Owens family were not. They had their own cottage, their own vessel. Possessed the means of making a living for themselves. *Perhaps,* Joff thought, *he should tend a little more closely to those things.*

His grandfather had been a free trader, a smuggler fifty years ago, before the water guard were formed to oversee the shore. The old man was famed up and down the coast as one of the best sailors Cornwall had ever produced. He outwitted the water guard for years before finally handing over the reins of the family business to his son. Grandpa Owen's daring exploits to the Channel Islands opened up routes that were still being used. Things were different then, though. The nearest customs house was in Exeter, over 60 miles away. It would take days to travel down to the Cornish beaches, with progress reports coming way ahead of officialdom.

As the years rolled on, the old man never tired of telling his grandson the stories of the good old days. How the demise of that golden era came in 1822 when the amateur water guard were transformed into the professional revenue and customs men.

This new force was given 121 permanent stations up and down the Cornish coast and things became far more serious. The new station masters and their men were experienced seafarers. They were now under the wing of the Treasury in Whitehall. Money was no longer an object. They were supplied with all the latest arms and equipment, whatever it took to halt the illegal tax dodging trade. Orders were issued for the first time to patrol the shores in rough weather. New, fast, six-man vessels were provided for the task. Serious attempts were finally being made to thwart the thriving free-trade. But Grandpa Owens and his friends barely noticed.

* * *

Squire Bradshaw was having difficulty containing himself.

"Those heathens did what?"

"Well, Sir, they took back the brandy..." Flynn began.

The Squire slammed his fist down on the table before him.

"I wasn't asking the question!" he thundered. "I was trying to understand how such a thing could happen. How they could be allowed to get away with such a thing!" He slammed his fist down again.

This time his rhetorical question received no reply.

"Well they will not get away with it, do you hear me, I don't care how long it takes I will have my goods returned!"

In 1836 William Lovett, a Cornishman born just a mile from Penzance, founded the London Working Men's Association, and in May 1838 he helped draft the People's Charter—a list of changes they, the Chartists, wished to make to the law books of the land that would, in their eyes, make England a better place for all.

They wanted to give all men the right to vote in a secret ballot and permanently improve conditions for the poor. Calling it the 'People's Charter' was an ingenious touch as it connected in the minds of the general public that this was a long overdue, progressive addition to the original Charter for justice, as they all understood the Magna Carta to be.

However, despite its overwhelming popular appeal, it was officially rejected in June 1839, causing widespread rioting and civil disobedience throughout England. After a whole week of violent national defiance, Lovett and his small band of dedicated activist friends started the laborious process of collecting names for a second, longer petition. It had taken three long years but now they were back. It was May 1842 and the original petition of one and a quarter million names was now three million names long.

1842

It was two years ago now since Betsy had fallen so cruelly to her death. Joff still thought about her every single day and still dreamed of her on far too many nights. He would wake up in a cold sweat and see her horribly contorted body lying on the sand. He would have to force himself to breathe calmly and try to remember the good times they had shared before fate had taken such a cruel turn. He was fifteen years old now and had been promoted to playing at weddings and funerals unsupervised. Every single funeral still put him in mind of Betsy. Old man Boscombe knew that, knew he could be trusted to hit the right notes every single time in memory of her. He was still around afterwards to take a cut of the fee, though.

Joff's pa had fallen in deep with the Chartists and fallen out badly with the Squire. He was still smuggling, still making use of his contacts and his vessel. He took advantage of the properties in the village containing the old forgotten spaces, relics from Grandpa's youth when the press gangs had landed around here and local men had hidden themselves away to avoid being forced into the navy. These spaces had always been there and where they once hid men they now hid barrels. Now, though, Pa refused to pay the Squire's cut and that concerned Gramps.

They had no need to take such risks, to antagonise the Squire so, but his headstrong son couldn't help himself. He didn't appreciate London's efforts at controlling every aspect of his life, didn't like the way that paperwork was becoming more important than anything. He was falling in with some bad company, and they wanted revolution.

It was no surprise to anyone when he was finally trapped and taken away in irons. Ironically, he was accused of importing brandy without paying the duty. Naturally they had produced a witness, an old lush from the neighbouring town who swore blind that she saw him firing on a revenue man some nights previously. That was enough; they whisked him off to somewhere called St.

Katharine's Dock, and then to Newgate for a trial, and that was where they hung him.

* * *

A few weeks after receiving the news of the hanging, Grandpa and Joff were awaken early by the sound of horses neighing and fidgeting in the lane at the front of their cottage.

"Owens!" a man was calling. "Owens!"

Joff went to see who it was, still rubbing sleep from his eyes. Any number of his pa's friends could be making a surprise visit under cover of darkness. It wasn't an unusual occurrence.

He was none too pleased to see Jimmy Flynn, though, leading a delegation of half a dozen masked men.

"What?" he asked, suspiciously.

"Where was you last night?" Flynn demanded.

"What's it got to do with you?" the boy sneered, safe in the knowledge that he had been at home with his grandpa all night.

Flynn's men circled tighter and the boy instinctively backed away.

"Last night one of my men was attacked and thrown off the point. He was found this morning washed up on the beach. So I will ask again, where were you last night?"

Joff stared at him open-mouthed. It seemed as though he was implying that Joff might be in some way responsible. He could barely believe his ears. The horsemen edged closer.

"What, you think I had anything to do with that. That's not me, you know that," Joff objected.

"So where were you last night?" Flynn repeated.

The boy stood open-mouthed as the horses closed tighter around him.

"Seize him, men!" Flynn instructed and two men approaching silently from the rear of the cottage grabbed him as the horsemen before him rushed to assist them. In seconds Joff had four burly men ensuring he would not be running off anywhere soon.

"Where is your brandy?" Flynn wanted to know.

Joff declined to answer, just stood helplessly as two guards lifted his grandpa from his chair and marched him to the wagon.

Flynn slapped the boy across his left cheek. "Where is it?" he demanded.

Joff spat a mouthful of blood onto the dirt by his feet.

"Take 'em to the farm!" Flynn ordered.

So the old man and the boy were bundled into the wagon as the guards clambered all around them.

At the farm Joff wasn't surprised to see the Squire waiting on his horse as they came into the yard.

Squire Bradshaw owned three tin mines, eleven farms, and half the homes in Penzance. He employed almost everybody who worked on the land. He was a justice of the peace and chairman of the Parish Council. To all intents and purposes Squire Bradshaw was an upstanding, respectable member of the community. He didn't look it as he sat in the moonlight staring at the prisoners. He looked more like the devil incarnate.

"So, I might have known you were involved!" the Squire sneered.

He frowned slightly then addressed his next comment to Flynn, "Where's the others?" he demanded.

"Still roundin' 'em up, Sir," came the reply.

"No matter," he said calmly. "You!" he swivelled his head to look directly at Joff. "Where were you last night?"

"At 'ome," he mumbled sullenly.

"The truth, boy! The truth now!"

Joff glanced up at him, and replied, "At 'ome, Sir, all night."

"Well if you don't want to tell me where you were last night, perhaps you will be able to tell me why your barn seemed a little full?" He was swishing his whip about him now, trying to steady his horse.

Joff looked at him with no idea what he was talking about.

He smiled coldly, then looking the boy straight in the eye, declared, "Surely that is my brandy you have hidden in your barn?" He asked the question with a raised eyebrow. It was purely hypothetical; he already had his answer, his sneer gave him away.

There had been no brandy in the barn, Joff was sure of it. If they had found any it was clearly a set-up, but he remained silent.

"You were spotted up on the cliffs last night!"

"I was nowhere near there last night." He spat out the words incredulously.

Joff licked his lips. The Squire wanted to teach him a lesson and now he had him. Evil intentions screamed from his every pore.

"You have been helping yourself to my goods, stealing from me!" he glared harder "There is a system in this country that will never be allowed to topple, Mr.

Owens." His voice wasn't loud but his rage was barely contained. "A system, and each must know his place within it." He prodded the boy in the chest with his riding crop. "You, Mr. Owens, seem to have forgotten your place within the system. You were useful to me once," he paused, breathing heavily, "but now you are a thorn in my side. You have grown too big for your britches. You were up on the cliffs last night after dark, and, as I shall be informing the sheriff, I have long held serious concerns about your self-control." He sniffed and looked about to berate the boy further when his monologue was rudely interrupted.

"That's enough!"

Joff turned to the voice he recognised instantly and there was his grandpa holding a pistol in both hands and pointing it rather shakily at the Squire. At that range he couldn't miss.

Flynn took a step towards him and Grandpa spoke without altering the aim of the gun.

"Get back! If any of you try anythin' 'e gets it! Right between the eyes! I mean it!"

Joff couldn't help smiling. He recognised the gun immediately as the Derringer pocket pistol that Pa had paid a lot of money for a few years ago because it was easy to hide, he had said. That was obviously true because Grandpa had concealed it from them pretty well. The old dog still had it in him.

"Let the boy go!" Grandpa was giving the orders now.

The Squire motioned slightly, a sideways movement of the head and they released their grip on Joff. He took that as a signal that he could go.

He moved cautiously to Gramps, who spoke again without looking round.

"Go son! You got to go, now!" he risked the briefest of glances towards his grandson and then his eyes locked once again on his target.

"Where will I go?" He tried not to sound too desperate.

The Squire's horse began to fidget.

"Just move yourself." He sounded harsh.

Joff turned without another word and headed through the gate. There was an immediate fork in the lane and he was out of sight as soon as he rounded it. He headed towards the village and wondered what to do next. In no time at all, for want of somewhere better to go, he was closing in on the pub.

Joff slowed down, sat on a wall feeling foolish and exposed. He had to leave, he realised that. You can't point a gun at the Squire and expect any member of your family to last long afterwards. He heard people coming across the stone bridge and jumped down from the wall. He was afraid to meet anyone. He moved into the Beech trees that grew down to the edge of the village and headed back. Somebody must have spotted him, they called out, instantly depriving him of the element of surprise. He ploughed on through the trees, breaking saplings and scratching his forearms repeatedly on the abundant brambles that grew so freely. He became extremely conscious of the noise his progress was creating. When he heard the barking of excited dogs mixing with shouts, he guessed Flynn and his men were coming. He guessed Gramps was a goner. He angled his run slightly, heading downhill to the stream. If they were planning to hunt him with hounds, he was going to use the water to cover his tracks.

Joff had a purpose now and it felt better. Then his foot hooked around a clump of ivy and without warning he was down, rolling heavily through the damp leaf mould and struggling to catch a breath. He saw the low branches of an old yew sweeping the ground before him. They grew closer and closer and then he was crashing through them and thudding to a halt against the dark knobbly trunk. He allowed himself a few seconds respite under cover of the branches then skidded on the bases of his feet the short distance to the stream and plunged into the water. He splashed uphill through the shallows, listening nervously for the hounds, every bark lending him an extra burst of speed. Within minutes he jumped from the stream and was moving across the hill, hidden from view by the vegetation, and thankfully, judging by the barking dogs, moving away from his pursuers.

Joff made the brow of the hill in record time and without so much as a backwards glance he left Penzance behind. His home town, his birth place, all he had ever really known, was fading into the background and he was so wrapped up in his immediate concerns that he didn't even think to take a final look.

When he could run no more, Joff walked as fast as the terrain would allow for three hours, intermittently angry then devastatingly afraid. One minute tears streamed down his face as he imagined how differently things might have been had Betsy still been around, and he forced himself to keep silent, stay unobserved. The next he was screaming profanities at the top of his voice, not caring who might be able to hear him. It was so unfair. All he wanted was to find a girl, a nice girl like

Betsy, and settle down with his own little family. That had always been his dream. He could fish and play and they could be happy. He had never wanted to get mixed up in politics and all the troubles that brought, never. Finally, when he was all cried out and his frown was actually hurting his face, the moon made a brief appearance through the fast-moving clouds. By its light he spotted the tall stone chimney stacks of the tin mines on the edge of Camborne and he decided it was time to rest. He gathered fern leaves and laid them out against the shelter of a hedge, then pulled another clump of ferns over himself, curled up in a ball, and watched the stars roll across the sky above. He tried, unsuccessfully, to stop feeling sorry for himself. He supposed it was his own fault, really. The older men had warned Pa many times about not getting too involved in politics.

"You will make enemies of the ones that feed you," they had predicted, and they had been proved right.

It hadn't been hard to see the wisdom in their caution. Fellow mariners regularly disappeared because of the views they held. Sailors from any number of European countries would talk of nothing but the revolutions they hoped would soon be sweeping through France, Greece, and the Germanic countries. Places that would be in the hands of the workers soon and, "You can have the same in England," they had said.

It had seemed so exciting at times, so pointless at others.

"Why do you break your backs and risk your necks for the good of the Squire?" Pa would ask in the crowded bar night after night.

Some weeks it seemed as though the Chartists were right, that big changes were afoot. The world was on the cusp of becoming a better place because enough people wanted it. Enough people were prepared to believe that it might be possible. Other weeks there were so many arrests the fleet would be halved in number.

* * *

Joff lay in his bed of ferns and tried not to think about what might have happened to Grandpa. He recalled how only yesterday he had been going on at breakfast. How the Chartists were being persecuted. It was outrageous that they were being treated as a danger to society. For daring to question the way things were being done.

"This new capitalist system will be the death of us all," Gramps had predicted over his eggs.

Joff shivered and pulled the ferns around him. As he attempted to get some sleep he took a sliver of satisfaction from knowing that he had been right. It was a mess. Pa was dead, Grandpa, poor old Grandpa—who knew what had happened to him? Joff could only imagine. He was alone, destitute, and a wanted man. Yet, he decided, it was strangely satisfying knowing at least they were right. There most certainly was something very wrong with the world.

The following morning Joff woke up cold and early. The grass was still wet with dew, the sun not yet in the sky. Soon the miners would be heading to work and he wanted to be gone before they arrived. Cautiously, he lifted his head and on the far headland, much to his horror, he saw two horses. They were moving at the speed he would be moving at if he was searching for somebody and wanting to cover a large area. The realisation they were looking for him filled his stomach with dread. He moved carefully away from the stone hut. He was so busy watching them that he slipped. His nerve cracked and he panicked turning and sliding hurriedly down the hill. He half-heartedly ran his fingers through the shards of grass as he moved, making them stand up straight as best he could, to blur the evidence of his passing. He knew the miners would gather here as they always did before heading underground. He prayed their tracks crossed his before the horsemen came his way.

As he moved, barking dogs could be heard behind him. To his right the voices of approaching miners were faintly audible. Straight ahead was a field of sheep. He resisted the urge to look about him. Crouching low and moving slower so as not to spook them, he headed for the flock. Surely, he reasoned, he could confuse his scent if he could get amongst them.

He heard the riders shouting towards the miners. The actual words were unclear but he was fairly certain that he knew what was being asked. The hooves of the horses shook the ground and he knew they must be close. The temptation to take a peek was almost unbearable but he resisted, kept low, and on hands and knees joined the flock of sheep. A few looked quizzically at him but they allowed him space and simply carried on eating. He crouched lower as a sharp pang of hunger stabbed deep in his stomach, and he knew he would be useless until he had something to eat. He had to find some food. He lay on the wet grass dreaming of food, shuffling a little when required, keeping him amongst the sheep, and trying to ignore the voices close by. Finally the men all left. The sheep had done him proud.

It was time to move again, though. Miners were renowned for not mixing well with strangers. They were also under the employ of Squire Bradshaw and Joff couldn't risk that. His stomach rumbled again but it was more important to remain wary. He would head east. At least then he would be sure to hit the coast somewhere not too distant from the port of Falmouth. If he got all the way there and still no food presented itself, maybe he would be able to forage something on the shore. Besides, he knew people who lived in Falmouth.

Slowly, cautiously, he crossed the field. Once back among the trees he set off in the manner of all early morning walkers, one foot in front of the other until he found his rhythm. He kept away from the high peaks as he didn't want to stand out on the horizon and give his position away to potential spies. Little flocks of sheep eyed him as he passed but they kept their distance. They watched him going on his way while their chewing motion never missed a beat. They were curious as to what he was doing on the moor but he was nowhere near enough of a threat to interrupt their constant breaking down of the rich moorland grass.

Four hours later he was crouched over, trying to ignore the now constant ache of his stomach. He was skirting a clump of elm trees, cautiously making his way to the edge of the copse, and as he rounded the final tree Falmouth came into view far below. He dropped to his knees and leaned against a thick tree trunk as he feasted his eyes on the sight. He could see the little town clustered around the harbour and beyond it, a line of ocean-going schooners lined up on the quay. Beyond them was the ocean. Far out from the coast white caps were dancing across the deep blue water and he longed to be dancing with them, heading away, anywhere really, but away.

Although he was completely ravenous it felt too risky to wander brazenly into town. There were too many people milling about. So despite every fibre in his body begging him to rest, he carried on. He skirted Falmouth and dropped down the steep incline a little further south. He chose the secluded little beach at Covernack, where not a soul was to be seen, and foraged in the rock pools. After a meal of shell fish that did little more than take away the more extreme pangs in his empty stomach, he rested in a little cave until he was ready for walking again. Four hours later and further along the coast once again, he fashioned a makeshift bed of fern leaves. Tomorrow he would head across land. He would go to Polperro and hoped that from there he would head to sea.

* * *

After a breakfast of more shellfish beneath a deep grey sky, he began walking. As darkness fell, light rain that had been threatening all day began making everything slippery. He reached the top of yet another hill and paused for breath. Looking through the trees, he finally saw the lights of Polperro twinkling in the distance below. That was the thing with Cornwall, always plenty of hills and valleys. And whenever it rained the footing could be treacherous, especially at night in unfamiliar territory. Although he knew the place, he had never arrived by land before. He headed downwards slowly and with great caution.

The village was built either side of a natural stream running downhill to the horseshoe-shaped harbour below. Here the stream ran out first onto the beach and then into the sea. The hills either side were dotted with cottages, barns, haphazard family homes, and a large wooden sardine cannery right on the dock. The buildings on the right faced those on the left and vice versa. Everything overlooked the harbour and beach. It was intentionally hard to arrive unnoticed so if Joff could he planned to creep through the trees. Anyone approaching via the only single-track road would be spotted long before they were even half way down the hill. He had to be careful—vagrancy was a crime that carried harsh consequences.

Joff set off stumbling in the darkness over the uneven ground while a cold, persistent wind blew relentlessly into his face. He was travelling blind but could taste the salt air and it gave him strength to carry on. He kept walking unsteadily downwards, ever lower with the wind in his face and the Atlantic calling him.

As he neared the coast the wind became gustier, its direction less easy to be sure of and then he saw the ocean. It had never looked so beautiful. Moonlight was reflecting off its angry surface. White caps danced across the vast writhing mass and the smell of it filled his nostrils. Joff leaned gratefully against the end tree of a row of cedars and below him the lights of Polperro danced invitingly.

Joff collected his breath and, ignoring his heavy heart he began the final ascent. He was in a desperate situation and in dire need of good luck. This could very well be his last shot. It had been a while since he had last passed this way but he had made a few friends. Of course, when they were needed, friends could prove to be extremely fickle.

Distracted by his thoughts he tripped on a hidden root. He cursed under his breath as somewhere below a dog barked deeply. The sound echoed around the natural amphitheatre and no doubt put all on high alert.

He waited, crouched low and trying to get his bearings while the dog settled. Trees and acuba shrubs grew all the way to the houses and when silence returned he used them as cover, making his way ever closer to other humans.

Joff reconnected with the stream that ran through the centre of town. Then using its right bank he guided himself through the dwellings. Ahead he could see outside lights and knew there was a coaching house. He slowed down, taking care not to pass too near it, realising that he must look suspicious and didn't want any encounters here where the revenue men were likely to have their most reliable spies stationed. No, he needed one of the smaller drinking dens nearer the beach. Somewhere that catered to the locals, the fishermen. Somewhere the lights were not too bright and he would stand a chance of re-acquainting himself with some of the characters around here who already knew him.

Joff needed somewhere right on the harbour, somewhere that also offered a clear view of anyone who might be approaching. In short, he needed 'The Blue Peter' or 'The Blue' as the locals called it.

He approached the pub ultra-cautiously. The dog had definitely been tracking his progress through the village and now he was barking again. Another mutt answered his call and Joff was worried the owners would realise there was a stranger on the prowl and unleash their hounds. He waited and hoped for the best and thankfully the dogs calmed down and the wind whipping off the sea took his scent away from them.

Slowly he worked away from the stream, forming a giant circle and approaching the Blue from above. He could hug the rock face and observe the comings and goings without standing out against the skyline.

It was a busy night down in the pub. The door kept swinging back and forth and he moved cautiously ever closer until crouching behind an overgrown hawthorn bush he could make out their features. He watched the figures in dark clothing scuttle in and out. Each and every one was caught by the lamplight as they passed. Each time the door opened his senses were assaulted by the light, the chat, the warmth, and the aroma of hot food that was released into the night. It was hard to stay focused but he managed to. Finally he saw a man he knew. Exactly the type of man he had been hoping to spot.

"Duggan!" he hissed. And the solitary figure about to push open the door halted in his tracks and turned, looking over his shoulder, trying to identify who was calling his name. As he turned towards Joff his face fell instantly into shadow. Joff dismissed all thoughts that he could be mistaken.

"Duggan!" he hissed.

It was Duggan Libby, a man he had worked shoulder to shoulder with not more than a year ago. He had been part of Pa's crew that day and they had unloaded 180 barrels of French brandy into Polperro harbour in broad daylight, hidden inside carts of coal. Duggan had been their man on the spot, responsible for the landing crew. He had delivered the haul to a more secure location away from the coast.

He and Joff had spent four days and nights in each other's company and he had said if Joff was ever back in town that he should look him up. Well, now he was back in town and it was time to look him up.

"Over here, Duggan!" Joff hissed again, hoping not to attract any other unwanted attention.

"Who's there?" he called, rather more loudly than the occasion demanded.

Joff was reluctant to reveal himself by name. Especially in a town such as this one, where you are always being watched by somebody from some darkened window or other. He stood up a little so he could be seen more clearly and called in an even tone, "Over 'ere."

Duggan saw him now and a shadow of recognition flitted across his face. Barely worth mentioning, it was present for the briefest of moments and then it was gone.

But he had seen it, it was worth mentioning. It meant that news had spread, he had heard already. The awful crimes Joff was accused of, whatever they might be, were no longer confined to the town he had left in such a hurry.

He looked as though he was actually considering turning back into the pub, but Joff was upright now so he started moving towards Duggan and to his credit, he waited for Joff to approach.

"Joff Owens as I live and breathe, it's bin a while, eh?" he observed, sticking out his hand to shake. He resisted any temptation to glance nervously about when they shook and Joff silently thanked him for that. Quietly he registered that at least the man wasn't ashamed to be seen with him.

"So what brings you to our neck o' the woods then?" he asked.

Joff shook the offered hand. He actually seemed calm, relatively pleased to see his friend now. Perhaps Joff had been wrong and his name was not yet mud in these parts.

"They're all lookin' for you, ya know," he said.

He was smiling as he delivered this information. So it was out, good to know, he supposed.

"Bin a naughty boy 'ave we?" Duggan was grinning now.

Despite the gravity of the situation, despite the horrific pangs of hunger that tormented him, despite everything, Joff couldn't help smiling along with him.

He shook his head slowly from side to side and, looking Duggan right in the eye, said, "No! I 'aven't bin anythin' like as naughty as they claim."

They grinned at each other.

"What are they sayin'?" Joff asked.

Duggan tutted and finally glanced around him, looking for any witnesses to their little reunion. He turned back to face Joff and still grinning asked outright. "So you weren't up on the cliff," he paused for dramatic effect, "smuggling?!" He was grinning like the proverbial Cheshire cat. He knew that sounded highly plausible.

"No I bloody weren't." His head was shaking now at such an accusation.

"So what 'appened then?" he wanted to know.

Joff hesitated but decided it was just as well to get his story out there. He was already homeless and destitute; there wasn't much else they could do. He decided to tell Duggan the truth.

"Well the truth of the matter is that Pa 'as fallen in with these Chartists. Mr. Lovett an' them, an' well the Squire 'as taken real offence at their work."

"So you was up there what, workin'?" he asked.

"Up where, what do you mean?"

"On the cliff, what was you doin' up on the cliff that night?"

"Forget the cliff," Joff replied.

"So you've been set up?" he wasn't smiling now.

"Yeah exactly," Joff replied.

"So that ol' Squire is givin' you a real problem," he decided.

"Yeah you could say that," he agreed as thoughts of Gramps flitted across his mind.

Duggan sucked in his teeth at this declaration. "It don't sound good." He tutted and grinned at Joff again.

He tutted again and smiled, "Sounds like you 'ave got a problem then."

Duggan was laughing, but in a sympathetic manner. He clearly believed Joff's version of events and Joff decided it was safe to ask for his assistance.

"Thing is Duggan, I 'aven't eaten all day an', well, I was kind of 'oping that you might be able to put some food in my belly." He looked down; he didn't have to of course. They both knew Duggan would be facing the beak if he was caught assisting his friend. It had to be his decision.

"Come on." Duggan grabbed Joff by the elbow. "Let's get you out o' sight an' fed an' we can decide what to do wiv you."

Duggan stepped in front of Joff as the door to the pub opened, shielding his face from view. A man came out and saw them standing there but he recognised Duggan instantly so didn't dwell on their presence. He kept moving with his head down. He was a local. If someone with Duggan Libby wanted to hide his face that was none of his concern.

Below them the wet sand of the little bay glowed brilliant white as the moonlight reflected off it. The night had turned clear with not a breath of wind. Beyond the harbour the surf could still be heard crashing onto the rocks around to their right. To their left, on the opposite side of the beach, houses were scattered haphazardly right up the hill. A lamp burned in only one window, the rest remained dark. Hiding who knew how many sets of prying eyes already looking down on them.

Duggan led him as the crow flies directly down the rocks and across the sand. They stepped through the shallow stream and worked their way straight through the boats pulled up on the sand. Joff followed closely as Duggan stepped confidently ahead, seeming to know where the rocks, lobster pots, and other potential trip falls were in the darkness. The man clearly wasn't bothered by who might or might not be observing them either. This was his village and it seemed he had no reason to keep Joff's presence secret. Joff, on the other hand, felt uneasy out in the open like this. He had spent the last couple of days creeping about, avoiding people, and he had gotten used to operating in that way.

There was a narrow gap between two houses that were built right onto the beach. A large dog growled from somewhere in the shadows as they approached.

They headed straight for it. Joff had no choice but to trust Duggan's judgement.

Joff was aware that only the best trained attack dogs growl quietly at approaching strangers. Untrained mutts bark their heads off at the slightest sign of an intruder; they were never a problem to deal with. The best dogs, however, the ones to worry about, ones like this, growled first as a warning and then they attacked. Duggan whispered a name that sounded like 'Jess' as they approached the gap in the houses. A shiny, black nose poked through the darkness and sniffed him as Duggan held out his hand. The nose disappeared and Duggan lifted himself up onto a granite ledge.

"Come on," he said, and Joff squeezed past a large black Alsatian as quickly as he could.

They climbed four or five steps and then were in a narrow, cobbled lane with fisherman's cottages crowding tightly on both sides. Duggan led him a few paces to the right then he darted left into another gap between houses. This time there was no dog, just a huge bramble bush. He held back a couple of lower branches and showed Joff with his foot where a path had been cleared through the thorny foliage.

This whole hillside was a maze of narrow, compact dwellings. The land was criss-crossed by countless alleys, lanes, and cut-throughs. Some led nowhere; others looked impenetrable to those not in the know. With so many windows you had the constant feeling that you were being watched. It was as though each house had been positioned in such a way that between them they could have a total overview of the beach, the harbour, and the whole village. So many of the fishermen's cottages had doors and windows that opened up directly onto the beach or the stream that it would have been possible to land contraband from the comfort of your own front room. This place truly was a smugglers paradise. No wonder they didn't like strangers in Polperro. *Thank God I am with Duggan,* Joff thought.

Finally after it felt like they had clambered across the whole hillside and back again, Duggan led Joff through a thick, heavy oak door and they were standing in a snug little room. Unsurprisingly its window looked out across the houses on the opposite side of town. Duggan crossed into a darkened corner and lit a lamp. Light flooded through the room and immediately Joff's eyes settled on a hunk of cheese and a plate of sardines resting on a table. He looked across to his friend and nodded towards the food

"Alright if I...?"

"'Elp yourself," Duggan replied.

Joff ignored the cloud of tiny flies that his movements sent spiralling up into the air and picked up one of the delicious little fish by the tail. He popped it into his mouth where a cacophony of sensations assaulted his deprived sense of taste. It had been a long time since he had eaten anything quite as good as this. At last all was right again with the world. He gulped the sardines down one after the other, then, picking up a knife from the table, cut himself a piece of cheese and took a massive bite of rich, delicious Cornish blue cheese. Duggan meanwhile had been pouring drinks; he came across the room and offered Joff a pewter goblet. The hungry young man accepted it gratefully, the huge mouthful of cheese binding to the roof of his mouth.

"'ere ya are, a nice drop of cider to wash it down with."

Joff smiled and took a few hefty gulps and the cider left a refreshingly cold trail down the inside of his chest as he swallowed.

Duggan lowered himself into a large comfy chair. He rested his feet on a wooden chest and watched with amusement as Joff greedily ate his fill. Finally Joff wiped his lips with the back of his hand and burped loudly.

"That is the finest cheese I have ever tasted," he declared.

"Glad to be of assistance," Duggan replied, smirking.

Joff allowed himself a few moments then attacked the food with renewed vigour.

Outside a dog barked and automatically they both looked through the window, towards the sound. The joy of eating again had caused Joff's predicament to slip his mind for a few joyous moments, but now it all came flooding back.

"Someone's comin'," Duggan declared.

Joff moved away from the window. "You reckon?" he asked nervously.

"Oh I reckon all right."

Duggan's local knowledge was beyond reproach. Joff fought hard to stave off the waves of despair that were surfacing higher and higher, threatening to engulf him.

Duggan glided out of his chair and towards the window. Very slowly he pulled the drapes almost closed, just leaving a narrow slit of glass visible. He stood slightly to the side, looking out across the beach, across the village.

"See that light in that window?" he said, pointing to the opposite houses and moving his head back so Joff could see around him.

Opposite them at least half a dozen lamps were burning in different houses.

"Which one?" Joff asked.

"There, on the right. The one that's 'ighest up the hill."

"Yeah I see it," came the reply.

A solitary whitewashed cottage sat higher in the hills than all the rest. Its curtains were wide open and a candle burnt brightly on the interior window ledge.

"If it goes out..."

As he spoke the light went out and Joff knew instinctively that wasn't a good sign. "It just went out," he said, although they had both seen it.

"We better move then," Duggan said. As he spoke Joff watched the light in the next cottage down the hill go out as well.

Duggan noticed too.

"Somebody is creeping down to the village through the trees," he said. "Things 'ave bin pretty quiet around 'ere lately, so I reckon 'ooever it is might be 'ere because of you."

Joff's heart was racing now. Another dog barked somewhere below them as Duggan extinguished the lamp.

"Let's go!" he said.

Joff grabbed the remaining sardines and cheese and followed him out the door. Duggan fled up the hill, taking another series of turns and cut-throughs. This time, though, they were moving at a higher speed than Duggan had been inclined to show before. Joff stayed close on the other man's heels, determined not to get lost in the warren of dwellings. He could hear barking echoing off the walls with no idea where the sound was emanating from. He concentrated hard on keeping up with Duggan; everything else was secondary to his determination to not get lost in the darkness.

Finally they were over the top of a hill away from the town and into an orchard. They were on flat ground now, with the houses disappearing behind them. Joff could pick out the apple trees in the moonlight and then saw big lumps casting shadows. He started to detour around what he thought were granite boulders when one moved. He realised they were now in a field of dairy cows. The animals were scattered all around, some lying down, others standing. They ignored the trespassers as the men picked their way through the herd. It was an old trick, a ploy to fool any bloodhounds that might be on their scent. This particular herd were probably well rehearsed in their role assisting fugitives.

Once past the cows, the apple trees gave way to scattered prickly gorse bushes that soon became closer together, creating scrubland, then occasional trees turned into woodland. Finally Duggan stopped in the shadows beneath an old yew tree and crouched down on his haunches, breathing hard. Joff followed suit.

Safely below the skyline, Duggan whispered, "See this openin'?"

He was holding up the lower branches of the yew and had wiped away a clump of wet, decaying leaves. He had revealed a wooden door of the type one would expect to find over the beer cellar off a big public house. Unbelievably, this was a working stash hole, surely, so far from the village that nobody would ever think to look for it here.

He pulled the door open and hissed at Joff, "Get in!"

Joff hesitated, searching his face for signs of an alternative plan, but this it seemed was the only option. He lowered himself into the dark hole, hitting his shin against a metal step ladder. Cursing under his breath, he put his feet on the steps that led further into the dark interior. Any sense of foreboding he was beginning to experience quickly vanished as somewhere not too far away came the unmistakable sound of a bloodhound. Those dogs and their human handlers would be cresting the brow of the hill soon and then they would be in the cow field.

"I'll lead 'em a merry chase, don't you worry," Duggan whispered. "Follow the cave to the coast. Wait at the opening 'til sunrise an' I'll send a boat for yer."

There was nothing to say that could sufficiently express the gratitude Joff felt towards his friend. He struggled for the right words but couldn't think of anything worthy so he simply nodded and mumbled, "Thanks!"

Duggan nodded back and half smiled. "It's been fun!" he said.

The bloodhound's deep call came once again out of the night and Joff lowered himself down a few more rungs. Duggan handed him a lamp and a piece of flint.

"I'll come", he insisted. "Don't worry, just wait, I'll come," he was trying to reassure Joff as he pulled the trapdoor across and what little light there was vanished from above and he was alone. He took a deep breath and descended in total darkness and utter silence, not the distant crash of waves against rocks, not the bray-like barking of the hounds, not even the drip, drip of water somewhere.

The further he sunk below ground the colder the temperature became. The hairs all over his body rose in response to the chill as his ears strained for something, anything. There was nothing like a descent into the unknown to heighten the senses. At the base of many steps his feet suddenly made contact with solid granite. One minute he was rhythmically descending and then without warning he had reached the bottom; it jarred his feet. With his arms extended like a blind man, he groped the space. Solid rock surrounded him except for one place. He almost fell at the suddenness of touching empty space but managed to stay on his feet. He was in a tunnel, he realised. The path only led in one direction. He crouched down and lit the lamp, then followed the track through the solid rock as it twisted and turned its way towards the sea.

Every so often ledges had been hacked out of the granite. Someone back in time had carved shelving into the stone for items that were never going to appear on any invoice. Joff kept walking and only when he had the first faint smell of saltwater in his nostrils did his shoulders begin to relax, the tension of feeling trapped underground begin to leave him. It was time to extinguish the lamp. The smell of the sea grew stronger with every turn of the path now and then he rounded a corner and felt a breeze upon his face. It was advisable to slow his pace. Without warning he was looking out over the sea. The cave was halfway up a sheer cliff face that dropped vertically to the ocean. The rock seemed to double back on itself like a fold in a piece of paper. He peeked around it. He was ten feet above sea level in the sort of place one never stumbled across by accident. In fact, unless you arrived at the peak of the high tide you weren't going to stumble across this particular cave at all.

He peeked around the entrance and stared out across the water. He could see no boats or ships but that didn't mean they weren't out there. *I should be out there,* he thought. Not hiding in a hole like a rat. If anyone was forced to hide for safety it should be Squire Bradshaw or Jimmy Flynn, not Joff. It was so unfair. He imagined what it would feel like to barge into Squire Bradshaw's home in the middle of the night and drag him off to answer for his sins. Anger screwed Joff's face up into a grimace and a powerful desire for revenge soared through his blood. He ducked back into the cave and slumped down, then leaned back against the stone. He had to wait and see whether Duggan was able to deliver on his promise and send a boat for him. If not, well 'if not' didn't really warrant dwelling on. He would worry about that if and when the need arose.

Joff sat with his back against the oddly smooth rock and prepared to wait until sunrise. He knew he had a face like thunder but was completely alone, so there was no need to temper his expression. He let the bitter feelings of self-pity wash over him, relishing the feel of it, determined to remember this moment, using it to feed him, to give the strength he would need. To give him a reason not to succumb but to carry on, to continue the good fight.

Now that he had eaten he felt strong again. Now that he had time to think, it was so incredible. All his pa had wanted, all the Chartists had wanted, was a little more fairness in the world. They hadn't demanded that the toffs—what they disparagingly called the wealthy landowners—should forsake their fortunes or even their privileges. They had just wanted a little more fairness to spread around, and the aristocrats had gone ballistic. Squire Bradshaw had destroyed them and four other families simply for speaking their minds. Of course it was unfair, he could see that, but what good had come of saying so? His pa had been convinced that the masses would rise up and join their ranks, but they hadn't. They had done nothing. So perhaps his first impressions had been right. Maybe not getting involved was the best course of action. It would certainly lead to an easier life.

A month ago he was contented. He had his music, had food in his stomach and somewhere to rest his head. Now what? Now he had nothing and life would never be the same again. He wished his pa had kept out of things and left the politics to somebody else.

Then he wondered if he would ever see his grandpa again, and wanted to avenge the treatment they had both endured. It was so confusing. These must be the big decisions they talked about. The ones you had to make when you were all grown up. This must be what it was like in the adult world. Well, he was here now and they weren't, and he supposed that made him a man. *Is this the precise moment when I change from a boy into a man?* he wondered. *Will I remember this moment for the rest of my life?*

Joff shuffled into his back rest and the rock was surprisingly comfortable, no doubt worn smooth by the backs of many men who had sat there before him, waiting, no doubt, for their own particular ship. He wondered how many of them had wanted to change the world for the better, like his pa had, and whether any of them had managed even a modicum of success.

He picked at his food in darkness, listening to the waves crashing into the rocks below. Shearwaters skimmed the tops of the waves and made their blood-chilling nocturnal calls.

He found the sound of the coast soothing, and soon fell asleep where he sat.

He slept with his head in his hands. It wasn't ideal but it was comfortable enough. Every time his head slipped he was suddenly jerked awake. But he deemed it safer that way; he didn't want to lie out, get too cosy, and risk missing Duggan's boat.

Joff needn't have worried about waking up in time. The early morning dew made sure that he was wide awake and shivering with cold, long before the sun rose in the sky. He was reduced to shivering and fidgeting until he could take it no more and crept to the cave opening. Keeping low, he watched as the darkness slowly lifted, as shapes became objects and night became day. Far out to sea the dawn breeze was whipping up little whirlpools that danced across the surface and told him which way the wind was blowing. Gulls swooped in a noisy, unruly mob on a small section of the water, and he knew they were having sardines for breakfast. A shoal of the little silver fish must have raced to the shallow surface water to escape some predator from below, only to find themselves getting picked off by the seabirds. A flock of Gannets appeared and immediately set about joining in the feast. Joff watched them tucking back their wings as they dove below the surface. Their hunting technique was far superior to the lazy seagulls, and as always Joff was impressed at their skill. He scanned constantly for vessels as he marvelled at the antics of the birds, and wished he was as wild and free as they were. He watched in fascination as they feasted to their hearts' content whilst always leaving the huge shoals barely dented, before finally moving back towards their roosts. Breakfast time in nature was over before most humans had even started their day.

The morning wore on and the tide continued to rise, and still he waited. He knew he shouldn't expect Duggan until high tide, so there was nothing else for it. Another lap of the cave and then continue waiting.

As the light grew stronger the wind picked up and people began to stir. The first signs of life were a fleet of trawlers. Joff surveyed them for signs out of the ordinary, signs that perhaps they were Duggan's men, but they were innocently following a mackerel shoal along the coast, working, not pretending to work. A movement further out in the deeper seas caught his eye and instinctively he ducked from view. A cautious peek revealed the unmistakable sleek lines of a revenue cutter on patrol. It was speeding across the waves, all sails flying. Joff watched, begrudgingly impressed as the vessel skillfully reduced speed.

He instinctively ducked deeper into the shadows. The cutter slowed to a crawl as they surveyed the fishermen through their brand new government-Issue binoculars. Joff hid his face in his smock to break up his silhouette, and peeked from behind a large rock. He was no more than a slit for eyes as he watched closely for any obvious signs of imminent danger, any cause for alarm. But they drew no closer; they were no threat to him, at least not at this precise moment. Duggan, it would appear, had not given him away to the authorities, which strongly suggested that he had evaded them last night. Joff was beginning to hope that his friend would manage to live up to his word and come back for him. They were more than just friends, after all. They were both Cornish, which meant ties that ran far deeper than any loyalty to London or the rest of England. It was already strongly implied that he was obliged to not give Joff away at the very least, even though there was nothing in it for him except the satisfaction of getting one over on the authorities. There would be severe penalties if he was caught playing a part in an escape, but he almost had to help.

Duggan was a Cornish rebel through and through. He couldn't resist what Joff's predicament offered. The free trade provided the only scrap of pleasure to most young men throughout the county. Without it you had to get your fun where you could. London still had a lot of work on its hands to install respect for the law and compliance with the rules around here.

There were workers in the mines at Morwellham Quay who were paid in tokens, not money. Tokens that they could only spend in the mine shop where the prices were extortionate and the choices very limited. They were even forced to buy tallow to light their way as they worked underground. Tallow was the cheapest item to be had in the store. On occasions when there were no ships on the horizon and consequently no extra income to be earned, they were reduced to eating tallow. Not the Squire and his family, of course. No, that would never do. But for the children of the miners it was absolutely fine.

Joff sat there shivering with the early morning cold and rather surprisingly he was dwelling on the injustices of the world.

But if the truth be told those miners did very little to help themselves. Sometimes it seemed as though the Cornish would go out of their way to make their own lives harder in the long run. They could improve things to some degree tomorrow if they so desired. All they had to do was swear allegiance to the King in London, but they were Cornish, not English. And they would rather stubbornly stay Cornish and suffer for it. The authorities may have finally taken control of the land, but they had an awful long way to go before they could truly say the locals no longer saw them as some kind of foreign occupying force.

Joff caught sight of another vessel rounding the far headland and he slipped further into the shadows. He watched a majestic three master heading far out towards the horizon, and as always he wondered where she was going and as usual wished he was aboard.

On the far cliff he saw the miniature shape of a horse. It was being ridden slowly along the coastal path, and Joff knew it must be a revenue man on his patrol. He wondered if the man was looking for him and ducked down a little lower.

A wave crashed against the rocks and a little of its spume splashed his legs. The tide was almost fully in now. It was the moment that the water level was high enough to send a boat for him, but it was far too busy out there and he knew if it was his decision to make he wouldn't be sending anybody until the next high tide, when it would be dark.

Fortunately Joff still had cheese in his pocket. He nibbled at it as slowly as he could and forced himself to be patient. It was extremely unlikely that the horseman on the far side of the bay would be able to see him from such a distance, but he slunk deeper into the cave just in case. There was no point taking unnecessary chances.

He leaned back against the rock and imagined a world where children didn't have to eat candle wax, where a man worked at feeding his own children, not wasting his time making profit for somebody else. He half smiled as he realised some of his pa's dogma had washed off on him after all.

Joff must have dozed off because when he opened his eyes all was dark. He moved position so he could look out over the sea, and watched the moon as it rose in the sky. Heavy, dark rain clouds drifted across it and Joff chose their cover as the moments to risk exposure and peek further out to sea.

Blackness and shadows danced across the cave and he could literally feel moisture in the air. He risked another glance outside. The sea was more choppy than it had been a few hours before, and the clouds much thicker and more numerous than yesterday. Conditions were much better suited to clandestine operations, and soon the tide would be at its maximum. If Duggan was going to come, it was going to be on this tide, Joff was sure of it.

As he sat there alone he felt the adrenaline of the coming adventure tingling through his whole body. He had no idea what life had planned for him next but he could at least be ready when his rescuers arrived.

Joff heard them before he saw them. The sound of water slapping the underside of a wooden boat, then the water rolling off the oars between strokes.

He crouched low and kept reassuring himself over and over that it simply had to be Duggan, surely it couldn't be anyone else. He couldn't be that unlucky.

There was the unmistakable dull thud of wood touching rock and he heard a voice hiss: "Joff!"

He didn't have to call twice. Joff scrambled on to the bow of the craft before Dugganknew what was happening. There was no need for unnecessary words. Sound travelled a long way at night across the sea. Duggan put all his strength into the oars and they slipped away, beaming widely at each other. They kept tight to the cliffs, working east away from Polperro. Up above them a few lamps burned in the houses on the edge of town, but Joff knew they had no need to worry about being reported.

Joff maintained silence, content to let Duggan do his thing. He had done Joff proud up to now and knew what he was doing. If the truth be told, Joff was just grateful to be back at sea.

Slowly the little town of Polperro faded behind them. They maintained silence whilst Duggan rowed rhythmically. He was used to such work, gripping the oars firmly, his strong shoulders bunching with each stroke. He set a steady pace as he expertly skirted around each nook and cranny of the rocky coastline. It was too dark to see the lay of the land but Duggan pre-empted each treacherous, rocky contour as he kept a consistent distance between them and the sharp, jagged rocks.

He had brought along a beef and onion pasty and Joff lay back in the bow savouring every mouthful while watching the stars and wondering about his grandpa and Betsy.

After what must have been a good hour they cleared the headland that separated Polperro from the slightly larger town of Looe. Duggan's smooth rowing style created no chop that could give them away to a keen eye. Before they closed in on Looe he gently altered course, taking them further and further from land. Joff relaxed in the bow and watched the stars peeking from behind the clouds.

What felt like at least another hour passed and Joff wondered what they were doing back home. Perhaps they should have been more discreet in their opinions, been a little more sympathetic to the way things worked, a little less sympathetic to the Chartists. Maybe if they had, he wouldn't be in this situation now. Perhaps he would still have his family and their cottage. Perhaps it was better to just plod along keeping quiet, not making any waves, just playing the organ and minding his own business. Keeping their heads down and doing what was expected of them for the peace and quiet of all. Yet how could that be right? Once his pa had learned things from the sailors of Europe, once they had filled his head with strange, exciting, new ideas, he couldn't unlearn them, couldn't keep silent and watch people he loved get taken advantage of time after time. No, Joff was certain now, despite his current predicament, his pa had really not had a choice. He was sure, if a thing wasn't right it was wrong, and if he knew things that others didn't it was his solemn duty to bring it to their attention. How they dealt with that information, whether they chose to act on it or not, was of course a matter for each and every individual to make for themselves. It wasn't his pa's fault that most people chose to do nothing. He had been held responsible for the weakness of others, it seemed.

A mile out to sea from the town of Looe there is a small uninhabited island little more than a puffin colony, and slightly further beyond that there is an even smaller island, little more than a rocky outcrop really, but at the back there is a small v-shaped inlet. It was here that Duggan brought them. A fishing gaffer was innocently casting sardine nets at the mouth of the inlet.

"Right Joff," Duggan whispered, "get ready to go aboard."

With no bag, no belongings, it wasn't likely to take him long.

"I'm ready!" Joff hissed.

He felt a massive sense of relief that he had managed to evade Squire Bradshaw, and smiled in the darkness. He was excited to be getting on a decent-sized vessel and moving at last even if she were only a Polperro fishing gaffer. No doubt about it, this was the next step on the rest of his journey through life, and quite frankly, he was itching to get started.

"'Ere we are," Duggan whispered as he drew quietly alongside the fishing boat.

"I'm grateful," Joff whispered back. "Thanks for everything, eh."

He knew the words were nowhere nearly enough for all that his friend had done for him, but now wasn't really the time or the place for long, heartfelt platitudes of gratitude.

Duggan's white teeth flashed as he grinned.

"Don't mention it, it's been my pleasure."

Even so he had just taken an enormous risk to do Joff a massive favour, and Joff knew not when he might see him again.

"Thanks anyway," he repeated quietly.

"We got one over on 'em, eh?" he muttered.

They smiled at each other, a shared knowledge that they had managed to get the better of those who would deem themselves their betters. A victory was rare indeed so the taste was extra sweet when they did manage to triumph.

Joff's pa and grandpa had given Squire Bradshaw just the excuse he had been hoping for and he had gone after them with a real tenacity. Joff understood why the Squire had deemed it time to break up the little family. They had gone from being a slight irritation to the organisers of chaos. If the miners at his mines started listening to the Chartists he would have a real problem on his hands.

Of course Flynn and his motley crew would come down like a ton of bricks on any of his actual employees who started to make noises about workers' rights. The Europeans might be overthrowing their superiors, but Squire Bradshaw was doing his utmost to prevent equality spreading throughout the county. Tin, wool, beef, timber—he had interests in them all and he was quite happy with the system that was already in place. It had been good enough for his father and his father before him, and with the added profits that capitalism promised it was damn well good enough for the present Squire. He longed for the railway to make it down to Cornwall. When it did, his profits would grow even bigger.

Maybe one day Joff would have the strength to return and resolve some issues with him.

Duggan brought them alongside the fishing boat and a thick-armed crewman hauled Joff aboard in one fluid movement. Then in the brief time it took him to climb to his feet, he turned and Duggan was gone. Slowly, methodically, already heading away, back the way they had just come. It was a round trip of six or seven miles, a real herculean effort for most men. Duggan, however, probably would not even break a sweat.

There was no opportunity to watch him fade into the night. Joff was taken rather briskly below decks where the stench of fish was overwhelming. There were always revenue men in their speedy cutters patrolling the waters in this area. One head too many might well be noticed if they were unlucky enough to attract attention.

As Joff scurried below they abandoned all pretence of fishing. The nets were hauled in and they set sail ever further from Polperro, from Looe, from Cornwall. Joff flopped down onto an empty sail bag and waited. He wondered who Duggan had handed him on to and what they intended to do with him, but he tried to dwell on only the more positive thoughts. Sometime later a crewman popped his head through the hatch and spoke a few words to him. His was the first voice Joff had heard in all the time he had been aboard. He was longing for conversation but had not really expected any here. He did not take it personally; he knew how these things worked. He was not a friend of theirs; they would probably never see him again. If they knew nothing of him they would be less likely, less tempted, to feel the need to discuss him at some later date. They were professionals. They were paid to off-load Joff and promptly forget that he ever existed.

"Plymouth light'ouse is on the 'orizon. Youm be goin' ashore in an hour," he said.

It had felt as though the boat was making some good speed, but Joff was impressed that they were nearing Plymouth so soon.

He nodded his thanks and the man disappeared from view, not even bothering to return Joff's smile, and leaving him once again with only the empty bags and the stench of fish for company. He imagined Flynn and all the Squire's men angrily searching for him. He hoped they didn't make life too uncomfortable for those he had left behind.

CHAPTER FIVE

Squire Bradshaw sat astride his magnificent jet-black thoroughbred. He was patting the horse on its neck as it snorted from the strain of galloping across the fields.

"What have you found?" the Squire was asking the scruffy urchin at his feet.

"It's a pouch sir, like you would put baccy in." He held it out for the Squire to see for himself.

It was indeed a leather pouch specifically designed for the transport of smuggled tobacco and quite possibly a clue. Maybe it had belonged to Joff Owens and in his haste to get away he had dropped it. If so, that would mean he had come this way, had headed across the fields towards Hayle. The Squire eyed the two boys before him with deep suspicion. They for their part smiled sweetly up at him.

"Alright, well done," he managed to say through gritted teeth.

The taller urchin held out his hands in the shape of a begging bowl.

"If you could see your way to 'elping us..."

Squire Bradshaw thrashed the stallion's rear quarters with his crop. He turned before the boy had finished his sentence and was gone, galloping across the fields, the horse kicking up clods of mud as he raced away.

The boys turned to face each other.

"Do you think 'e bought it?" the smaller of the two asked his comrade.

"I 'ope so," came the reply.

"What if 'e did come this way? Won't we be makin' it worse for 'im?" The younger of the two boys could not have been more than six years old, but he showed a grasping of events far beyond his years.

"'E wouldn't do that!" The elder boy wagged his finger enthusiastically in his young colleague's face, mocking the very suggestion.

"'E won't go inland, 'e will 'ave put to sea. Joff Owens's not one for walkin' across the moor. You just wish you 'ad thought of it instead o' me!"

He poked his young companion in the midriff and began to run away back towards the town nestling in the bay below them. The six-year-old followed close behind.

"I did think of it!" he shouted.

The elder boy slowed down, allowing himself to be caught up to. "Yeah, I know, an' it was a very cunning plan indeed." He ruffled the child's thick, matted hair.

The little boy looked up, "I 'ope 'e makes it!" he declared simply.

"We all do, Jimmy, we all do!" came the sombre reply.

CHAPTER SIX

Joff sat cross-legged on the sail bags in the dingy cabin and listened to the muffled voices and creaking floorboards as the crew busied themselves above deck. He could hear men walking about, gathering ropes, placing buoys, and generally preparing for something. They had to be reaching his drop off. After hours of nothing but his own thoughts for company, he was relieved to have something different to focus his attention on. He couldn't help wondering who these sailors were and how much they were being paid to assist him. Finally a head appeared in the hatch and addressed him.

"We's in Plymouth Sound now. Get yer ready. Youm goin' ashore."

It was obvious from his accent that he, at least, was Cornish. Joff wondered if the rest of the crew were also local. How would life be without such men willing to bend the rules? He silently thanked the man for his rebellious nature.

Joff stretched and, keeping low so as not to bang his head, followed him through the hatch. He stayed low and Joff followed his lead. They headed to the stern of the boat where they crouched in silence. A watchman had gotten there before them and he caught Joff's eye and raised an eyebrow. "Ready?" the eyebrow said. There would be no words exchanged.

In a few brief moments Joff heard the familiar sound of oars slicing calmly through water. A rowing boat was approaching and he planned to become a passenger on it in the minimum amount of time possible. He braced himself as the solitary rower emerged through the blackness. He touched the larger craft with the gentlest of kisses as Joff stepped lightly, as quietly as he could, across the gap. The rower barely had to break his rhythm and they were gone. Calmly, unobtrusively—and most importantly, unseen—they slipped through the night and Joff had no idea what fate held in store for him. Yet the sky was full of stars, the ocean was vast, and he was grinning like the cat that had gotten the cream. Perhaps he was in mortal danger but he felt relief at being out of the enclosed cabin, one step closer to something. He didn't know why but it felt great to be alive. He kept low and glanced up at his rescuer. The man glanced back at him, winked, and smiled infectiously at Joff's happy face. Joff winked back and silently wondered if there was a piano where they were headed.

All too soon he could see the lights from a little town ahead. As he watched they grew ever closer. Then he could make out the whiteness of a little sandy beach and as he stared a group of about thirty men tumbled from a pub he hadn't noticed at the back of the beach, right onto the sand.

The loud group of men proceeded to lark about whilst surreptitiously heading noisily in the general direction of the boat, of the sea. Right towards the far corner of the sand they came, where the lights of the village did not quite reach, exactly the same spot towards which the boat was silently heading. It was a gently sloping shoreline with a number of small rowing boats pulled up onto the sand. These, Joff knew, were used to get out to the larger vessels anchored offshore.

His rescuer was clearly unperturbed by the revellers. They were obviously friends of his and Joff was impressed at the simplicity of the plan. As they maintained their course directly towards them, they shadowed skillfully, clearly nowhere near as drunk as they were pretending to be.

Only when the water beneath was inches deep did Joff's rescuer raise his oars. They glided onto the sand as the joyful, drunken crowd wrestled noisily with each other around them. The rower stepped smartly from the boat and instantly he became part of the crowd. They were perfect cover. Joff slipped up the sand and onto the narrow, cobbled street. He followed closely at his helper's heel. Very soon they reached a junction and the men dispersed and were swallowed up by the dark streets.

The rescuer popped the latch on a little old cottage door and it opened quietly. Joff followed as the man slipped inside. He padded quietly up a narrow flight of stairs and still Joff followed. Ever upwards they rose until they came to what could only be described as a tiny attic room. He pushed open the door with a creak then stood back, allowing Joff a glimpse into the rooftop space. Joff could see boxes piled high, all stamped 'Property of the Royal Navy.'

The man spoke now, but in hushed tones. "Be'ind them boxes you will find a space. Get some kip an' stay 'ere 'til we comes an' gets you."

Joff nodded and asked, "Where are we?"

He hesitated before deciding that it was probably alright to divulge that particular piece of information. Joff wasn't a prisoner, after all.

"Youm's in Cawsand, boy." He looked at Joff properly for the first time since they had met. "Know it?" he asked.

"I know of it," Joff admitted as he attempted to push past his host, past the boxes to the promised comfort behind.

The man blocked his path with a hand across the door and repeated, "'Til we comes an' gets you, mind!"

Joff nodded again with more vigour and reached out to rest his hand on the other's shoulder, lending solemnity to his words.

"Don't worry," he replied. "I'll stay put."

The other man nodded, satisfied, and moved his arm so his guest could enter the room. At last Joff was safe, albeit only temporarily.

For the first time since leaving home so abruptly, he slept peacefully.

CHAPTER SEVEN

Joff knew Cawsand was the first little town you came to if you approached the giant natural harbour of Plymouth Sound from the sea. The naval town of Plymouth was only three miles to the north in the cup of the harbour, where the rivers joined the sea, where they carried the tin from the mines to the ships. The dockyard at Devonport had recently been expanded and was busier with each passing year. Ships and sailors from all corners of the Empire and beyond would be in dock on a constantly rotating basis. There would be thousands of foreign men in the city one week, only to be replaced by a thousand more from somewhere else the next. In those heady days of Empire building, there was always another vessel in need of repair work and there was an inexhaustible number of men killing time before their ship went to sea. Those men were ready customers for contraband goods. Good profits were there to be enjoyed by those who dared take a chance.

Cawsand was a respectable little town. The chapel was always full on a Sunday and the revenue men had little cause to venture down the long winding track that led there and nowhere else. If officialdom ever did see the need to pay the town a visit, their presence was announced hours before they actually arrived. Whenever they landed, be it by sea or by land, the locals were always at the beach or at the foot of the hill, waiting for them. This was not a place that one could easily creep up on, but like all places, there was a weak spot.

Cawsand was not completely isolated. It had another town of equal size just one field's width away. This place was called Kingsand, and the feud between the two towns was on-going and relentless. Occasionally it developed into something serious before eventually settling down again into a longstanding local rivalry which nobody could remember the true origins of.

However much the two communities disliked each other though, all was forgotten when the revenue men showed up. Rivalries would be put to one side and forces joined against the common enemy. The Cornish valued their feuds but like a bickering married couple they would always join ranks against outsiders. Life in this hard-to-get-to, hilly piece of England's green and pleasant land moved at a slower pace than London, and they liked it that way, even preferred it. Yet always the ever growing naval port of Plymouth was visible across the bay. It could not be ignored and so it wasn't. It could always be relied on when employment opportunities were hard to find on the Cornish side of the river. The villages of Cawsand and Kingsand might well appear respectable, but the truth was, they were free-traders there, each and every one of them. Smugglers descended from long lines of smugglers stretching all the way back to their Celtic ancestors.

Joff awoke with a smile on his face and a song in his heart. It was the perfect morning for sitting in the church playing scales faster and faster as the sun rose over the hill. There was no piano here, though, nor a giant window to stare through. Here there was a tiny window throwing light across him, and he had to stand on his tiptoes just to gaze through a little slice of it. He could see the crisp blue sky and a jumble of mismatched roof tiles. In the distance he could see the giant cranes above the docks of Plymouth, a place that he knew employed thousands of men. It was the largest collection of workers for miles around. Perhaps they would have a leader, someone who would be sympathetic to Joff's plight, maybe even have the means to assist him in his quest for justice.

After a good night's sleep, Joff felt much more positive. He wanted to get out there and feel the wind on his face. Get moving; get started on clearing his name. The impatience of youth was burning brightly.

Finally he heard the sound of footsteps climbing the stairs and then a face appeared around the door.

"Alright are you?"

Joff nodded and came around the boxes towards the stranger in the door.

"Yeah, alright thanks. I slept like a baby." The man wasn't smiling, Joff quickly noted. "Everything alright with you?"

"Well the thing is, there's a ship leavin' tonight. We can get you onboard an' you can work your passage to London."

"I don't want to go to London," Joff replied. "I need to stay 'ere an' clear my name, so I can go back 'ome."

The man looked at Joff sadly. "That isn't goin' to 'appen, son. You are a wanted man. You must 'ave upset somebody pretty 'igh up, judging by the amount of men out there looking for you."

"Well," Joff began, "I thought if I could find a Chartist man in Plymouth, in the dockyard maybe, well then I could get the might of the workers to 'elp force 'im to improve the lot of those that works the tin mines."

"That isn't clearing your name. That sounds more like revenge to me."

Joff shrugged.

"Well I thought if the Squire is busy dealing with labour trouble..."

The sentence trailed off. The man was right; Joff hadn't really thought this through.

"'Ow do you know about 'labour trouble'?" the other asked with genuine astonishment written all over his face.

"I know 'cos I've listened to William Lovett 'imself speakin'," Joff replied, hoping to get him on his side.

The man frowned before answering, "There isn't much labour power in Plymouth. It's a naval town, you know. Any unrest 'ere an' they got the Queen's army, the royal marines no less, in barracks just down the road. All they got to do is jog up the 'ill from Stone'ouse and bash a few 'eads. They soon take control. If you got an interest in politics, you would be better served gettin' yourself safely up to London."

"But I don't know no-one there," Joff began, but he was already rising to leave.

The older man stopped, and holding Joff's eye, added, "An' the boat leaves tonight."

"I'm 'ungry," Joff said just before the door closed.

"I'll bring somethin' up," he replied without turning around.

Then he was gone and Joff was left with a dilemma. Why should he want to go to London? What would he do there? But then again, what would he do here? Maybe he was right. If they were already looking for him this far afield, how long could he seriously expect to retain his freedom? He laid back on the bed and tried to imagine a new life in London. Tried to think what he could do there. He could play, he supposed. They must need piano players in London. No, that would never work, he decided. He needed to stay where he was. He rose up again and peered out through the window. He could only see roof tops but knew all those little boats would all still be dragged up on the sandy beach and he wondered how easy it would be to row one to Plymouth. He didn't think it would be worth mentioning to his kindly mentor, but he liked the idea much more than he liked the idea of going to London.

When Joff heard footsteps heading back up the stairs, he got off the bed and stood waiting, acting casually. The man entered the room carrying a tray, and Joff smiled when he saw it. A big, genuine smile at the sight of such a feast.

"Thought you might like a little cider!" the host announced, "an' some sardines an' some bread." He smiled and Joff smiled back.

He wasn't trying to be hard on Joff, the smile said.

"Looks lovely," Joff replied, meaning that he understood.

He made a fuss of finding room to put down the tray and finally placed it in the only spot he could, the floor.

"Food looks lovely," Joff repeated, "so I suppose I'll just eat and have a sleep an' stay put until tonight then?" Joff smiled again, asking the question with a raise of his eyebrows.

"That sounds like a good plan to me," the other replied.

He kicked a tin pot towards Joff, "If you need to go. I Think it's better if you just stay 'ere out o' sight an' I'll come for you around the hour of ten."

Joff nodded, "That's really good o' you, much appreciated."

He smiled uneasily. He was doing it for the money and no other reason and they both knew it.

Once he had gone, Joff wolfed down the food and drank half a tankard of cider. It was encouraging to know that he had until ten. By his reckoning, that would give him at least three or four hours to make good his escape. He tried the door latch and it lifted willingly, allowing the door to open. He was not locked in, but why should he be since he was not a prisoner. He listened hard for any sounds of life emanating from elsewhere in the building but heard nothing. He knew his tatty smock would not look out of place on these cobbled streets but also knew the deep Cornish suspicion for outsiders. He gently closed the door and sat on the bed to wait for dusk.

As the sun neared the end of its day and the shadows were long enough to aid him, he slipped from the cottage and stepped sharply towards the beach. In just a few moments he had reached his destination. He could see the tenders still lying haphazardly on the sand. Any one of them would suit his purpose. He crouched low and used the rocks that ran down the edge of the beach to keep him in the shadows. He headed towards the cluster of boats nearest the water's edge. He selected a deep blue one because it had a pair of oars lying inside it, and slowly dragged it across the wet sand. He heard a dog running down the track towards the beach and froze, crouching low behind the boat. But the dog didn't get on the sand. Somebody in the village called out and it went running back towards the sleepy little cluster of houses. As soon as it vanished, Joff doubled his efforts and dragged the little rowing boat into the shallows. He waded alongside it, then swam, steering it into the darkness. Only when the beach was gone from view did he haul himself aboard and start to row.

There was barely time to break sweat and he was approaching Drake's island. He was a lot closer to Plymouth now but the little island was sheltering him from any looking glasses that might be, would surely be, on the lookout for approaching, suspicious, or simply unexpected vessels. Unfortunately, he fell into all three of those categories, so he opted to approach with great caution.

Above him, sheer granite cliffs rose for eighty feet. Hundreds of gulls were circling and squawking and generally announcing his presence to any that might be in the vicinity. He pulled hard on the oars and edged away from the island, and slowly the birds receded and returned to their nests. He was heading across the bay, not into it.

As he cleared the little island the lights of the city hit him and he knew that it would be impossible to approach unobserved. It could only be a mile or so, so he decided to swim for it. Making sure there was no splash, he lowered himself gently into the water. Then he made his way slowly towards the city, where he felt sure there would be somebody who could help. Small waves rolled across the bay and he let himself rise and fall with their motion. He knew that as long as he didn't splash around he would be very difficult to spot. Something the size of a human head floating through the vast ocean was notoriously difficult to see, especially at night. He would take his time and make sure he managed to slip ashore unnoticed.

Eventually he dragged himself onto the rocks at a little outcrop locally referred to as Devil's Point. It was a whirlwind of currents where two rivers joined the sea. The sort of place where you would normally expect a few fishermen to be gathered, but tonight something had mercifully kept them all away.

He crouched low on the wet, slippery rocks for a few moments, letting the water drip from him, and only when he was sure that wind and rain were his only companions did he scramble cautiously up the solid granite and head towards the cobbled streets that made up the hard-edged town of Devonport. Few souls were abroad on this night and it was relatively straightforward to hug the shadows and keep himself from those he did see. Finally he entered a street that contained lights. Raucous noise could be heard coming from a public house. He shook himself dry as best he could and entered the packed room just as the noise abated. The crowd were quietening down, turning to face a low stage. He stood quietly at the back, listening as a man began speaking in powerful, passionate tones that ran with clarity to the furthest recesses of the hall.

"I believe!" he announced, "with all my heart, in liberty, equality, and justice for all!"

He paused to scan the sea of faces before him. "But most of all I believe in minimal intervention from the state!"

Loud grumblings rose from somewhere in the crowd staring up at him.

He ignored them and continued, "Why should one man take 'ome less than his colleagues for the exact same work?"

He spoke at length along the same theme, and Joff scanned about, trying to read the room. When the speaker had finished, loud cheers rose up from most of the ranks and loud clapping that went on and on, trying to drown out voices of opposition that seemed to rise from random quarters.

Minutes later a minister in a dog collar took to the platform. He stood facing the crowd, his hands outstretched, gesturing for the mob to quieten down. He waited for a silence of sorts to settle before he said, "Brothers, the personal votes guarantee that you already have access to the admiralty with any grievances, any at all. Nowhere else in the whole of England do working men enjoy such a privilege!"

A smattering of agreement rippled through the crowd.

The churchman continued, "You are in the unique position of being able to address the law directly with your complaints, and..." he paused for effect, "don't they listen?"

Uproar ensued at the number wishing to respond. Joff scanned the room again, uneasily. Slowly they quietened down again. Then one man said something they all seemed to agree with.

"Yeah they let us speak, but listen? When was the last time they acted on any complaint in a manner that suited us?"

Once again pandemonium broke out in the crowd and the minister wisely took a step backwards. These community meetings were supposed to calm volatile situations, were supposed to allow the working men to let off steam. But in the experience of recent months they did no more than reinforce the working man's dissatisfaction with his lot and allow the Chartists to peddle their literature through the crowds. Only six months previously a petition of one and a quarter million signatures had been presented to Parliament. The government had steadfastly refused to give it the time of day. There had been riots throughout the land that had needed military force to quell.

 Joff was unaware of much of the background, but as he hung back, listening, he was reminded greatly of similar meetings back home. He never really paid much attention to what was being said. He was usually only there to play a few tunes as the meetings wound up. He knew, though, that gatherings such as this one only took place when the men had genuine grievances. Like back home when the tin miners felt Squire Bradshaw was pushing them too far, when their children had been eating tallow. Nothing was ever achieved and dissenters would be mysteriously inconvenienced. Their families would fall on unexpected hard times in one way or another. This, however, felt different. Joff was used to a roomful of men who all felt the same way. Here it was blatantly obvious that the room was divided into two groups. At the front, near the stage, the men seemed to be on the side of the workers. Towards the back of the crowd stood serious-looking, thoroughbred representatives of the establishment. Joff edged closer to the front.

 He listened as a member of the high admiralty took to the stage and droned on about the importance of the work in a dockyard such as Devonport, where the men, in times of war, were called upon to do what was nothing short of essential to the military effort and the very existence of the empire. He stressed that he personally was always there to listen to any legitimate concerns his valued workforce might wish to voice, and reminded them that the system of retaining favours worked to the benefit of all.

He stepped down and the counter-point was made.

"Look at the rise of the co-op," the new speaker said. "A noble way of conducting business. Indeed were we to have cooperatives in all fields, the State would have no reason for existing!"

Loud cheers rose all around.

"You, 'ere take this." A boy of about sixteen thrust a pamphlet into Joff's hand and moved on before he could enquire as to what it was about. He glanced down at it but it was no more than a jumble of meaningless shapes he took to be words arranged around a picture of a giant warship launching down, presumably, Devonport dockyard slipway. He held it openly in his hand, hoping to convey that he belonged and that clutching this piece of paper hot off the press somehow made him one of them. He squeezed himself closer to the front so as to leave no doubt where his allegiance lay. He clapped enthusiastically when the workers did so. He cheered along with them when another speaker rose to offer a few more words of wisdom. The cheers and applause rose to another level, announcing that he was clearly a favourite, one of them. Well now he was also a favourite of Joff's.

"Brothers!" he declared, "all we ask is the right to an eight-hour day!"

Loud cheers greeted his sentiments and all around Joff tankards were banged enthusiastically on wooden bench tables. These men were well aware of events unfolding across Europe and they wanted a piece of it. They wanted to be treated as equals, they wanted rights and, unlike their brethren in Cornwall, they were prepared to stand up and say so.

Joff stood steam-drying as he listened. His enthusiastic joining in had not gone unnoticed. At the end of the bar a tall man in a thick black jacket nodded warmly in his direction and a serving girl came over and thrust a tankard into his hand.

"From 'im!" she said, looking down the bar. A stranger at the end of the bar raised his drink in salute and sipped, all the time watching Joff through his dank, greasy fringe.

The barmaid spoke again. "You look as though you could do with a little warming up," she offered in a manner both exciting and terrifying. Then laughing at some unseen merriment she turned on her pretty ankle and with a swirl of her skirts was gone, swallowed up by the massed ranks as she went on her merry way distributing drinks and breaking hearts.

She was the most beautiful girl Joff had ever seen. The speakers were forgotten now as his eyes followed her around the room.

Chaos and pandemonium appeared to reign supreme but beneath the surface this was clearly a well-oiled business. Under the watchful eye of the stranger in the long coat, the owner's apron was filling up with coins and the whole thing, despite its chaotic appearance, was well under control. Devonport was a hard town, full of thieves, whores, and tough dockyard workers. There were garrisons of Marines placed strategically within and without the dockyard walls. Service personnel and locals went drinking in the same locations. Places where an abundance of girls would engage in conversation with whoever was buying the drinks and potentially rival confrontations between the civvies and the services often spiralled out of control. This particular girl disappeared somewhere out the back and Joff's attention returned reluctantly to the stage.

Right here, in this public gathering, there were no uniforms on display in the crowd. Joff was witness to events he never would have thought possible. A group of workers with direct access to those at the very top. He wanted in. If here, why not in the tin mines at the heart of his home county. Why not a gathering that could put second thoughts, maybe even serious doubts, into the old Squire and his selfish ways.

Joff decided he was, more by luck than judgment, in exactly the right place at the right time. He grasped the tankard and made regular sips to allow it to pass down his dry lips. He spotted a fire on the far wall and went and stood next to it.

Then he heard a voice he recognised. His head swivelled towards the stage and there was Mr. Lovett again.

"We formed the Chartist Movement!" he announced passionately, slamming his right fist into the palm of his left hand to emphasise the point again, "to improve conditions for all men!" He laid special emphasis on the word 'all.'

He stood with his head hung modestly and allowed a moment for the applause to die down.

He raised his hands and a sea of silent faces stared up at him.

Then the spell was broken by a heckle. "Fool!" went up from a solitary dissenting voice.

Joff watched from his vantage point as angry faces all turned in the direction of the voice. On the stage Lovett was shouting now.

"You may call me a fool but for what?" He scanned the sea of faces, "For what? For wanting a fair day's pay for a fair day's work! For expectin' the bosses to let us take the Sabbath as a holy day. For wantin' the vote for every man once he reaches twenty-one. A vote in a secret ballot, mind, where members choose who can represent them in parliament. Does that sound like the ramblings of a fool?"

Loud cheers of 'no' drowned out those at the back.

"We are none of these things yet all o' these things. We are jus' normal men like you. We 'ave members from as far afield as Sheffield and Yorkshire. Men who have had enough of making their masters wealthy whilst they can barely afford to feed their own children!"

Pandemonium was breaking out left, right, and centre.

"The Charter is to be presented again, gentlemen!"

Cheers filled the rafters.

"We will collect even more signatures than we did in '39. Now is the time to rise up an' be counted, brothers. The bosses need us as much as we need them and we will have fair pay for an eight-hour day."

A heckle rose up again from the crowd. "We don't need no Chartists down 'ere. We got the ear o' the Admiralty!"

Murmurs of agreement rippled in places towards the back. The mood had changed again. Joff glanced about and saw that the personnel had changed as well. Clubs and lengths of wood had appeared from somewhere and the two gangs were moving towards each other almost faster than he could take it all in.

Glancing about the room, it was clear that the time for talking was over.

Beside Joff a voice whispered in his ear, "Ooh, it's gonna get ugly!"

He turned to take in the same lad who had been handing out pamphlets. He was not much older than Joff, dressed in black with an explosion of dark curls bursting out from beneath a flat cap perched on top of his head. With sparkling, lively eyes he took Joff in and with a welcoming grin spread across his face he held out his hand to shake, "I'm Davie," he declared. "Davie Clarke."

Joff took his rough hand and they locked eyes, grinning wildly, caught up in the moment, the rhetoric, the danger, the possibility that the world was changing and they were there to witness it.

"Joe," Joff lied, "Joe Penrose."

"You from 'round 'ere, are you, Joe?" he asked, still smiling although not quite so broadly.

Joff shook his head in the negative.

"Come to 'ear Lovett then I suppose?"

He nodded, thankful for the excuse Davie was offering him.

"Yeah, I ain't surprised you came." He was giving Joff a cover story. "It was well publicised for miles around, weren't it." He delivered the sentence as a fact. But they both understood he was giving new information.

"That's true enough," Joff agreed.

He nodded, "Talk o' little else these last few weeks on the shop floors o' the yard an' in all the pubs from Devonport to the Barbican, an' even across the river into Cornwall." He looked at Joff, still smiling. "I expect that's where you 'eard talk, in your local pub was it?"

Joff nodded gratefully, "Yeah, that's right."

At that point the circling was over and the two groups of men flew at each other.

The workers were a fairly even split of young apprentices and older dockworkers. The apprentices were supposed to consider themselves fortunate to have jobs. Supposed to be grateful that if they kept their noses clean they could see themselves maintaining a steady life until the day they walked out or until they shuffled off their mortal coil having kept their noses clean, performed their duties, and left barely a mark on the world.

These young bucks wanted more and they had been drinking.

At the back of the room off-duty marines had been drafted in by the authorities to make sure things ended violently. If the meeting caused enough of a social nuisance there would be a good excuse to ban them in the future. These were the same squaddies that flashed the cash to the local girls of Union Street every weekend. The apprentices didn't need much goading to fall into the trap. The older dockers on their own would not have fallen for it but now that their younger colleagues had already started throwing punches, they too joined in the affray.

Davie grabbed Joff's arm, and looking him straight in the eye, he said, "I better be off. You comin'?"

Joff nodded and followed him through the melee, across the stage, and gratefully out through the back door.

Behind them all hell was breaking loose as the marines gleefully laid into the dockyard apprentices, who happily gave as good as they got.

It was true that the dockers in Plymouth were considerably better off than the tin miners back in Cornwall or those employed in the private factories that scattered the north and the midlands. Here in Devonport they worked directly for the government, in the form of the Admiralty. Strikes could never be tolerated at work sites on which the nation depended so greatly, and both sides knew it. It was true to say that workers here were treated less harshly than those in the employ of private enterprise, though, and these two factors combined made it extremely difficult for the newly fledged Chartists to take root. In a city where jobs were plentiful and the common belief of 'if it ain't broke, don't try and fix it,' coupled with the old system of retaining favour with the bosses, meant any agitators could be kept firmly in their place. Then, if all else failed, the authorities could simply use the marines to bring meetings to an abrupt end.

Joff followed his new-found friend out into the night air where he approached a group of men in the shadows and tried to hand them pamphlets.

One of the men thrust the piece of paper back at him.

"We ain't interested!" he declared with a scowl.

"Do you even know what it's about?" Davie challenged him.

"Get out of my way!" He pushed Davie in the chest and in a split second the fight had followed them outside.

Davie took a couple of serious punches. He got one to his left cheek and another straight behind the first, smack in the centre of his stomach. Joff practically saw the air whoosh out of him at that one. Now they were pinning his arms back and he was about to take a beating with a very sturdy-looking cosh. Joff dived on top of the man wielding the cosh, kicking out at the two holding Davie down as his would-be rescuer sailed through the air. Joff took a rabbit punch from behind and pain shot through his kidneys. Someone who knew where to aim had caught him just right. A sharp searing pain raced through his whole body and he spun around, lashing out at the source of the punch. He connected with a decent right hook and as he did so another whack caught him across the cheek. Davie managed to break free from his captors. He ran, head down, into one of the men who was raining punches on Joff and they both fell to the floor. Joff had the feeling that more men were joining in the fight, caught a glimpse of somebody diving through the air out of the corner of his eye. But a cosh came flying at him from the other side. He never even had time to look up before it hit him. That was the last thing he remembered.

Joff came to his senses and knew without opening his eyes that it was daytime. Light was playing behind his eyes. He lay still, pretending that he was still asleep or unconscious or whatever. Just pretending, buying time. He could definitely feel the rolling motion of a boat. Somewhere not too distant a seagull was calling. He was on board a vessel and it was daylight. He lay still and listened for the sound of any movement that might reveal if he was alone or not.

Listening intently, he detected the unmistakable sound of wind in a sail. It seemed as though they were making good speed. But around him, within the cabin he guessed he must be in, he heard nothing. He figured he was alone and so risked a very slow opening of his eyes.

"Captain, Captain, 'e wakes, 'e wakes!"

Joff was just in time to see a small boy disappear through the cabin door. It slammed shut behind him and Joff heard his bare feet slapping the wooden boards as his skinny little legs took him swiftly away.

"'E wakes! 'E wakes!" he called.

His shouts faded then stopped and Joff groaned slightly. He rubbed his head gingerly and felt two lumps barely contained beneath his hair. His head was throbbing and he was in no condition to attempt any form of escape. But he wasn't restrained in any way so he guessed things could have been worse. He slumped back and awaited the arrival of whatever fate had in store for him.

It wasn't long before Joff heard footsteps coming closer. The cabin door was flung open and a pair of muscle-bound sailors squeezed their considerable frames into the small space, just about allowing enough room for the man Joff assumed to be their captain, to stand between them, blocking the entrance.

"'You're awake!" he observed in what Joff thought sounded like a foreign accent.

It wasn't really a question so by way of reply he simply smiled sheepishly.

He stood there waiting for an answer.

"I'll be fine," Joff said.

Of course he wanted to know where he was, but decided that the captain was asking the questions at this stage, not him.

"Think you can walk?" he asked.

Joff nodded.

"Come on then." He turned on his heel, his sailors following at his back. With Joff's head pounding, he brought up the rear.

On deck, sitting at the starboard rail, was Joff's new pal Davie. Joff was rather surprised to see him; surprised but pleased, and it must have shown on his face.

"Are you feelin' a bit better?" he asked, smirking.

Joff wasn't but nodded anyway.

"Thanks for jumpin' in like that," he smirked before adding, "you're a terrible fighter, though. It was lucky for you that my friends came along when they did."

Joff realised he should offer his thanks so he did so now. He didn't want to start offending anyone.

"I don't really remember what happened, but thanks, thanks a lot," he said.

Joff scanned around to include them all, even the skinny little boy, watching intently from behind the main mast. "Thanks a lot, I really mean it."

Smiles were out in abundance. These were tough men who probably enjoyed the scrap and they seemed satisfied that their guest was suitably grateful.

"Why are we at sea?" Joff asked, rather bravely he thought.

"Well once we 'ad gone to the trouble o' draggin' you away from those 'eathens, it didn't seem too wise to leave you for 'em to finish off. So we decided to bring you with us. We can always get you ashore if you wanna go back to Plymouth, though."

"No," Joff replied rather too hastily. "No thanks. Plymouth wasn't quite what I was expectin'."

The waves were sparkling and deep blue as they flashed all around. "I'd much rather be out here."

"Always good to be at sea, eh boy!" said the heavily tanned face at the helm.

Joff nodded in complete agreement and went to sit next to Davie.

"So where are we headed?" he asked Davie.

"Is Joe your real name?" Davie replied quietly.

Joff could stick to the story and keep pretending to be Joe Penrose, or he could come clean. He shook his head. He felt the time was right to put some trust in Davie. If he had intended Joff harm it would have already happened.

"My name's Joff, Joff Owens," he exclaimed.

Davie looked him up and down. "Not Joe anymore then." He laughed a little and looked around the crew. "Are you sure now?" he asked again, amusement overshadowing his sarcasm.

"Look, my real name's Joff alright, I lied 'cause I got no end o' trouble following me around an' I didn't wanna take no chances, so I said I was Joe." He shrugged.

"Alright easy, I'm only playin'." He held up his palms in mock surrender.

"Anyway Joe's a good name, maybe it suits you!"

Joff shrugged and nodded.

"So where are you from, Joe?" he wanted to know next.

"Penzance," Joff replied sheepishly.

"An' what's your livelihood, Joe?" his questions were delivered with a smile.

"I'm a piano player." Now it was Joff's turn to smile at him.

Joff's initial thought on waking was that he was being press-ganged into the royal Navy, so it was kind of a relief to be in the situation he now found himself. Things, at this precise moment, could very easily be a whole lot worse. He decided that his problems with the Squire probably wouldn't seem too serious when compared with whatever this crew were up to, so he decided to come clean.

Davie was smiling at him still. "A piano player?" he said and sat back patiently waiting for Joff to elaborate.

Joff liked Davie, trusted him even. He had no friends in the world right now and these men had saved him. He wanted to be honest with them.

"Hey Tin, you 'ear that? We got ourselves a piano player!" Davie said loudly whilst Joff dithered.

They all stared at him anew and he smiled sheepishly.

The captain looked directly at him. "Well I never!" he said, laughing, and the sound was deep and good natured.

"Well that's good boy, cos you can't 'ave a revolution without music, can yer, lads?"

The crew laughed along as they changed tack. Joff watched them pulling in the heavy ropes with ease. Their laughter was good for his soul and he felt like he was amongst friends for the first time since Betsy had been his friend.

Joff had spent enough time listening to his pa and gramps, so he knew these men were obviously Chartists, agitators, trouble makers in the eyes of the Crown. Yet he felt like he belonged. So what if they were prepared to bring down England? Maybe it needed bringing down.

"But my pa he was a free-trader an' well 'e taught me my way around our little patch o' coast, you know," Joff said as their laughs slowly faded in the wind.

They were interested in that as well; a hush had fallen over them.

"What did you say your family name was?" asked one of the men before him.

"Owens," he replied. "The Owens of Penzance."

"What's the name o' your Squire?" the captain instantly wanted to know.

"Bradshaw," he muttered, "Squire Bradshaw."

He told them how Betsy had died and how the Squire had set them up because of his pa's political leanings. He thought they would appreciate that. He told how he had made his way across Cornwall to Plymouth. Not mentioning that he had cried himself to sleep on the wilds of Bodmin moor, wishing Betsy had still been alive and things had turned out differently. Finally he got to ending up in the wrong place, at the wrong time, in the wrong town just as the marines had started the brawl and the next thing he remembered he was waking up aboard their vessel.

They listened in silence and when he had finished they retreated to the stern, leaving just the boy on the helm, ignoring Joff as he steered them into the starlit night. Joff slumped down on a sail and watched the stars sparkling above. The thought of food grew stronger and stronger as the rumbling of his stomach grew louder. He reminded himself they hadn't run him through with cold steel and dumped him over the side, and it helped to think of his hunger as a small victory, as proof he was still alive.

He could hear snippets of conversation. Sometimes he imagined that Dutch was the language being spoken, sometimes bad English. And always the vessel cut through the waves at a rate of knots. Wherever they were heading they were making good speed. The boy changed tack and each wave they crashed through caused them to shudder a little more than the last. They were heading into deeper water, out to sea. To France, or Holland perhaps, or God alone knew where. Joff didn't care because it felt so good just to be back at sea.

Eventually Davie returned and sat beside Joff.

"They'll be bringin' us some food shortly," he said, "I expect you're a bit hungry by now."

The understatement was of immense proportions. Joff managed a smile at his weak humour, though. Davie flopped down onto his back beside his new friend and they watched the stars pass by as they waited.

Shortly the smell of cooking wafted across them.

Finally, Joff was given a bowl of fresh fish broth that smelled like heaven. He accepted gratefully and tucked in, beaming. Nothing tastes better than a fish fresh out of the sea whilst still aboard the boat it was caught on.

Between mouthfuls they spoke in hushed tones.

The language they spoke was not foreign as Joff had presumed. They were in fact as English as he was, but they were from deep in the Black Country. Their heavy midlands accents were interspersed with a healthy dose of colloquial slang. They might as well have been speaking in a foreign tongue.

These men were Chartist rebels through and through, members of Brian's first ever nationwide political movement for the poor. They firmly believed that the world was fast dividing into the oppressed and the oppressors, lords and serfs, haves and have nots. So dire did they consider the situation to be, they could no longer do nothing. They believed the proletariat had nothing to lose but their chains and they were prepared to match authority's overuse of aggression with a little aggression of their own.

They were five in number, followers of the Frenchman Pierre-Joseph Proudhon. Their leader, Tin, used to be known as 'Captain,' but that was not always sensible when they were ashore in some of the unsavoury ports where they called. So they had begun referring to him as 'Tin' when on dry land, then the name had followed him aboard a few years ago and now he was Tin, on dry land and at sea. Behind him, huddled into a corner of the stern, trying to keep away from the salty sprays that kept splashing over the side, was Benn. Benn was six feet of pure muscle. He still felt bitter at the treatment his father suffered when he had dared attempt go on strike and as a result had been hounded to death. Benn carried this resentment with him as a source of strength. Had done so ever since he was a young boy, through his teenage bare knuckle boxing championship years back home in the Midlands, and now into young middle age. Ever since he could remember he had seethed with injustices both real and imagined, and he desperately wanted to change the world.

Tila, the other muscle man, stood mid-deck seemingly oblivious to the salty shower he was enduring the brunt of. Using Tila's huge frame as cover was the fourth crew member, Davie. Finally there was the boy Bobby. Joff watched him tucking into his meal.

Since announcing to the world that he was awake Joff hadn't heard the boy utter a single word, but his eyes were everywhere at once, and Joff got the distinct impression that he missed very little.

"We buyin' 'is story?" Benn asked, not bothering to lower his voice.

Tila scowled and shrugged, "'E certainly ain't like no government spy that I ever seen before."

They looked towards Tin for his opinion on the matter.

"'E ain't no spy, an' he seems to be tellin' the truth. That Squire an' all, sounded all too true to me."

"So what we goin' to do with 'im now?" Benn wanted to know.

Back in Devonport they had all noticed the scruffy young stranger as someone who had potentially come to spy on the agitators. Once the fighting had started, however, it was blindingly obvious Joff was being branded as a stranger in town, being lumped in with them. On the spur of the moment they had decided to take him with them and if they didn't like his story it would have been a simple matter to dispose of his body out on the waves. But there were always unexpected consequences in these situations and this time it was that they all believed him. That he was, like them, someone operating outside the law. They felt his injustice, understood things that most men didn't readily grasp. It was highly plausible that he was too young to realise the Squire had been using him and now that he was starting to show a little enterprise, a bit of initiative, the Squire had done what form would expect. He had framed the troublemaker and more or less banished him from the kingdom. These men had been fighting such injustice their whole lives. They knew only too well how heavily the odds were stacked against the ordinary man when power and money combined to destroy him. Yet somehow the boy before them had escaped from the Squire's kingdom and had crossed the border into Devon.

Tin nodded towards Benn. "Let's 'ear 'is story again," he said.

"Tell us again about this Squire Bradshaw," said the captain.

So Joff repeated his story and this time they listened straight-faced and appeared much more sympathetic.

"Seems to me like you do all the work an' the bloody Squire gets all the profit, is 'ow it seems," Benn offered up by way of opinion.

Joff looked at him with shock written large across his face. It was incredulous, "That's exactly what Pa used to say an' they all said that was crazy, an' we 'ad no idea 'ow much work men like the Squire do on our behalf an'—"

Tin interrupted his flow. "We don't think you're crazy." He looked around the motley crew before continuing, "We think there is wisdom in such words."

Joff felt his cheeks blush red; such praise, such praise indeed. These were real men of the world. They knew things, had seen things that, in his eyes, gave their words far more credence than the locals in his sleepy little home town. He was told he should respect adults regardless of the fact they all seemed incapable of verbalising anything of any meaning. These men were different, unafraid to hold and explain opinions that Joff had secretly wondered about but had never heard uttered aloud. Their conclusions made far more sense than some of the explanations he had been asked to swallow over the years.

Joff couldn't take in enough. He wanted to know everything. As night became day he greedily devoured their anecdotes and stories. Tried to memorise every name, every detail.

"What's 'moral force'?" he wanted to know, rudely interrupting in his enthusiasm.

Tin stopped mid-sentence and glanced across at him. They had only just met and Joff knew nothing about the man except he was his superior. Of that there was no question yet Joff couldn't help himself. Rudely butting in again and again. He was behaving in exactly the same way that had earned him countless reprimands over the years, yet Tin and these men were different. They didn't take offence at being disrespected. Tin smiled paternally and patiently explained it to him. The way one would make allowances for a small child.

"It's the opposite of 'physical force,'" he said. "You know what that is, don't you?"

Joff paused momentarily, mentally making sure it wasn't a trick question. "Of course," he replied.

"So what is it?" he asked patiently.

"It's when you fight to decide who wins an argument," he announced, fairly sure that he was correct.

"That's right," Tin declared, smiling. "An' 'moral force' is when you just try an' persuade someone to do the right thing, just because it is the right thing to do."

Joff must have frowned. "That don't sound like it would work too well," he declared doubtfully.

Broad grins broke out, even little Bobby was in on the joke. They glanced around at each other, clearly sharing some private moment.

"It don't!" Davie said, shaking his head in exasperation as he spoke.

It had been no more than a passing remark. An insignificant comment, slipped into the overall conversation. A phrase given no extra importance or afforded no special meaning, yet when accompanied by the knowing glances that came with it, one that spoke volumes.

If Joff had been more experienced he might have seen it for what it was. A declaration, an admission almost, that these men were determined to create change and had long ago lost any confidence or faith they might have once harboured for the use of 'moral force.' They had decided that 'physical force' was the way to get things done. That was how one achieved one's aims in their opinion. But at the time Joff had been too caught up in the moment to read such signs. He would get better at reading body language.

"Do you know what the 'Reform Act' is then?" Tin asked him next.

He shook his head. He could vaguely recall hearing his grandpa mention such a thing. He doubted that they had it in Cornwall.

Tin rose from his seat and grabbed the rail firmly with both hands, his eyes sparkling with the belief one might see in a preacher convinced he was doing the Lord's work.

"Are you not aware that last year in parliament, they discussed the right to vote for all men? Imagine votin' on 'oo gets to represent us in the 'ouse of Parliament?"

Joff shook his head and pursed his lips. Surely he was talking nonsense. Where Joff came from, the Squire was their representative in London and when he died his son would take on the huge responsibility.

"I think that may just be a London thing," he ventured. "I don't think we 'ave such things down in Cornwall."

Tin smiled triumphantly at this, letting go the rail with one hand and spinning his body to face the newcomer. He wagged his long finger and said, "But you do, my boy, you do. All Cornish men, those men who pour through the gates at the dockyard in Plymouth every mornin' come rain or come shine. You should all," he corrected himself. "We all should have such rights!"

"We should?" Joff asked doubtfully. It seemed highly unlikely. He wondered who would represent them if they chose not to vote for their squire.

"They should indeed." Tin looked mightily pleased to be the one divulging this information. Joff's brain went into overdrive as he tried to digest issues of such magnitude.

"But that would mean the workin' men would 'ave a say in 'ow things is done," Joff ventured doubtfully. Certain he was missing some important part of the equation. Yet they were all nodding enthusiastically once again. A circle of smiling faces that seemed to be confirming the truth of the words exactly as he had understood them. It still seemed too incredible to be true.

"Nah," Joff said with confidence. "That can't be right!"

Tin really did have the look of a preacher in the pulpit now. "It's true, my lad, an' you better believe it. One day soon all men, not just landed gentry, but all men, even those 'oo work on the land, will all have the right to vote." His eyes were shining brightly again. He turned to face Joff directly and added with such passion, such belief, such confidence in his own assertions, that the boy never doubted its inevitability for a second.

"In a secret ballot!"

The words hung in the air like magic. All Joff's life he had been surrounded by folk who would never even dare to imagine that things could improve for the good of all, with the consent of all. Yet here was a man not only prepared to put such thoughts into compelling words, it was abundantly obvious he actually believed that it was inevitable.

They talked for many more hours and for the first time Joff felt alive, truly alive. Here he was at the age of 15 just starting out on the journey of life and he was at sea amongst men who not only understood how he felt, they felt the same way, knew how to articulate those strong feelings, and were not afraid to do so.

This was nothing like the small community he had known. This was more like the stories he'd heard about from his pa and the smugglers of Europe. Where men were rising up and taking control of their own destinies, where politics and fairness mattered. Not a place like Cornwall where everybody was too afraid to speak their minds for fear of upsetting the Squire. That place already seemed a world away, one that he was leaving further behind with every slap of the sea on the hull.

They were cutting through the dark water at a steady pace, when finally the words dried up and they were all left to ponder. For the first time in hours Joff registered the sound of the wind in the sails again and realised they had been talking all day and all night.

Bobby was dangling a line over the side. Expertly, with no fuss, he was reeling in mackerel and placing them in a wooden bowl. Soon he had sufficient fish to feed all of them. Joff watched as Bobby scampered below decks and before Joff had time to take in the return of the stars the other boy was back with a large wooden chopping board and a very sharp-looking knife. Joff watched, his stomach rumbling, as Bobby gutted the fish and threw the heads, tails, and entrails over the side. The conversation started up again as everyone waited.

"I was wonderin'," Joff ventured. "Where do you learn so much?"

Tin smiled easily. "London," he replied. "The only place in the whole of Europe these days where men can learn about the world." He looked at Joff with an unreadable expression. Somewhere between concern and envy. "London is where it all 'appens, son."

The very word, the very name of the place held such promise. It was the capital of the greatest empire ever known to mankind. It was where the Queen herself resided and apparently it was where someone such as Joff could go to learn the ways of the world. He could see that now. It was the place where ideas fused and working men had a voice to be heard.

"It's also a place where a man can easily come to harm," added Tila rather darkly.

Joff ignored him. What did he know? London was a place of excitement, not danger. Joff felt certain of that much. He would find work at the piano in one of the swanky hotels and a year from now he would be the talk of the town.

Silence settled again as the moon peeked through the clouds.

"An' where are we headed?" Joff wanted to know.

"St. Katharine Docks," came the answer.

"Where's that again?" Joff asked.

"London," Tin answered, smiling. He looked across at Joff. "Is that acceptable to you?"

Joff grinned enthusiastically. "Oh yes," he answered. "That's just fine by me."

Excitement coursed through his very veins. He hadn't thought London was the place for him back in Cawsand, but now, three days later, he had changed his mind.

"An' in London men talk openly of anything they wish to discuss, anything at all?" Joff asked, still not quite believing it, still finding such a world hard to imagine.

"They do," Tin said. "They do where we're goin'."

"I want to play at the top concert hall in the whole of London!" Joff announced. "An' you can all come hear me play!"

Joff scanned their faces. Benn and Tila stared back at him, Bobby ignored him completely.

"You might get work right enough but it won't be in one o' them places," Tin said.

"That's fine by me!" Joff declared, so pleased with such stunningly good luck that he completely missed any undercurrents.

Squire Bradshaw stood in the stable frowning as he brushed the sweat from his horse's flanks.

"Go on!" he hissed without turning around.

Behind him in the shadows a figure shuffled and then said, "That's it Squire. It was 'im. It was definitely 'im, at a meetin' in Devonport but nobody seen 'ide nor 'air of the boy since. I expect 'e's 'eading 'ome, hopin' to find an accomplice!"

"Do you now?"

"Yes, Sir, I do."

"Well I want him found." Now he stopped brushing the horse and turned around. "Found! Do you hear me?!"

"Yes, Sir!" came the only reply that ever comes during such conversations, right throughout the pages of history.

ST. KATHARINE DOCKS, LONDON, 1842

Twenty-four hours later the boat was thudding up against a wooden jetty in the noisiest place Joff had ever seen in his whole life. Veterans from the recent war in Afghanistan sat on the docks with stumps where their legs should have been. People of all colours, shapes, and sizes were everywhere your eyes rested. An indescribable variety of items were being offered for sale.

"London is what happens when free market capitalism has no constraints," Tin muttered.

Joff didn't have a clue what he meant but it was certainly the busiest place he had ever seen.

Alien smells assaulted his nostrils before he had even stepped ashore. He glanced across at Tila, and catching Joff's eye he nodded slightly. Joff smiled back nervously. Perhaps he had been too hasty to dismiss his warnings, and perhaps he was correct to be vigilant for danger.

They tied up nonchalantly to a metal ladder that ran down the side of the thick stone wall. The tide was low and the rusty old ladder went up and up, past the seaweed mark and up some more. Bobby was scampering ashore before the knot was tied. Tila and Benn quickly followed behind him.

"Go on, Joe!" Tin gave him a little shove.

Joff had no idea what to expect at the top but every fibre within him told him that his destiny lay at the top of this ladder. He tentatively grasped the rail and up he went with his heart racing. He felt it shudder behind him as Tin started climbing and Joff quickened his pace.

First he saw hundreds of pairs of hob-nailed boots, then tough-looking men all moving about purposefully, many of them shouldering crates or boxes or wheeling carts. As Joff stepped onto dry land he shivered as though somebody had just stood on his grave. He crossed himself whilst trying to take everything in.

This was the self-same dock to which men from Penzance, men like his pa, had been brought. When the authorities began clamping down on the free trade they soon realised no court in Cornwall would ever find their own guilty. So they had dragged men all the way to London to ensure the verdicts that the authorities hoped for were returned. Tin caught Joff's melancholy demeanour.

"Come on, Boy," he hissed, "No time for regrets now!"

"I'm fine!" Joff half smiled at him, and shaking off the sadness, hurried to keep up.

Although Joff was in London for the first time, the place felt as though it knew him well. In all directions he caught glimpses in the crowds that looked all too familiar—the back of a head or the cut of a jacket, and then they were gone amongst the melee. This was a city of two million souls.

Joff was used to living in a place where he knew everyone around him, where strangers were thin on the ground. His mind was trying to adapt to what was normal, that was all. Still, once he thought he had seen a certain person it was enough to get him thinking about them. Very quickly ghosts awaited him around every corner; long buried memories came flooding back with every step.

Joff caught a glimpse of a white dress that looked very familiar, but it disappeared into the crowd before he could be sure.

"Betsy!" he gasped.

"What?" Tin looked at him, slightly concerned.

"Nothin'," Joff said, making the briefest eye contact possible.

Perhaps there had been a mistake? He wanted that to be true but he remembered the funeral as though it were yesterday. There was no tricking himself out of that one.

As he walked, his surroundings seemed to fade, the voices grew fainter.

Of course he thought of her. He remembered the day that Betsy had worn her new white dress. She had twirled in the doorway as the sun had shone through it.

"You are so beautiful!" he had said, meaning it, and totally transfixed by her movements.

She had giggled coyly, averting her eyes. "You!" she had replied.

"You are!" he said.

Their eyes had locked across the room and his love for her had never been so strong.

They had both felt it. He had seen it burning fiercely in her eyes and they both knew it. Words would have cheapened the moment; nobody in the history of the world was ever in love like they were.

She had gone out in her new white dress to pick flowers in the churchyard. It had been a glorious summer day and the poppies, the irises, the cornflowers were growing in abundance between the headstones.

During the midday heat she had rested and fallen asleep behind the stones. He remembered her telling him how she had woken as the sun had been falling from the sky behind her. She had stretched and stood up, at which point her peace had been rudely shattered by a scream and a cry of "GHOST! RUN!"

A small boy pointed at her before turning and fleeing for all he was worth, two other lads right behind him. She had shouted after them, called out that they were mistaken as they had disappeared at a rate of knots. She admitted their high-pitched screams had easily drowned out her attempts to placate them.

How they had laughed when she had told him the story.

Before him now three small boys ran through the crowd.

Joff had called her his beautiful ghost that day, not realising that within a year she would be gone. He would give anything to have his beautiful ghost back to haunt small boys in churchyards.

"Joe! Joe!"

Joff felt a tug at his sleeve.

Those carefree days seemed long ago. He was "Joe the travelling vagabond" now. In a place he did not know. He would have to keep alert.

Tin was frowning down at him. "Stay alert, Joe!" he hissed.

"Sorry," Joff replied sheepishly.

On board he had listened to every word spoken by Tin and the crew and he knew they were totally committed to the cause. Knew they thought he felt the same way. He couldn't tell them yet that he didn't really want to get too involved. To help in the struggle to bring justice to the long-suffering downtrodden was fine, commendable even, but it wasn't for him. He had to take care of his hands.

He was downtrodden. He had suffered a terrible injustice, and it stung that he had been such an easy victim. But he couldn't go around fighting people, not if he wanted to play music.

They approached a huge, firmly-closed iron gate with an armed sentry standing in front of it. Tin headed straight towards him and to Joff's amazement the sentry opened a smaller wicket gate within the main one, and they were through. Joff heard it clang shut behind them, but he didn't turn back.

Outside the gate the crowds were even thicker. All around was a hive of activity. He had never seen so many people gathered together. A man was running alongside Joff calling a name over and over.

"Patch!" he called. "Patch!"

He looked Joff up and down and tugged at his sleeve in a frantic manner. "'Ave you seen my dog? Patch 'e's called."

Joff shook him off and replied in an unhelpful tone, "No, no I 'aven't!"

Joff quickened his pace, determined not to lose his friends. He was being accosted from all sides, all manner of things were being thrust in front of him for closer inspection, trying to delay his hurried step. Whispers and shouts came at him from the shadows.

"Fish, Mister! Want some fresh fish?" and a crate of rank strips he wouldn't feed a cat were thrust before him.

Tin led them to a wide road with tall buildings running up both sides. Carts, carriages, and horses were everywhere. The noise was turned up a notch, as were the bad smells.

"Girls?" muttered a shady youth loitering at the next turn. He was far less demanding than the fish traders, more sure of himself, almost certain he would be earning some money before the night was through.

All about Joff, goods fresh off the boats, were piled high, being offered for sale. Everything had a price, it seemed. The first in a chain, each a little higher, each allowing a modest profit to those whose paths it crossed.

Tin spat on the ground. "The worker's sweat is fueling an insatiable hunger for all this new rubbish."

He lashed out at a boy who tried to thrust something before him. "Keep that junk away from me!" he screamed.

The boy backed off.

The depression of the 30's was over. New shiny possessions were a possibility again. No regard was given to how briefly you wished to own a particular item before the desire faded out of existence and the treasure became worthless junk. An insane lust for ownership seemed to block out all logic or reason. Joff looked around himself in wonder at the vast quantities of crates full of things that had travelled thousands of miles, brought here from all corners of the globe. Goods destined to be unloaded as quickly as possible before being hurriedly conveyed to the west of the city. To be sold in the newly opened shops along the magnificently sweeping curve of Regents Street, or the slightly less grand Oxford Street.

The trail of commerce led from these very docks to the West End, to north London, and beyond. Landed gentry scattered the length and breadth of the country wanted the latest must-have gadgets as soon as was humanly possible without having to go and get them. They were the masters of the universe, leaders of the greatest system ever devised by man. Their reign would last forever and they wanted all the trappings the world could offer. Their factories and estates made money so rapidly that price was never an object. The prestige, the jealousy it provoked, that was the objective here.

However, goods had to first pass through the docks, through the filth and the squalor. Incredibly large numbers of people so poor they couldn't afford to feed their children were seeing all this magnificence with their own eyes. It was hardly surprising that things went missing and that people were beginning to harbour a sense of injustice. Envy and radicalism were growing amongst the discontent down here on the dock side.

"Make no mistake, Joe my boy, these are excitin' times!" Davie declared.

Joff beamed at him, the place felt so alive, so exhilarating. How could he not be right?

"Here," Tin said, raising his voice to be heard above the general hullabaloo. "Revolutionaries from all corners of the globe are here right now!"

Joff beamed along with them. He'd heard it all on the boat.

This little part of Europe was the one place where ideas could be exchanged and aired without fear of persecution. Charles Dickens, Edgar Allen Poe, and many other great thinkers, orators, philanthropists, and radicals. Men full of new and exciting possibilities to go with the new age, met right here. Joff felt an incredible sense of belonging. This was the world centre of free thinking. This was the place on the map that mattered more than any other. He was going to be the best piano player in the whole damn place. All accepted that here was a place where one could dream and that was his dream.

Slightly ahead of them he saw Bobby duck into a doorway. Tin slowed the pace but kept moving and they followed the boy into a coffee shop.

Tin went to the counter whilst the others joined Bobby at a table near the back of the room. Joff looked around him. The place held about twenty or thirty people, with room for the same number again. Joff couldn't help noticing that the vast majority of the patrons were men and not a single one looked up as they entered. He glanced over at Benn and Tila. They were also going out of their way not to catch the eye of anyone, including him. Joff sat down and studied his feet until suddenly Tin was pushing him along the bench, squeezing in beside him, and opposite him a stranger was sliding in alongside Tila.

A girl brought them a tray of drinks and Joff noticed the stranger nod towards her, although silence was maintained until they were alone.

"'Oo's this, then?" The stranger asked as soon as she had gone.

"This is Joe!" Tin told him and the man looked Joff up and down.

"Joe, eh?" he asked.

Joff nodded and averted his eyes.

He sat quietly as they whispered, their heads almost touching across the table.

After a while the stranger turned to Joff and asked, "So do you like London, Joe?"

"I think I'm goin' to," he replied.

"Well you've come at the right time!" the stranger declared.

He took a mouthful of coffee and Joff looked down again, thinking the conversation was over.

He was wrong. The man leaned towards him and said, "Do you follow a religion, Joe? Do you pre-suppose the superiority of one group over another?"

Joff shrugged and looked down. He already knew that fanatics tended to raise their favourite topics and supply their own answers.

"Well?" he pressed.

"No!" Joff said meekly. "No I don't."

"Are you here to trade, Joe?"

"I have no money in my pockets," Joff replied, looking up at him.

The man smiled and his long dark hair fell over his face.

"Here men without money in their pockets can trade. They can trade ideas and theorise on what might or might not be for the best. They can gather in coffee houses and on street corners and they can trade ideas," he said, "openly!"

Tila leaned forward and said, "Don't just see the trappings of wealth." He looked at Joff, full of seriousness. "That is what they see. You must look beyond the wealth!"

The stranger jumped in with his thoughts. "The recession is not over, boy, employment is not easy to come by. These men, they come like you, fresh from the rural counties an' marvel at what the empire offers to the chosen few. But now, after they have seen with their own eyes how ordinary these chosen men really are, these masters of the universe, they can't help but wonder aloud, 'Why you and not me?'"

He answered his own question. "'God chose me!' will come the inevitable reply!"

He stared at Joff for a moment, then spat out. "God chose 'em. Are you 'appy with that answer, Boy?"

Joff shrugged.

"Yeah." He was looking right through Joff now, "neither am I."

Joff said nothing.

The man continued, "Once here they meet with other intelligent men. Well educated men from as far afield as Russia and the Germanic regions who can help them see things differently. They discovered something the ruling classes have always understood. There is power in large groups of like-minded individuals."

They all banged their tankards in agreement and Joff marvelled again at how these people knew so much.

As the noise died down Tin leaned across the table and whispered to his crew, "'E ain't 'ere. 'E's gone across the city."

Joff was smiling at the stranger now, liking him. The man ignored Joff, who then looked around the room. Whoever they were talking about, it certainly didn't concern him.

Shortly they said their goodbyes and Joff followed the crew out into the night.

They walked past the large, imposing perimeter wall of the dockyard and up a slight incline. The famous Tower of London became visible to their left. At the top of the hill Tin peeled slightly to the west and Joff took one final glance at the solid-looking Tower before catching them. He was very conscious of not lagging behind. He did not know his way around and could easily, like a dog called Patch, get swallowed up and lost in the crowd.

They walked for an hour and the houses that they passed amazed Joff. He had never seen such detail, such scale, such contrast.

"'Ere we are," Tin finally announced, "Charlotte Street!" and he knocked on a solid, black door half way down the street.

It opened almost immediately and a man sporting a marvellously thick, jet-black moustache thrust his face out aggressively.

"Si?" he said.

"Quiermos, Oswaldo?" Tin replied, and the man opened the door further, allowing them all to enter.

They climbed a narrow wooden staircase to the top of the house and into a room with a slanting window.

Their host said something in a language Joff didn't understand and Tin nodded. Then he left them.

Joff crossed the room to the little window and looked out. Below, the lights of the houses seemed to go on forever. He felt real excitement coursing through his veins. He had no idea what was going on but it didn't matter. He was just glad to be here and content to leave everything to Tin. That was why he was the captain. Joff stared out through the dirty glass. He had never seen so many lights, so many houses. It explained why there were so many people.

"Joe! Joe!"

His name was being called so he turned around. Benn, Tila, and Davie were already stretched out on the floor with their heavy coats pulled over their bodies. Bobby was curled up behind the door. Tin, the only one still standing, was standing by the door still wearing his coat.

"Lay down," he said. "Get some sleep. We got a big day tomorro'."

"I ain't tired!" Joff declared.

He smiled at Joff, at his adoption of the word 'ain't.'

"Oh ain't yer now?" he put extra emphasis on the word, mocking him playfully. He had a soft spot for him and Joff knew it.

"Where are you goin'?" Joff asked. "Can't I come? You won't even know I'm there!"

He glanced around the room; the other four appeared to be asleep already.

"I ain't ever been to London," Joff said. "I'm too excited to sleep!"

"I'm only goin' round the corner," he said.

Joff took that as permission to come. He stood and moved towards him, towards the door.

"You won't even know I'm there!" Joff repeated and Tin's smile said Joff was coming with him.

Tin had meant it when he had said they weren't going far. They turned right within fifty yards at the very first junction they came to. They continued for a few hundred yards and he knocked on a big blue door. This time they stood and waited. After a few minutes Joff heard footsteps and a door being opened, but he was mistaken, it wasn't for them. It was the matching, neighbouring door to their right. A man in a top hat exited in a hurry, and ignoring them completely, headed up the street. A woman came out onto the step and briefly watched his departing figure. Then she turned, stared at the two of them momentarily, and went quietly back inside. Tin smiled at Joff and rapped harder on the door knocker.

This time it was opened and Tin was immediately wrapped up in a bear hug with a giant of a man. Tin was a big fellow but this man lifted him easily off his feet and fairly squashed the breath out of him.

They were whisked inside; more moustachioed men dressed in white shirts and black waistcoats flooded the narrow hallway. A vodka bottle appeared and was passed around and Joff found himself shaking hands and being introduced to a lot of men with foreign sounding names that he knew he would never remember. After a few glasses of the powerful spirit, his head was buzzing and he was feeling fine as they were led upstairs to a bigger room. In the corner there was a brand new stand-up piano.

Joff couldn't take his eyes off it. He was itching to run his fingers across the keys. He couldn't remember when he had last gone so long without playing. He looked around the room and they were all surrounding Tin and slapping each other playfully. Nobody was paying him any attention. His eyes fell back on the piano.

Joff stood there for a moment, his gaze darting between the piano and the boisterous group before him. Finally he could take it no more. Surely nobody would object if he just sat on the stool. Still, nobody was paying him any attention, so what harm could it do to open the lid and just hit that middle C, just to see if the ol' girl was in tune or not.

He glanced up and saw that one of the men was in a headlock and they were all crowding round him trying to slap his head, while he squirmed and kicked and tried to break free.

Joff hit the middle C and glanced across again. The man in the headlock had broken free but he was writhing on the floor now, kicking out as they were all raucously jumping about the room to avoid his flailing legs. They looked as though they were having a lovely time. Joff lifted the lid halfway and hit the middle C again. It sounded perfectly pitched and he couldn't help himself. He opened the lid fully and began to play.

Tin's long lost friends were mainly Italian. By midnight Joff had learned several Italian swear words and was so drunk he was reduced to belting out the popular Cornish drinking songs. They loved it, they screamed the harmonies back at him, some in English, some in their own tongue, and the raucous rivalry grew ever more boisterous.

By dawn they were all the best of friends and blind drunk. Joff thought he fell asleep at the piano, and he definitely woke up on the floor. As he woke, rubbing his eyes, he did that split second thing of not having a clue where he was. Then the floodgates opened and it all came back to him.

Joff lifted himself up on one elbow in order to survey the room. The first thing he set eyes on was Tin sitting by the door, smoking a cigarette, and half smiling at him.

"Mornin'," he said.

Joff propped himself up and grinned at him, although his head was humping and his stomach rumbling.

"Mornin'," he replied.

"Are you ready?" he asked.

"Ready for what?" Joff wanted to know.

"We got a go across the city." Tin looked into Joff's eyes more seriously now. "I got a message to deliver."

They were alone in the room. Evidently their hosts had retired to sleeping quarters elsewhere in the house. There seemed no shortage of space in such a large property.

Joff shrugged. "I'm ready," he declared.

"Good lad, let's go!" he replied.

Out on the pavement Joff stepped backwards into the middle of the street and looked up. The building they had just come out of was four stories high, as were the neighboring properties and those in the street behind. Never had so much brickwork and timber towered over him, so many dwellings so closely packed together. Greyness surrounded him on all sides. He scanned left and then right. There were no trees, no greenery at all, in any direction. He could barely believe his eyes; he had never before experienced such a thing. Last night when they had been walking through the streets he had just assumed that there were fields and trees on the edge of the darkness. It was amazing that man would build so many houses, so closely packed together.

He turned to look towards Tin, who stood with his hands thrust into the pockets of his shabby pantaloons.

"I ain't never seen so many buildings!" Joff said to him.

He smirked, "London's a big ol' place!" he replied.

Joff nodded. "So where are we?" he asked. "I mean, what street is this?"

He smirked again and starting walking, Joff following in his wake. "This is Cleveland Street," he said over his shoulder.

They were turning left as he spoke and Joff repeated the name, just to feel it on his tongue.

"Cleveland Street!" he repeated as they turned left again.

"Yeah, and this is Charlotte Street." Tin glanced back at him, then stopped, allowing his little friend to catch up. "Remember them names, 'cos in this little slum on the edge of Fitzroy Square, we got a lot of friends!"

Tin moved forward and within a few more paces was climbing a front step and knocking once again on the door of the house they had gone to first last night. It was that close. Joff stood on the bottom step, repeating the words 'Charlotte' and 'Cleveland' over and over so he would be sure to remember them.

The others were awake, waiting for them. "Where've you been?" Benn wanted to know.

"With the Italians," Tin said. "An' they 'ad a piano in there." He took a step back and threw an arm around Joff's shoulders. "You should a 'eard 'im. The boy can play a bit, I can assure you!"

Joff stood there smiling sheepishly. For some reason he felt a little smug having what he'd told them confirmed.

"Did you speak to Oswaldo?" Tila wanted to know.

"'E's moved, gone over to the East End. They said there's a meetin' in Whitechapel he'll be at. We can go look for 'im there."

"What, now?" Benn asked.

Tin nodded and they rose as one and soon they were moving again, through a series of streets that all began to look the same after a while. Joff kept up, repeating the words 'Charlotte' and 'Cleveland' quietly to himself.

* * *

Joff had heard the stories, but they had all, each and every one, neglected to mention that walking through the streets of the East End, of Aldgate, Spitalfields, and Whitechapel was more akin to a stroll in a pig farm than a walk around the capital of the Empire. Mud and filth were everywhere. At first Joff tried to step around it but very soon realised he was wasting his time. Every single person they passed was thick with mud up to the ankle and some beyond that. Clearly this was an inevitable consequence of walking in this area. Fortunately his clothes were not particularly clean to begin with and growing up in the countryside had prepared him well for those situations in life when filth was accompanied by that old familiar stench, fresh manure.

All around him men, women, and children were going about their daily business. All in their own way adding to the noise and unhealthy odours, adding countless more layers to the multi-challenging, and ever-changing hub of humanity that was their capital.

Tin walked with a purpose to his stride, the gait of someone familiar in his surroundings whilst also moving too fast to allow any of the beggars time to approach or engage him. Tila and Benn were formidable looking enough to deter all but the most determined troublemaker, and Joff took the lead set by Davie and Bobby. They kept their eyes fixed on no one and they kept moving. It was darker in the East End than the streets they had passed through to get here. The sun didn't seem to penetrate down in the same way. The streets were narrower and at ground level the buildings seemed to be in permanent darkness. Ragged people kept materialising through gloomy fog on all sides before quickly fading away.

All around shadowy figures tracked their progress in a way that would have unnerved Joff had he not got such suitable companions. People in rags were everywhere he looked. He had the impression that their every step was being monitored. He would never have thought it possible that such an atmosphere of hopelessness and menace could exist here in the heart of England's fabulously wealthy capital city.

Finally Tin ducked around a pile of rotting vegetation and into a dark alleyway. The others followed close behind him. Within a few yards they walked out into a public square where gas lamps lit a feeble trail to a large wooden hall at the far end. Paths and alleys on all sides were bringing men together. They were all heading towards the hall from all over the square. Once again they quickly became part of a throbbing, bustling crowd. Became a collection of individuals from whom a combined sense of purpose, of pride, seemed to fill the very air around them. Joff had barely a split second to register the sight and savour it before he was getting condensed closer and closer to his fellow man. Joff jostled a little to make sure he fell in directly behind Tin. Their little group instinctively bunched together as they were swallowed up by the whole and the sense of power he had seen was no longer to be admired from a distance; he was in the thick of it, was part of it, and could feel it flowing through him until he was almost giddy with the strength of it.

"See!" Davies' face was full of pride. He shouted to make sure his words reached Joff across even such a small distance.

"See what the workers have in their grasp, Joe! Power! Real power!"

Joff beamed at Davie as the crowd carried them forward, towards the great hall and then into it. As soon as they crossed the threshold the excited chatter became louder, bouncing back at them off the walls and ceiling. By sheer coincidence Joff was at his very first meeting of the International Working Men's Association. At that precise moment there was nowhere on Earth he would rather be. He stared in awe at the stage. It had been decorated with huge flags representing the unity felt by working men everywhere. All internal squabbling had been put to one side. The time had come for change, and the flags indicated that men all over the world had got the message. Joff filled with pride, although he had no idea why. Centre stage the American Stars and Stripes hung proudly. Workers from the US had travelled in large numbers. In 1842 they were the undisputed pioneers and the powerhouse behind the concept of workers having 'rights.'

Beneath the flags a handful of men sat in a row shuffling papers and glancing about them in the manner of people waiting for something to begin.

As though on cue a small hammer was banged on a table to get everyone's attention.

"'Ere we go," Tin observed. Instantly the volume dimmed, excitement filled the room to bursting, and on the stage an elderly man rose to his feet.

Joff listened transfixed as speakers rose, one after another, to describe the world as they saw it.

"We want to turn ideas into actions!" shouted one hot-headed man not much older than Joff was himself. Joff was mightily impressed at his commitment, his confidence.

His speech ended to the sound of thunderous applause and hearty shouts of agreement. Then the crowd fell silent in anticipation of hearing the final speaker of the day and what he had to say.

Joff was amazed; it was William Lovett, he was about to hear the man speak for the third time, only this time Joff was ready to receive his ideas.

"Tomorrow," he began, "we shall present to Parliament for a second time. As you all know they rejected the first Charter despite it containing over one and a quarter million names." He used his hands to quell the hisses and boo's that inevitably started up. "Gentlemen, I can inform you that tomorrow we shall be presenting another list of disgruntled citizens." He paused for dramatic effect. "This time we have over three million signatures!" He raised his voice over the cheers. "One third of the adult population of England, Scotland, and Wales have signed. It truly is an outstanding achievement!"

By now the crowd was going wild.

Never had Joff witnessed such enthusiasm for a speech, such passion. The words Lovett was speaking mattered deeply to each and every man in the hall. Hell, they mattered to him now.

Joff felt a tug at his shoulder and, still clapping for all he was worth, turned his head.

"You see, Joe. The world is changin', things are gonna get better!" Tin was also clapping with all his might. Joff actually dared to believe it.

Outside they fell into conversation with a group of Whitechapel men whom Tin and the others seemed to know.

"So you're a piano player?" one man repeated incredulously, eyeing Joff up and down. "I don't fink I ain't never met a piano player before!"

He was dressed in the heavy, black overcoat of the dockworker. Hobnailed boots peeked from beneath his frayed trousers.

"We've got a piano back at our local." He threw his giant arm over Joff's shoulders and continued, "Why don't you boys come wiv us?" he declared.

So they all walked the short distance to a public house and without too much ceremony Joff sat and played. He started off with a few tunes that were popular in the Sloop back home and very quickly moved into 'entertainer' mode.

"Are you gonna take the offer from las' night?" Tin asked as Joff's fingers flew across the keys.

"What offer?" he shouted up at him without missing a note.

"Las' night? The Italians?"

Joff shrugged mid-song, having no idea what he was talking about.

"They said they could get you a deal in number 19 Cleveland Street," he smirked. "Still don't recall?"

Joff shook his head.

"They said they could get you a live-in gig there 'til you can get yourself sorted, an' you told them you was goin' to be a big star in the theatre an' didn't need their 'elp!"

Joff cringed inwardly. "Do you think I missed me chance?" he asked.

Tin laughed at his young friend. "Naw," he said.

"What 'appens at number 19?" Joff asked him as he broke into the opening bars of *The Rose of Allendale*.

Tin laughed again. "Finish up, let's go sort you out. Besides it's much nicer over that side o' town!"

Joff played three more tunes and they then set out for the hour's march back across London.

* * *

The next day the 'People's Charter' was paraded through the streets of London. It was a giant scroll containing three and a half million signatures and needing three carts to transport it on. It was accompanied all the way from the East End to the palace of Westminster by marching bands and crowds of well-wishers numbering into tens of thousands of people. It was the biggest parade, the most important day in London since anyone could remember. Unfortunately Joff missed the whole thing. He was being shown his new sleeping quarters in the attic space of 19 Cleveland Street.

"This is your room," Emile told him, showing him the grubby little space at the very top of the house.

Joff ignored the room and looked through the little window down on the street below. He took in the countless grey rooftops of London and beamed and thanked his lucky stars.

He moved closer to the glass, scraping his head on the slanting ceiling as he did so.

"Alright is it?" Emile asked.

"It seems perfect," Joff told him, rubbing his head and inspecting his hand for blood.

He smiled warmly. "Good," he said. "You will be sharing it with two pot boys. You will be playing every lunch time between eleven and three and every evening from six o'clock until all our guests 'ave left the premises, whenever that might be." He smiled again. "Alright?" he repeated.

Joff hadn't even been in the big city for twenty-four hours and already he had work and a place to sleep.

"Alright by me," he said.

It soon became apparent that number 19 was far from a respectable establishment. Debauchery and carnal desires of all persuasions were catered to there. The rich and famous mixed with East End postal boys. Relationships between consenting adults were formed that would have been impossible in wider society, sometimes for money, other times for pure, good old-fashioned lust. The public would have been absolutely horrified if they had known even half of what was going on behind the closed door. Joff played the piano and kept his opinions to himself.

* * *

As the 1840s progressed the authorities in Britain became increasingly concerned with the revolutionary upheaval sweeping through mainland Europe. As always, this concern manifested itself in heavy-handed crackdowns. Each year the police came down harder and harder on known agitators, their associates, and the places in which they gathered.

For Tin, danger was a constant companion. He insisted on careful planning and varied routes for every little journey. By the end of the decade each one of them visually swept every street they stepped onto. Taking in all the occupants at a glance, trusting their instincts as to whether any might present a threat.

Assessing people surreptitiously became second nature.

Tin made sure they were all aware, one day someone would surely be sent to bring them down.

The People's Charter was again rejected by Parliament.

1849

Squire Bradshaw felt he had invested a lot of money in finding that damn boy over the past few years and he wasn't satisfied with the return he was getting on his capital.

"How can you not have found him yet?" He stared at the two men sitting opposite him. "You said he left Plymouth with a known group of rebels and that you would have him as soon as they docked. You assured me that nothing would go wrong." He was glaring more than staring now. "That was seven years ago!" His temper got the better of him at this point. "SEVEN YEARS! And nothing!" He sat back a little, trying hard to compose himself, then he hit them with his latest idea.

"I want you, both of you, to get into the backstreets, the courtyards, and search again. Do what you must, just find him!" His face was deep red. Not trusting his voice, he dismissed them with a wave of his arm.

* * *

Joff followed Tin and the crew through Spitalfields and across Commercial Street. Davie had fallen foul of the law but the rest of the old gang was still together. They moved towards Whitechapel weaving in and out of the slow-moving carriages and carts.

Since Joff had arrived in London seven years previously, the population had doubled. Rents were now four times higher. Wages, though, hadn't increased at all and families were being forced into smaller and smaller living conditions. Flats had become rooms that became shares of rooms and in seven short years sewage and sanitation facilities in Whitechapel that were designed to take care of fifty thousand people now provided for two hundred thousand. Inevitably infrastructure and people began to break down.

Meanwhile every day more descended on London looking for work. Most were quickly spat out east of the city walls.

The East End was no easy place to find yourself when the chips were down. Many seethed with resentment and injustice and they found the Working Men's Association. Membership numbers swelled as rural men from all over Britain, survivors of the vicious Afghan War, and politically ambitious individuals from all corners of Europe and the Empire, found the roads to the Association's door. A sense of grave injustice deep in your heart felt the same in any language.

Joff was still in his Cleveland Street residency and earning extra cash writing tunes. It worked rather well. He penned the tunes and gave them to Benn, who was now overseeing a printing press. He produced thousands that were sold in the streets and the pubs. Joff would then play the same songs each evening to a good old sing along.

"Joe, are you comin'?"

"I'm comin'!" he called.

They were across Commercial Street and back in Whitechapel.

"Oi Mister, where yous lot goin' in such an 'urry?" a scruffy urchin wanted to know.

Benn glared at him and he slunk back into the shadows.

Very quickly they were back in the hall where Joff had attended his very first political meeting all those years ago. The flags had been replaced by banners now, though. The red flag of the Socialists was taking centre stage where not so many years ago Joff remembered it had been the Stars and Stripes.

Joff was the guest entertainer today and took his seat at the piano.

"'Ere, Tin, what do you think o' this?"

Joff slammed out the opening bars of *The Ratcatcher's Daughter* and Tin grinned at him over the piano.

"Very nice, very nice." Tin was a real music fan.

"Good job. You are on form today," Benn offered up. "See that old fella on the stage?" He pointed and Joff followed his finger with his eyes. "Second from the left," he added helpfully.

Before them, centre stage, seven men sat in a row behind a long wooden table.

"Him with the beard?" Joff asked.

"That's Karl Marx hisself," Benn said, and Joff looked with more interest at the famous figure.

"'E don't look all that special does 'e?" Joff ventured.

"That remains to be seen." Benn had raised his voice to be heard above the crowds beginning to pour into the hall.

"Play somefink!" a steward called.

It was time to go to work. As the hall filled Joff played and when the speakers were ready to begin he stayed in his seat and listened with total concentration, like everyone else.

"The Tories and the Whigs see us as a threat to their cosy little arrangement. Pretending to debate but just holdin' hands under the table and..." He spoke for a few more minutes then paused. Looking out across the hard-working, lowly-paid mob before him, he screamed at the top of his voice, "One man one vote! One man one vote!" And the cry went up with great enthusiasm.

Joff wanted to know who this firebrand was, but trying to conduct a conversation under such conditions was pointless. He had come to know most of the regulars at these halls but had never set eyes on this man before. He liked his style.

Finally the meeting was brought to a close and the men on the stage all rose. Realising Joff was not about to hear Marx speak, he contented himself with playing for all he was worth as they filed down the steps to the side, through a curtain, and disappeared back stage. Loud applause persisted until they had all gone completely from view. They clapped a little more until gradually the crescendo of hands slowly abated and all around him men began to file out through the doors.

Tin and the crew didn't seem in any great hurry, so neither was Joff. They hung back as the great hall rapidly emptied. Only then, with a bit more elbow room, a bit more breathing space, did Tin lead them out into the night. Joff happily followed along, dreaming about taking the same rights these men talked about back down to the West Country with him. Dreamed of standing up to Squire Bradshaw and making him realise that he could no longer treat them as dogs and get rich off the backs of their labour. Oh, to be alive at such a momentous period in history. He had to literally stop himself from bursting into song. The world was changing and he was right in the epicentre.

Tin led them through the narrow streets. Poverty surrounded them on all sides. It wasn't just the shabby figures that watched through dead eyes as they passed. It was the actual buildings, the streets themselves.

Ingrained dirt coated every single surface; the stench of filth had been allowed to accumulate over a long period of time. It assaulted their nostrils at every step. They sort of got used to it, but they never really got used to it.

Open sewers ran parallel to the pavement, broken pipes distributing as much effluence over the street as they transported to the evil-smelling river. Joff might have lived in a slum near Fitzroy Square, but it was nowhere near as bad as the East End.

Joff was glad when Tin finally led them into a tavern where the smell was bearable and they could eat, drink, and finally discuss the meeting. Joff was desperate to hear their opinions.

The tavern was busy but Tin led them towards an empty table near the back of the room. They passed through groups of men speaking a variety of languages. A few nodded greetings towards them, and the flag of the International Working Men's Club hung behind the bar. It would seem as though they were amongst friends there. Joff slid in beside Tila on the bench and they waited for the serving girl to make her way to them. Tin opened the conversation, and Joff listened as ideas were exchanged and observations made whilst they waited for their drinks.

"The Reform Act will double the size of the electorate, 'e said."

Tila seemed to think this was a good thing. "The Tories ain't goin' to get things their own way no longer!" he agreed enthusiastically.

"Maybe, maybe not," Tin replied.

"Liberals, Tories, it's like being offered a donkey or a cart when what you really want is a horse," Benn said, and they all nodded in agreement.

"If they don't pass the Act then I say we blow up Parliament!" Tila hissed.

He was high on euphoria but they all knew he was at least fifty percent serious.

"Ssshh." Tin glanced about the room, although there really was no need. Each group there was hatching its own plots. They were far too busy to listen in on another group's plans.

"Never mind that," he continued, trying to veer the conversation away from explosives. "We 'ave got to sort out this smell. Revolutions all over Europe and we can't even sort out the bleedin' drains."

"Yeah, but look at the French." Tila was passionate in the way he interjected. "They didn't mess about. I say we blow up Parliament an' hang the bleedin' lot of 'em!"

"What do you think?" Tin asked Joff, who leaned forward before speaking softly.

"I think the Communists are wrong. I think a man deserves to benefit from his own labour, not work for master or state."

"Exactly!" Tila raised his voice.

"Society is a giant lie! We are a collection of individuals! Why should they make such a livin' through loans and rents from those that can ill afford it?" He motioned with his arms to indicate how things were beyond the pub walls.

"Takin' advantage of those that must work themselves into early graves. Why should we break our backs for someone whose income relies on the misery of his fellow man? Let's string 'em up and face the future head on!"

Joff listened to him droning on about how he planned to inflict misery and suffering where it was most deserved. Joff had heard it all before. He re-focused his attention slightly over Tila's left shoulder. To all intents and purposes he was listening, hanging on every word, but in reality he had noticed a flash of colour behind him.

It was the swirl of a long, deep-purple skirt. He glanced up into the face of an angel, the most beautiful girl he had ever set eyes on, and his heart was doing somersaults, his face was turning bright crimson, and an emotional thunderbolt shot to pieces everything he thought he held dear.

Joff was instantly, hopelessly, totally in love.

"Bobby," Tin spoke across him, breaking his line of sight. "Go get some more drinks!"

"I'll go!" Joff announced, and was up like a shot.

So engrossed in conversation were they that they all missed it when he didn't head towards the bar. He veered right of the serving area, towards where his angel was running a cloth over a table.

She looked up when he was still approaching, looked directly at him for the very first time, and he thought his heart was going to burst. So intent was he on her that his foot caught the leg of a chair. He stumbled slightly and she laughed, and fireworks exploded in his head and he knew, beyond doubt, this was the girl he was going to marry.

"Hello," he said, leaning on the table, trying to look nonchalant.

She stared him straight in the eye and smiled, and her beauty took his breath away.

"Hello," she replied.

"I'm Joff," he told her.

"Manda," she said, casting her eyes bashfully downwards, and he wanted to gather her in his arms and protect her forever more.

"Such a beautiful name," he said, meaning it sincerely.

Her eyes were the deepest shade of green he had ever seen in his life. He could barely take it in. She spoke again.

"Thank you," she said. "What's your name 'd'ya say?"

"Joff," he repeated.

That's so unusual. I've never heard it before."

"It's Cornish," he somehow managed to get the words out. "I'm Cornish!"

"Oh," she replied.

He looked up to see she was smiling, and he loved her all the more.

She glanced across towards his associates.

"Are you a rebel, Joff from Cornwall?"

"No!" to his horror his voice squeaked. "I'm a piano player!"

"Oh really." She raised an eyebrow.

Manda was from Ireland. She had come to London three months before when the potato harvest had failed again and quite simply she had the choice of leave or starve. Her family were all dead and this job was a vast improvement over her previous employment of stripping chicken carcasses.

Joff listened to her speak as waves of desire washed over him. The only Irish he had ever heard were the hard-drinking Fenians. Her accent was so soft in comparison. It was a pleasure to listen to and it was rather a rude awakening when he felt someone tugging at his sleeve.

"Joe! Drinks?"

He had taken so long that Bobby had come to find out what was keeping him.

"Oh yeah, sorry," he mumbled.

But Bobby was no longer paying attention; Joff was forgotten as Bobby looked Manda up and down, grinning at her in what he considered a rude, unwelcome manner.

"Alright, you can go sit down. I've got it all under control here," Joff told his friend.

Bobby grinned wickedly, doffing his cap towards her, and Joff pushed him a little.

"Nice to make your acquaintance, miss," he said around Joff, who did his utmost to block his view of the girl of his dreams.

"Yeah, yeah," Joff said with bravado, terrified Bobby was going to mess this up for him. "You go sit down, that's it."

Joff guided him in the general direction of their table, returning his attention to Manda as quickly as he could.

"Sorry about him," he offered, hoping his face hadn't turned red.

"That's alright, I understand." She smiled and said, "Joe!" She had him now.

"They call me that but it ain't my real name!" Joff protested.

"You're a mysterious man," she said in her beautiful, sing-song Irish lilt, and he was transported instantly to a place where he could finally leave Betsy in the past, to a future where all his wildest dreams could come true.

"Manda!" called a voice from the bar.

"I'm working for the moment," she said, glancing around to check the position of her boss.

"Can I see you after you finish?" Joff blurted out.

He simply had to see her again. It suddenly dawned on him that she might say 'no' and if she did he wasn't sure life would be bearable.

The worry was short-lived.

"I'd like that," she said.

To Joff it sounded as though she sang the words.

"I finish at mid-night," she added.

Joff felt as though he floated to the bar and then floated back to join his friends.

The conversation was still in deadly earnest, the way the working man was being treated was still deplorable, conditions in places of work were still disgusting, but it didn't bother him like it had ten minutes before. He couldn't feel strongly about life in the rookeries or the gruelling conditions on the docks right now. He couldn't think that way because he was head over heels, desperately, totally, absolutely in love. All he could concentrate on was her hair, her eyes, her smile, meeting her at midnight. Joff felt that his mind was no longer his own; it had been hijacked, he was a prisoner to do some other person's bidding and he could not have been happier.

"Joe! Joe!"

He heard his name and snapped back to reality.

"Yeah, sorry, I missed that. What did ya say?" He looked from one face to the next; they were all grinning back at him.

What?" he demanded. "What is it?"

"Who was that?" Benn asked.

Benn draped one of his giant bear paws across Joff's forearm and flashed his gold-toothed smile at him. Tin slapped Joff playfully across the back of his neck whilst announcing for all to hear, "He's been hit by the thunderbolt!"

They started banging their tankards on the table and laughing.

Joff didn't care. For the first time since Betsy he was in love and no amount of teasing was going to alter the fact that she had agreed to meet him.

They milked the moment for all it was worth and he let them have their fun. He sat back, a giant smile stretching from ear to ear, revelling in the chance encounter he felt sure was going to change his whole life.

Finally the noise died down. Tila caught Joff's eye and said, "Here's to ya Joe. She's a beautiful girl an' no mistake!"

Benn threw his big arm around Joff again, squeezing the breath out of him. "Yeah, we're only playin'. We're really proud o' you, you know," He paused and added, "At last, eh!" He followed his words with loud, booming laughter.

It was playful, affectionate banter. Joff could tell they were pleased for him, really.

The conversation eventually turned back to the main subject.

"The time is right for the working man to rise and put an end to the capitalist bourgeoisie," Benn declared solemnly.

Joff knew he truly believed they could make a difference. Felt as though the premise that 'all men were created equal' was finally being allowed room to breathe.

Between them these men had spent many long nights telling him why failure was not an option, slowly convincing him change was inevitable.

Obviously he welcomed this better world, but now he had met the girl of his dreams. Romance trumped politics in his mind.

"I'm off," he announced at the next lull in the conversation.

"Where you goin'?" Tin asked, and Joff glanced towards Manda.

Tin smiled as his young friend rose from his seat.

"Be careful!" Tin warned.

"Always!" he replied over his shoulder.

Weaving through the tables, he headed for the door. He paused on the threshold and scanned outside. Even at night places like this were usually teeming with urchins playing their games, old men hanging about, unfortunates passing by. So where were they all?

Joff moved on high alert, crossing the open ground and ducking into the first cover that presented itself. He stood with his back to an old, tatty door and listened. Almost immediately the distinct sound of boots on the ground was definitely approaching. He tried the door handle, praying that it would open. It did and just in time. He slipped into a courtyard as a block of policemen appeared from the left. There was barely time to shut the door. Heart pounding, he managed to pull it closed as more boots crunched across the ground beyond. They were trying to be quiet but in the now abandoned streets they were all Joff could hear. It registered that his heart was beating frantically, and then he heard the whistles.

All attempts at stealth were abandoned and on the other side of the door they started running. He could hear them racing through the alleys as fast as it was possible to do so.

Whistles and shouts of "Police!" soon became intermingled with the opposing shouts that inevitably followed.

Joff panicked and fled west, towards Cleveland Street. But as he put distance between himself and the pandemonium, his panic subsided. Soon all he could think about was his date with Manda. He slowed his pace to a jog, then a walk. Soon he stopped and turned back.

As he walked he formulated a plan. He decided to be bold. He would stroll up nonchalantly, and if they asked he would say that he was just passing.

As he entered the square he began to have second thoughts. Police were everywhere, stopping everyone.

"Oi you!" a voice said, and a giant of a man in the blue cape of the metropolitan police stepped in front of Joff while others moved to box him in.

"Where you goin'?" he demanded to know.

"Jus' goin' 'ome officer," he said respectfully.

He looked Joff up and down, 'Ome from where?"

"Work, Sir, I'm the piano player at the Savoy!" he lied.

"An' you live round 'ere?"

"Yes, Sir!" he said, lying again.

They seemed to be deciding if he could possibly be telling the truth when shouting started from inside the hall.

"Go on, then," the officer snapped, stepping aside for him, and with his heart pounding he headed closer to Manda's place of work.

"Oi! where you goin'?" The same officer called after him.

He stopped and turned back to face him.

"I thought I might 'ave a quick one officer, you know, after an 'ard night's work."

"That place is closed tonight," he said. "Now move along wiv yer!"

The police were swarming all around. Joff had pushed his luck far enough; it was time to leave. He turned around and headed towards Cleveland Street. Where, much to my surprise, Tin was already waiting. Benn and Tila turned up shortly after, but Bobby was never seen again.

Joff returned to the East End, to the bar, night and day for the next three days, to no avail, until finally, on the fourth day he walked in the place and there she was. His eyes fell on her straight away and he couldn't stop himself racing forward and lifting her off the ground.

"You're safe! I can't believe it!"

He blurted out how scared he'd been, how worried, how he never wanted to lose sight of her again.

"You mean it?" she asked, a shadow of a smile on her beautiful, pink lips.

"I do, I do, every word!"

They stood there in the middle of the busy bar, clutching each other tightly. She had felt it too. They were soulmates who had found each other against all the odds. They were destined to be together and they both knew it.

1860

Joff's musical talents were very much in demand. He was flitting all over the East End from music hall to music hall. The sing-along was now an integral part of a good night out. New venues were springing up from Hoxton to Bethnal Green. The most unlikely of taverns were getting in pianos to keep abreast of their competitors. It was a real boom time in the music industry. So much time spent tickling the ivories ensured that he was at the top of his game.

A fortnight at the Shoreditch Empire, a month in Hackney, six weeks over Christmas, and the New Year at Wilton's music hall down near the docks.

He would get a pound a week and all he could drink during shows. After a long, exhausting day he was usually so hammered that he didn't want to travel all the way back to Cleveland Street every night. He had gradually lost touch with Tin and the others. Sometimes he slept backstage wherever he could find a space to lay his head, with or without permission of the theatre owners. He liked the theatre when everyone had gone and he was left alone.

1860 turned into 1861, the cold winter passed into spring, and one day he walked into a pub in Whitechapel. As he approached the bar, he heard somebody shout, "Hey if it ain't the piano man!"

Joff looked up and there was Tin as large as life. He smiled and called him across.

Gladly, Joff went to join him.

"'Aven't seen you for a while," Joff said as he lowered himself into the chair.

"Ain't bin around much!" Tin replied. "Livin' up west now!"

"Oh really, that's nice!" he smiled, taking his first sip of the day.

"Still in Cleveland Street are yer?" Joff asked.

"There and Soho!" came the reply.

"That where the action is these days?" the pianist asked.

"You still like a drink then," he said, ignoring Joff's question and glancing at the clock over the bar.

"I'm a musician!" he said. "It's a rule that if we're awake an' we ain't playin' we gotta be drinkin', you know that!" Joff smirked at his old friend while raising his tankard.

Then they were off, laughing and drinking and ribbing each other without mercy.

It turned into an epic lunchtime drinking session that ran well into the evening.

"I gotta go," Joff managed at last. "I'm on in an hour!"

Much laughter followed that comment.

"You can't go to work, look at the state o' you!"

"I'll be fine," he managed, and started heading to the door.

"See you!" Joff called over his shoulder.

"Drop in an' say 'hello' next time you're up west," Tin called to him as he staggered out the door and up the street.

"Yeah I might just do that!" Joff replied.

Tin was spending more time in Soho now, mixing with a new generation of activists. It had been over ten years since the original Soho roundup and now it was safe for those of a bohemian persuasion to return to the part of the Capital in which their forerunners had resided. French and Italian radicals in particular were arriving in London almost by the day. They had all heard of Soho, of Cleveland Street and Charlotte Street, from their fathers and grandfathers, and they all headed there. It was becoming a society within a society.

The area held fond memories for Joff and he was glad of any excuse to go back.

One night a week later he happened to be playing at a little dive in Frith Street, Soho. It was only a ten-minute walk to Cleveland Street. When he finished he decided to stop off and say 'hello' to Tin.

It was well past midnight as he entered Cleveland Street but the pavements were still busy. Little clusters of foreign-looking men, most with a preference for thick, bushy moustaches, were conversing in hushed tones every few yards, it seemed. Joff recognised none of them so avoided eye contact as he passed through them, heading to number nineteen, where he soon spotted Tin standing at the front step smoking a cigarette. As Joff drew closer he spotted some men sitting on the step talking with him. His friends saw him approaching first and a look of suspicion passed across their faces. Tin immediately spun around to see who they were looking at. His eyes fell on Joff, who smirked at him in return.

"Joe my boy," he called loudly. "'Ow is it? Been ticklin' them ivories?"

He gestured with a flourish towards the three men sitting on the steps, "Emile, Raul, and Patrick, may I introduce my good friend Joe!" He leaned closer to them and added, "We go way back." He tapped his nose conspiratorially, "To the old days!"

Joff walked down the line and shook all their hands, each nodded at him in the Mediterranean manner of greeting as they shook.

"So is he with us? Raul asked Tin as though Joff wasn't present.

"'E's a Libertarian," Tin said. "An' a piano player."

"A piano player, eh?" the central figure said to Joff pleasantly enough. He was slightly more interesting now.

Joff raised his eyebrows and nodded.

"Where do you play? The music halls?" Raul was curious.

Joff nodded, then trying to be friendly, asked "Do you play?"

The man seemed flattered, "Well you know, a little," he admitted.

His friends broke into fits of laughter.

"Better you play for us?" Emile said and Joff shrugged.

"Of course, I'd be glad too," he replied.

Do we 'ave time for music?" Patrick asked, frowning.

"There is always time for music, an' dancin'," Tin decreed.

"You cannot 'ave a revolution without music!" Emile added.

The mere mention of the word 'revolution' caused the very atmosphere around them to change, to grow serious.

"Did you hear there's a revolution started in America?" Patrick asked Joff in perfect English.

"Yes," he said. "Was it a revolution or a civil war?" He didn't want to contradict the other man outright.

"So in London even the piano players keep abreast of current affairs!" He smiled slightly and Joff knew he was accepted.

"Perhaps the workers in America will benefit in the long run," Joff offered up hopefully.

Someone down the street coughed as Patrick shook his head.

"Those poor people are doomed." He looked so sad. "Their whole lives controlled by the vested interests of a small handful of Presbyterians." He spat on the floor before adding, "And they don't even know it. That government controls the natural riches of half a continent yet their own people are starving." He spat again then said, "It's disgusting!"

Joff should have known he would have strong opinions.

"Americans can never be free under that constitution." Patrick glared at him now, the smile seeming a long time ago. "Do you know why?" he demanded.

"Well," Joff mumbled. "Er…, no, not really. Why?"

"That constitution can only ever strengthen the grip of authority. Who knows what the future has in store for those poor souls."

At this point a constable came around the corner and the conversation died. Patrick glared at him as he approached. The officer made a point of slowing his pace to imply that he wasn't intimidated, but he kept moving. He was fooling nobody. Joff avoided eye contact anyway.

"Imperial lackey!" Patrick muttered as he passed, loudly enough for the policeman to hear. Others were glaring at him from positions on both sides all the way down the street. It was going to be a long walk for him.

Joff smirked but kept his head bowed. He missed the sudden bouts of tension. You never knew what was just around the corner, in this case literally. It was nice to be back.

Joff's musical engagement in Soho was a two-week run so it was no problem for him to pop in and say 'hello' the next night and the next.

Within a few days he realised that things were far from the same as before. These men were second-generation radicals. They had taken William Lovett's Charter and adapted it to suit the needs of the new urban workforce. They had a large captive audience at St. Katharine Docks and many willing ears scattered throughout the metropolis. This time they would not be satisfied with handing over a list of demands. They had plans, big plans, and they expected to be listened to.

Joff kept his mouth shut, played their favourite tunes, and they got very drunk together. He was making new friends, foreign friends, and despite the propaganda about dirty foreigners, they were getting on like the proverbial house on fire.

On the surface they were hard-drinking bohemians, seeking out thrills and debauchery, but behind the facade they were working hard, creating a manifesto to rival the one of Marx. They all hoped events would culminate in violent revolution.

Some of the members, the French in particular, had plenty of first-hand experience of the treatment they could expect if the ruling elite got wind of their plans before they were ready.

The commanding officer for Soho, Chief Inspector Melville, had, against every rule in the book, allowed the French force to operate covertly right in the heart of London. The area was swarming with undercover French police these days, all running up huge expenses for the French taxpayer while keeping tabs on their fellow countrymen. Watching Leon run his grocery shop and seeing who came and went from the comfort of surrounding restaurants. They and the metropolitan police were doing all they could to blacken the perceived threats in any manner possible. If they got wind of actual plans those efforts would be doubled.

Instead of a strong public launch the members would be forced to start the campaign by defending themselves over petty, trivial, irrelevant matters.

As long as the establishment controlled the newspapers they could always make life difficult. With such a formidable weapon, the propaganda war would be a sure-fire victory for them. Surprise was one of the few elements the rebels had and they were determined to make the most of it.

Then in January '63 came an unexpected piece of luck.

The International Working Men's Association called a public meeting to show support for the uprising in Poland. After all, the workers there needed all the help they could get and the organisation did claim to be international.

Despite very public opposition to any reform from the Prime Minister, Lord Palmerston, the government, anxious not to appear draconian, granted official sanction for the meeting.

After years of forced secrecy this truly felt like a momentous breakthrough.

Like-minded men all over the capital were daring to take heart. Further meetings were arranged throughout the summer. From Soho to Whitechapel and back to Cleveland Hall, many were inspired to turn words into actions.

Joff was back playing in Wilton's Music Hall that summer of '63, so he missed most of the meetings. The management began to hold all-day charity concerts on the day of political meetings. It raised funds but they still sold plenty of drinks and Joff still got paid. After work one day he had arranged to meet Tin at the White Hart on Whitechapel High Street.

Joff spotted his old friend immediately, slouching on a stool at the bar.

"You should o' been there, Joe," he slurred as he saw him.

"It went well then?" Joff asked with a smile.

"You should o' seen it," he drunkenly rephrased his original statement before adding "flags from all corners o' the world flying together."

Joff was next to him now and Tin gripped his arm and thrust his face closer. Brandy fumes assaulted his nostrils as he exhaled, "Workers from everywhere." He shook Joff's arm and pulled himself closer, "Working together, joining forces." He rose to his feet, stood in the centre of the room, wobbled slightly, and then delivered his overriding observation.

"Workers United!" He wiped his lips and smiled more broadly. "What do yer think o' that, eh?"

"It's brilliant, Tin!" Joff raised his glass and repeated, "Brilliant!"

"We're nearly there, my boy, nearly there!" he slurred.

CHAPTER EIGHT

Eighteen sixty-three turned into sixty-four.

Clandestine meetings regarding the ways of the world were still occurring regularly for those with the most to lose, in a variety of rooms, both public and private, right across London.

In Soho they didn't care so much.

Societies that were only recently secret were now all out in the open and gathering pace relentlessly.

In Whitechapel they were even more blatant. The Freedom Press was openly churning out an impressive amount of literature and an army of men, women, and children were distributing it all over London. Something big was happening and everyone, on both sides of the divide, knew it. You could feel the winds of change in the air.

Joff was back in the East End. It had been a hard, cold winter and he had been lucky to get a residency spot at the brand new Hoxton Hall where it was easier to doss in the derelict houses of Whitechapel than traipse through the snow all the way back across town every night. Nobody thought his behaviour suspicious or wondered why he was there one day and gone the next. He was just the piano player. He was either playing or he was drinking somewhere. They all knew that, and most importantly they knew he could be relied on to keep any secrets he might pick up.

Then late in the summer of '64 he was playing at the Hall to a particularly boozy crowd. A soloist was belting out the latest hit, "Any, Any, Any, Any, Any ol', any ol' iron!"

Joff was at the piano watching closely, waiting for his cue to the key change, when he caught something moving in the corner of his eye. He swivelled his head to make sure it wasn't a glass flying through the air, and who did he find standing at the end of the front row, frantically waving a bright red scarf, looking every bit the revolutionary? None other than his old mucker Tin. Joff nodded at him and glanced back to the soloist just in time for the key change.

Joff hadn't seen Tin for a while and it would be good to catch up. Also it was warm in the hall that evening and he could use a cool, refreshing drink. He caught the singer's eye. "One more, Stan, and take a break," he mouthed at him.

Stan winked at him to show he had heard, and then turned forwards to face the crowd, "One two, one two three four!"

Stan was in and Joff's fingers flew across the piano keys. Sweat was pouring off the pianist's brow and the damn singer was stopping and starting for all he was worth. They held it together and finished with a flourish, and everyone cheered and clapped as Joff made his way down from the stage.

Tin grabbed his hand and pumped for all he was worth. They smiled at each other and years of history flashed between them. When you had been in as many scrapes together, over as many years as they had, words were not always necessary. Their paths might not have crossed for a while, but they were still connected, still watched each other's back until they should meet again.

The old friends clasped each other and smiled again, and then Tin looked down. It was the smallest of eye movements, barely noticeable amongst so much noise and clamour, but Joff caught it and knew well that something was wrong. Joff dragged Tin by the shoulder towards the exit and out through the swing doors into the foyer, where there were a few people milling about, but at least they could talk.

"How are yer?" Joff asked.

Tin looked up at him; he knew something in his body language had given him away. He cleared his throat as though about to speak, looked Joff in the eye again, smiled, and shook his head. "Don't you worry about me," he said. "Come on let's 'ave a quick drink!"

"A quick drink? Why a quick one?" Joff asked, and they both knew Joff wasn't letting him off the hook that easily.

"'Cos you gotta get back for the second 'alf, don't ya?"

Whatever it was he wasn't telling, Joff let it rest. "Come on then, you're buyin'!" Joff punched his friend playfully in the kidneys and the man fell against the swinging door.

Tin ordered a couple of whiskeys and they stood at the bar smoking and drinking while all around them men poured alcohol down their throats as quickly as they could.

"Still livin' up Soho?" Joff asked, raising his voice to carry the short distance to Tin's ear.

"Yeah sort of. You know," he replied.

Joff knew all right. It was hard to settle with the authorities constantly on your back.

"All changin' now tho', in'nit?" the younger man said.

Radicals, Socialists, Communists, Anarchists even, were allowed to meet these days, to gather legitimately.

He nodded, "It's all changin' an' we are gettin' new ideas, fresh ideas from all over." He moved his head closer and lowered his tone, although the chances of being overheard were minimal at best.

"We have solidarity with workers all over the world. This is an international movement now an' nobody can stop us. The emancipation of the workers is coming!"

Joff listened as Tin outlined the ideas they were putting in place. Then listened some more as his friend ridiculed the manifesto Karl Marx was working on and which he would soon be making public. Joff realised there was a race of sorts taking place between the two camps. As Tin spoke his old passionate style of delivery returned. Perhaps Joff had misread the earlier signs; there was nothing wrong with him. He just looked the way he did because of the life he was leading.

All too soon the manager's large bulk was filling the doorframe.

"Joe!" he called, signalling Joff to return.

Joff drained his glass, studying Tin as he did so, waiting for him to look at him. His gaze stayed firmly fixed on his feet.

"I'm headed back inside," Joff said. "You comin'?"

Tin shrugged and half smiled as he rose to his feet. Once inside, he stood in the shadows, half hidden by the curtain on the end of the front row. Joff caught his eye one last time from the stage; he raised his glass and smiled.

"Welcome back, ladies and gentlemen," the compere' announced.

"One two, one two three four!" and Joff was in. Eight bars of fast cadenza, his hands were all over the keys.

At the chord change, when he looked down again, Tin was gone.

Tin had watched his old friend climb the stage and sit at the piano. He finished his drink in time to the count then he slipped out through the door.

He turned left down Kingsland Road, heading away from Hackney, south towards Shoreditch. At the junction of Shoreditch High Street he barely paused, continuing south into Commercial Street. At the junction he waited for a passing carriage before he crossed over onto Whitechapel High Street. Once he was safely on the south side of the street he ducked into an alley between two shops. Instantly it was darker, quieter, and terrible smells wafted through the air.

At the end of the alley was a maze of dark, muddy openings. Little more than gaps between the buildings that led further into the shadows. He chose one with the confidence of a man who had passed this way before. Many eyes watched him from the shadows. Tin was walking as the crow flies, heading towards the river, cutting across the edges of Whitechapel, merely to get to where he wanted to be. Somewhere in that labyrinth of dirty back lanes he crossed into the district of Limehouse.

Now he was close. At the next filthy, narrow junction he stepped onto a rickety old plank to his left. Using his hands against the waxy walls, managing to keep himself upright, he stepped off the plank into a grubby courtyard much like others he had passed through. Black was the predominant colour. Black mud, black walls, piles of black stinking rubbish, and a handful of black, scruffy doors. He tapped lightly on one and it opened immediately. A warm smile greeted him, and the door was held open just wide enough for him to squeeze through.

"Mr. Tin, come in, come in!" the gentle voice politely insisted.

* * *

A few weeks later on September 28, 1864, Joff was at a meeting in St. Martin's Hall on the edge of Soho.

They were taking advantage of the new laws recently passed through Parliament. Men were allowed to meet no matter what their political leanings might be. On that day, in that hall, an international organisation for the benefit of the workers was formed. Only this time it was no clandestine operation whose members risked persecution. It was so legal, it was almost respectable.

Many who attended swore the world changed that day and would never be the same again.

Joff spotted Karl Marx sitting unobtrusively on the side of the stage. Not talking but listening avidly as others spoke the words he had carefully prepared for them.

Joff knew that Marx was desperate for his ideas to be adopted and quickly—before the capitalist system was so firmly entrenched it would be impossible to dislodge for a hundred years or more, or before the Anarchists were able to gain widespread support for their ideas of tolerance to all. Most of the power here today already lay with Marx and his inner circle. Joff also knew it wasn't public knowledge yet, so he kept that information filed with all other secrets picked up at the piano stool.

Surreptitiously Joff watched the great man. He seemed confident and the way he shuffled his papers suggested meticulous organisation. He was unobtrusive but first to lead the applause after each and every speaker. Overall Joff was begrudgingly impressed at the way he conducted himself.

In comparison, Tin and the Anarchists were too disorganised, too willing to resort to violence. They were no contest for Marx and his efficient, well-orchestrated methods, Joff decided.

By the following year Marx and his brand of Socialism were gaining popular support, especially on the London Docks. Tin and his friends disagreed with and disapproved of this version of the future as much as they always had.

Joff was playing in the evenings while they did most of their drinking and bickering. He was glad to be well out of it.

Tin and his cohorts strongly believed that work, work, work was not the meaning of life. Pleasure, music, art, and philosophy were equally admirable usages of one's time.

Marx and his followers meanwhile argued vehemently that all should work hard, devoting the fruit of their toil for the good of the state, and the state would grow ever more powerful, allowing it to thrive and prosper for the benefit of all.

To Tin it was just another version of the capitalist system already in place where the minority ruled over the majority and he thought if they could get the message out there most other people would see it that way too.

Back home in Cornwall some of the villagers worked as pickers. It was hard manual labour from dawn to dusk that ultimately benefited the Squire and his family far more than it benefited them. Those pickers had to be whipped to make them work any faster.

Yet the fishermen and the free traders, men who owned their vessels or were masters of their own destiny, would gladly put in many extra hours without feeling the need for complaint. These men did not have to hand over all they caught for some middle man or squire to profit from. These men were happier, more confident, better neighbors, less sickly, better members of the local community. Joff had seen such things with his own eyes. He knew it made sense. Working for the state or the chosen few at the top seemed no choice at all to him.

Then one morning he was walking down Fleet Street when he glimpsed the front page of a newspaper.

"Anarchists meeting in Whitechapel!" screamed the headline, nicely linking them with that part of London where danger, poverty, and crime were the first things people brought to mind. For those readers who might not have picked up such a gentle hint, the first four pages of the tabloid spelled out in great detail how the Anarchists intended to burn every official building to the ground and allow the law of the jungle to prevail. It was ludicrous; nothing could have been further from the truth.

Peace and mutual respect were at the very heart of Anarchism. Obviously they were rattling the old guard who seemed determined to quash the perceived threat, publically, once and for all.

Ironically there wasn't a mention of the opposing view—their colleagues the Socialists, who now wished to be referred to by their new name, the Communists.

The public were systematically bombarded with negative views on Anarchists. There was no mention of what they stood for or what they wanted to achieve. There were plenty of lies bandied about and suddenly they were the enemy within, to be despised and ostracised.

Benn was convinced he knew who the traitor was and, without waiting for proof, had beaten the man to within an inch of his life, and now it was war.

War with the Communists, war with the police, and war with the citizens who believed every word they read in the newspapers. It amazed Joff how quickly things changed. One minute they were celebrating the freedom to meet in public, the next they were at war on all fronts. Every time he entered a pub it was like the dark days of looking around the bar for trouble.

One evening they were drinking in the White Hart. Joff drained his glass and rose to leave.

"So I'm off then," he said.

"Yeah go on then, leave us to do the men's work. Take care o' them fingers, mind!" Benn called after him, but he was smiling and Joff smirked back.

He meant no harm by his little comment. They all made allowances for the fact that his fingers were his livelihood. He was never expected to join in any fights or operate any printing presses or modern machinery. He was expected to provide the soundtrack to their lives and little else.

Tin glanced nervously around the bar. They now had the full attention of the authorities. It was imperative to be far more wary as they moved around in public.

Joff headed east away from Whitechapel, over to Limehouse, where he figured he would get one of the Chinamen to give him a proper shave. His confident gait made him difficult to approach. Through the alleys and side streets he made his way as half-seen figures watched from the shadows and judged that he was no easy target. They let him pass.

* * *

Squire Bradshaw listened to the hooded figure standing before his horse. It was a cold, frosty night high on Bodmin Moor and the Squire's horse was blowing hard. He had been galloping across the frozen moorland and was keen to be running again. As the horse snorted, the figure spoke louder.

"'E's callin' hisself 'Joe' now an' 'e's playin' at a music 'all in the east End o' London, Squire!"

"A music hall," the Squire repeated distastefully. "Which one?"

"Well 'e moves about but it was a new one, 'oxton 'all last I 'eard."

"Hoxton Hall," the Squire repeated, as though the pronunciation was an affront to everything he stood for.

"Where's he living?" he asked the hooded informer.

"Whitechapel, Sir, although again 'e does like to move around."

"Anything else?" the Squire asked, digging his heels into the horse's sides to stop it from taking off.

"'E's 'anging about wiv a load o' foreigners, Sir, Anarchists!"

The Squire kicked his heels into the horse's flanks and the animal moved forward half a step. He dropped a bag into the informer's hand and it chinked satisfyingly.

"Much obliged, Sir. Want me to stay on it, Sir?"

"Yes."

The man nodded his understanding and stepped back as the horse reared slightly in response to the Squire's knees, then narrowly missing the man on foot it got a grip on the icy surface and was off across the moor, building speed rapidly, its muscles pumping hard and fast, eager to race for home.

The horse knew the way. Squire Bradshaw rode with a relaxed rein, letting the animal make the decisions. He was thinking about the Owens boy and the information he had just been given.

1865

Back in a Limehouse pub the Anarchists ordered another round of drinks.

Tila leaned back and declared loudly, "To Lord Palmerston!" He raised his tankard as though in salute and the other men around him fell about laughing.

Lord Palmerston, the Prime Minister, had died that very morning. Church bells had rung his passing as the union flag on the palace of Westminster flew at half-mast. The nation was in mourning but here in this pub they were celebrating. Palmerston had been avidly anti-reform but he would now be replaced by his deputy Lord

Russell, who was at least in favor of giving the vote to skilled workers.

"At least wiv Russell we got some room for maneuver, eh!" Tila observed happily.

Benn looked to their skipper for guidance. He was undecided.

Tin spoke again, "Things look much rosier wiv Palmerston out the way."

He glanced around the circle of happy faces.

"Right?" he repeated.

They all agreed heartily.

"What about the tailors?" Benn asked.

"I 'ear Karl Marx 'as 'ad a big success wiv them," Tin muttered.

That was another fly in the ointment. A group of East End tailors had gone on strike over wages and working conditions and their masters had tried to farm in skilled craftsmen from Belgium and France to break the strike. Even though the wages were higher in England the tailors from the continent had refused to help the factory owners after Marx had used the full force of the International Working Men's Association for the first time. He had foiled the factory owners' plans and they had been forced to meet the workers' demands. For Marx and his followers it was a publicity coup. He was using the international aspect to good effect by convincing the foreign tailors to have empathy with their English brothers. They listened and agreed, Marx courted the publicity the victory brought him whilst simultaneously wasting no opportunity to slander the 'Libertarians,' as he called Joff and his friends. For the Anarchists, his public success was a real kick in the teeth.

As always, when it rains it pours. London had just received an influx of yet more Anarchists escaping the Tsars of Russia and these boys played rough. After the Socialists' success with the tailors' dispute, the Italians decided they needed to make a statement of their own. They were tired of waiting to be understood, of watching their political views sidelined. They had decided that the time for action had arrived and they intended to start by blowing up a series of police stations in synchronised unity, right across the city. If the operation was successful they would be the undisputed driving force for change. Working men throughout the land would look to them, not Marx, for answers. They needed to wrestle control from their more Socialist brothers, from Marx. They might not agree on much but this was the one point on which they all agreed.

The Italians had been busy.

All around London and as far afield as Camden and Kentish Towns, pockets of radicals waited for the signal. They had been provided with sophisticated bombs and were delighted at the opportunity to use them. Any faith in Marx and his patient approach had long ceased and they had absolutely no interest in standing for election themselves.

Tin had been approached by the Italians and asked if he and his men could be counted on when the day of the uprising came. This evening they were to meet and give their answer.

"Never mind Marx, with this show of strength, we are about to win the revolution once and for all!" Benn slammed a fist down on the table. "It can't come soon enough!" he added.

"Benn, sit down," Tin hissed. He knew there were spies everywhere and the last thing they needed was somebody reporting back that they looked as though they were planning something, getting worked up about something.

"Let's not draw too much attention, eh," he said to Benn by way of an explanation, and they all glanced towards the door as it opened. This time they were rewarded.

"That's 'im!" Noah hissed, jumping down from his seat as he spoke. He had noted there were three men and he wanted to get the necessary extra chair before they arrived at the table expecting to sit down.

"Who's the third one?" Benn whispered behind what he thought of as a welcoming smile.

"Dunno!" muttered Tila behind his hand.

Such a clumsy attempt to act casual was the most suspicious behaviour seen in the bar all evening and the place was full of shady-looking characters planning all manner of revenge and treason.

"Oh oh," Tin sighed. "We got company!"

They had all been watching the approaching Italians. Only Tin, the wily old fox, had possessed the foresight to glance instinctively back towards the door, just to make sure the Italians had not been followed.

He saw police, loads of them, moving forwards in military style units, and passing through the door in ever greater numbers.

Pandemonium broke out all around. Patrons keen to escape for a variety of reasons were scattering in all directions. An oak table was upended by a group eager to put a solid object between themselves and the long arm of the law. Whistles and shouts made the whole situation confusing for those being forced to suddenly react.

Tin spun his head left and right, searching for a chink in the armour. The police had now formed a ring around the back perimeter of the room and they pressed forward with military precision. There were so many that there wasn't room for a man to squeeze between them. The whistle blew again and they began a solid, steady march towards the centre of the room. All in their path were forced backwards, corralled together. Still more officers could be seen streaming through the doors. *Every bobbie in London must be involved in this exercise,* Tin thought, quickly estimating the occupants of the bar at about sixty or seventy people. Then he tried to do a head count of the ring of police forcing them back. They were outnumbered at least three to one. There was the best part of two hundred police here, he realised as he shuffled back to avoid a truncheon swinging inches from his face.

They police tactic was proving very effective. A few hotheads very quickly felt the kiss of the cosh and the rest were starting to succumb to common sense. They were out-maneuvered and severely outnumbered. They retreated unwillingly, further and further back to the bar.

"Back! Back I said!" shouted a policeman with a scowl on his face.

He lashed out with his truncheon and Tin saw that it was Benn who had taken the hit across the forearm.

Tin saw Tila doing what he would have done, pulling their friend away from the risk of further injury. He was too late. Benn had already put himself forward as a troublemaker. Tin watched helplessly as four officers charged into the crowd at the shrill order of the whistle and grabbed his comrade by the arms, the hair, and the scruff of his neck. They administered a few short whacks to keep his feet moving and whisked him through the crowd. The snatch was so quick and so smartly executed, Tin realised that many hours of training had been put in. He crouched down a little, trying to avoid getting noticed, and inched back as far as the wooden bar would allow.

The police pushed the crowd back with absolute control. Holding their truncheons across their bodies they were acting as a solid living barrier. The snatch squad went in time and time again. After Benn, they took three Fenians, then Tila, in rapid succession. The crowd ebbed and flowed from side to side and individuals were beaten back if they appeared to be trying to break through the cordon.

Tin could see from his half-hidden position that they were not just choosing faces at random here. They had a list and he knew he would be on it. He had to cause a distraction, had to try and escape, and time was running out. They might have both exits covered, but he knew a way out of here if he could only get to the stairs. He scanned the crowd at waist level and saw what he was looking for almost straight away.

"Noah! Come 'ere, Boy!" he hissed.

Noah was an orphan, a street Arab, who hung around feeding off scraps.

The boy crouched down and somehow moved through the legs and feet. He was with Tin in a flash. He looked up at the grisly captain.

"What?" his expression asked. No time for wasting words.

"Move to the far end an' make a distraction."

The boy nodded and he was gone.

He quickly broke through at the far end of the bar and actually succeeded in making it past the first two truncheon swings, but they caught him with the third. The blow whacked him high in the chest. He collapsed with all the wind knocked from his lungs.

He went down under a pile of blue capes and black truncheons and the crowd bristled at the treatment of one of their own. Skirmishes broke out right across the battle line.

As they did so, Tin leaped one-handed across the bar top. He landed behind the cash register as a truncheon flashed through the air a split second behind him. Keeping low, using the bar as cover, he took three giant paces and was out through the serving hatch, across the narrow corridor, and flying up the stairs as fast as his legs would carry him. At the first turn of the rickety old stairway, four empty beer barrels were piled on top of each other. Tin pushed them as he passed, sending them rolling down behind him.

He figured the barrels had to help but dared not waste even a split second looking back to see just how much, or how close at his heels they were. He bounded upwards two stairs at a time, breathing hard, taking the bends with his shoulder, bouncing off the narrow walls and feeling every bit the quarry he had become.

They were so close he was sure he could feel their very breath on his collar, the wind as they snatched at his ankles. He refused to look around. He could just manage one more step, hit one more bend in the wall. Arms pumping and neck muscles bulging, he kept moving ever upwards. Up two flights, three, and now he was closing in on the attic

Each stair was marginally narrower than the one before it, the curved walls on either side ever so slightly closer together.

He shot past the rooms of the serving girls, up the very last section of damp-smelling hallway, whilst behind him whistles, shouts, and clambering footsteps were so loud they had to be almost upon him. He focused on each new step as it came into view, and blowing hard, passed lightly across it whilst already focusing his attention on the next. Constantly expecting a hand to close around his tunic or grip at his ankle, or to hear the whistling of a heavy truncheon flying through the air before connecting solidly with his very vulnerable bones.

He flew onwards as the gods smiled down on him, then without warning he was in the gables of the old coaching house, racing towards a dead end, the window at the very summit of the building. There was no time for thinking. He flung himself through the glass. Shards of crystal and splinters of wood exploded outwards. Legs flailing, Tin flew through the debris, landing heavily on the neighboring roof and racing across it, hardly breaking stride. He knew exactly where he was and he ran the full length of the long building, ignoring those on the roof behind and all at ground level.

The stable boys, the weary travellers, the hangers on, the police, their upturned faces focused on the figure above them while he looked for a glimpse of the warehouse that he knew would soon be appearing to his left; and there it was. He injected an extra spurt of speed into his willing legs, crouched, and jumped.

He flew through the air for long enough to feel he was practically flying. The air turned silent, the wind raced across his face, all was at peace with the world. The moment was real for just the time it took to register and then it was over and the warehouse was closing in on him very fast.

He extended his arms, braced, bent at the knees, and with a thud landed on the drainpipe. Pain jarred through his shoulders and down his arms. Ignoring it, he grabbed onto the cold metal and shimmied his way upwards. He raced across the roof of the warehouse and the noises of the street returned to assault his ears. Whistles and angry shouts no longer seemed to dominate the general din. He didn't bother to look down. Decrepit blackened chimney stacks pumped black soot into the night sky all around him. Cats of all shades watched as he passed through their secret, high-up, feline world.

Tin ran the length of Old Montague Street, using close proximity of its giant warehouse roofs to cross from one side to the other. Then he ran and jumped across the even more closely packed rooftops of Limehouse as his pursuers grew smaller and smaller somewhere far behind.

* * *

After Palmerston's death in 1865, Lord Russell had indeed been the next prime minister and he was, as expected, willing to at least discuss the possibility of giving the vote to free men. Although he meant only skilled men, he saw absolutely no reason whatsoever why the unskilled, or God forbid, the poor, should be allowed a say in how the country was run.

In the same year, the politician John Mills mentioned the women's suffrage movement on the platform of the House of Commons for the very first time. Simultaneously, across London, but in the East End especially, the popularity of the music halls was going from strength to strength, creating a system, unintentionally and unforeseen, that was making the headline acts, very wealthy indeed.

Sell-out shows were bringing in vast sums for working-class entertainers, despite their less than humble backgrounds. With money came influence and these rags to riches 'stars' were not accustomed to the 'establishment' way of doing things.

After only twelve months in office, Lord Russell resigned and was replaced as prime minister by Lord Gladstone. Here at last was a man the people could do business with. All they had to do was wait for the next election. So alarmed was Disraeli by the prospect of a liberal government at the next election that he decided to out-liberal the liberals. He surprised everyone by accepting the need for change and in 1867 the Reform Act became law. As is often the way, when the time came it all happened rather quickly. Overnight the electorate doubled in size, the cosy old boys' network could be no more. All it needed now was a secret ballot and yearly elections and the Chartists would have succeeded in all their aims. Aims that those in Cornwall were told were no more than impossible dreams, yet here they were only twenty-five years later living that dream. It had been worth waiting for, sort of.

Now, some thought, the time was ripe to elect a man who would have their best interests at heart. A political party with Karl Marx at the helm was what they had set their hearts on and it suddenly looked a whole lot closer.

THE EAST END BECKONS　　　IAN PARSON

*　*　*

After the police raid, the popular press had made a huge deal of how Anarchists and the Irish Republican Brotherhood wanted to blow up society, wanted nobody to feel safe as they slept. They were all lumped together and labelled as terrorists and the public fell for the media propaganda.

Slowly news of Joff's friends filtered through. One by one, he learned of their fates. Most of the Russians, French, and Italians had been deported after a short time in jail. On returning to their home countries, they were never heard from again. The British and Irish amongst them were given hefty jail sentences. The ringleaders were all, whatever their nationality, hung by the neck until dead. It made no difference; new clandestine meetings started up again almost immediately. The White Hart in Whitechapel became, once again, an unofficial headquarters for men who were neither enthralled by the new capitalist system nor agreed with the views of Marx.

They were the dissident Anarchists and they came from all over Europe.

Joff had been extremely fortunate not to have been arrested on the night of the raid. In truth it was a bit of a wake-up call for him. As a musician, his working day started later than most and he had fallen into the habit of filling the daylight hours with boisterous alcohol-fuelled sessions.

Naturally Joff's choice of drinking companions was limited during the working day, but as Tin was his oldest friend in the whole of London and he didn't hold down regular hours either, it was only natural that the two of them had gravitated together and that Joff had met Tin's acquaintances. As it turned out, he liked them. He knew they financed their lifestyles by crime but by and large they had some memorable sessions and that was all that really mattered to Joff. He chose not to stop and think too hard about the company he was keeping. At least, not until the raids happened; then he was forced to think on it. That night he decided to find some new drinking pals. Tin was on the missing list anyway. It was time to find a new pub he could call his local.

Joff knew only villains and radicals would be drinking in the East End during the daytime and he'd had his fill of crime and politics. So despite being on his doorstep, the local pubs held no appeal. Soho or Cleveland Street were a bit of a hike on a daily basis and besides, the clientele over there were just as likely to get him into trouble. After a few trial runs he eventually settled on The Coal Hole, a little boozer on the Strand right in the heart of all the new theatres rapidly being built. It was where a lot of the musicians and actors passed the time of day and it was the perfect place if he wanted to pick up a gig. There were fixers in from all over London every lunch time and every evening. They could bestow concerts on the worthy, gigs on promenades in parks or pleasure gardens. Appointments in cafes, taverns, or assembly rooms. Boosy ballad concerts, and for the chosen few, a long-term show in a brand new west end theatre.

Only a ten-minute walk from his room in Whitechapel, once he had discovered the Coal Hole he was very soon a regular, playing the house piano every chance he got. Belting out hit tunes whenever someone told him a producer or a musical director was in the place. It got to be a bit of a joke at his expense but it wasn't meant maliciously and he didn't mind. Then one day it paid off in spectacular style.

"Hey there, I heard you playin' just now. You're pretty good."

Joff was in the gents', standing at the urinal and was being addressed from behind by someone who sounded German to his discerning ear.

"Thanks!" he said without turning round.

When he did turn, the fellow was standing by the door, as Joff knew he would be.

"I'd like to buy you a drink," he said, holding open the door.

Joff shrugged and followed him back to the bar.

As he waited to be served he reached out to shake hands.

"Meyer," he introduced himself.

"Joff," he replied, taking the offered hand and shaking it.

"What do you drink?" he asked.

"Half an' half," Joff replied.

He frowned slightly but repeated it to the barman or as close as he could manage.

Carrying their drinks, Meyer led Joff towards the back of the pub where they joined another man at a little table fashioned from an old beer barrel.

The stranger stuck out his hand before Joff had even taken a seat. He seemed keen, eager to please.

Joff smiled and shook. "Joff!" he said.

"John Hollingshead at your service!" the man replied.

After they had all taken a sip and gotten comfortable in their seats, Meyer spoke up.

"John here," he motioned to his colleague who dutifully allowed a smile to flicker across his face, "is about to become the manager of a brand new theatre, one of which you may have heard. Soon to be opening a little further down the Strand."

"The Gaiety?" Joff hardly dared ask.

They sat there nodding and beaming broadly.

Joff had indeed heard. The old Strand, it was the talk of the Coal Hole.

The Gaiety Theatre, or Strand Music Hall, as it had been called until recently, dominated the busiest four-way junction of the Strand, dominating all other buildings on the thoroughfare. Everyone at the Hole had heard about the vast sums of money being spent on the current refurbishment. It seemed no expense was to be spared.

They were installing the latest gas lighting throughout the whole building in a way that had never been done before. Ornate saloons and restaurants were to be on site and the actual theatre held an auditorium that seated two thousand patrons.

Vast armies of builders and tradesmen seemed to be crawling all over it every time Joff passed. It was to be the most opulent theatrical experience the world had ever seen and on top of all that it was less than a ten-minute walk from his room in Whitechapel.

"Yes, I've noticed it," he said.

John smiled, "Good, because in my capacity as musical director I would like to offer you the position of resident pianist at the soon-to-be-opening, brand new, Gaiety theatre!"

He raised his glass and the others both followed suit. The word 'yes' must have been written all over Joff's face because although he never actually, literally uttered the word, they both knew at that moment that he was officially accepting their once-in-a-lifetime offer.

"Where are you playing at the moment?" John asked.

"I'm at Wilton's," he managed to say, "another two weeks."

"That would be, what November the 7th? Then it'll change over for the Christmas show?"

He knew a run always finished on a Saturday night. Either that or he had been checking up on Joff.

"Yes, that's right, Saturday the 7th."

John smiled at Joff, who glanced at Meyer, who was sitting back, allowing his manager to do all the talking. Meyer smiled as well. They must have looked silly all sitting around a too-small table grinning at each other like Cheshire cats. Joff was smiling because this was the gig of a lifetime. He didn't know about them, why they were so happy.

"We will mostly be doin' burlesque shows and something new that we think will turn out to be huge. Are you familiar with musical comedy?"

Joff relaxed visibly. "Yes, it's very popular in the music 'alls." He refrained from adding "and I can play those tunes standing on my head."

"So you can finish your run at Wilton's and be with us in plenty of time for opening night," Meyer noted.

"Opening night will be on December the 21st, 1868," John said, all gruff and business like, "so that fits in rather nicely."

Not for Joff it didn't, but he knew something would turn up in between gigs, even if it was just a few nights a week in a dingy pub.

"Obviously there will be rehearsals through most of December, and," he said, clearing his throat and glancing at Meyer, who nodded encouragement, "we will have you on the payroll from December 1st. Would that be agreeable?"

If Joff had understood correctly, they were planning to pay him for rehearsals. He had never known such a thing. If this was the new, professional, musical theatre that everyone was talking about, he was all for it.

* * *

A few days before Christmas 1868, two thousand people packed the Gaiety theatre for the opening night of a four-hour extravaganza. The highlight of the show was Nellie Farren's burlesque dance, for which Joff accompanied her on piano. The people loved it, she was an instant sensation and, by association, so was he.

They performed to packed houses at the Gaiety six nights a week. Meyer and John's gamble paid off handsomely. Burlesque and musical comedy were exactly what the public wanted. Life had never been such fun before, and Joff was glad to finally be free of politics. It had caused him no end of trouble in Cornwall and had nearly done so for him here. No, he decided, he was better off sticking to the music—much better off—and besides, that was all he really wanted anyway.

It was such a pleasure to be working at the Gaiety that he would go in earlier than was needed just to hang about, have a few drinks with the cast, and soak it up.

There were so many interesting people and beautiful girls in theatre land it was a pleasure to get to work. They were well paid, and all doing the job they had always dreamed of. It was easy to leave the real world at the stage door.

Everybody was so polite, so kind. Why would any of them possibly want to be anywhere else? But it wasn't long before the inevitable happened. The thunderbolt struck Joff backstage. Once again he fell hopelessly, instantly in love.

She was a dancer of course, a real beauty, Irish by birth and her name was Aimee.

The two of them flirted for a whole month before he finally plucked up the courage to ask her to accompany him for a stroll along the Strand.

That autumn and winter they spent all their free time together and Joff couldn't have been happier. She was lodging with a nice family south of the river in Vauxhall, and so they would spend Sunday afternoons together strolling along the new Waterloo embankment, stealing kisses when they could.

Then one fateful day she looked up at him and asked in all innocence, "Why don't you ever take me to meet any o' your old friends?"

Joff should have told her they were all dead, that she was his only friend. Anything would have done, really, so why he chose to reveal the truth, he would never know.

"Most o' my friends now are at the theatre," he mumbled.

They were down by the Thames, near Shakespeare's Globe. He remembered the wind was howling through their clothing and the water was racing downstream, and she was leaning against the stone wall. On the opposite bank he could see the dome of St. Paul's. The sky was blue and crisp.

185

"What about yer old friends?" she asked.

"They're mainly political; I didn't think they would interest you." He tried to read the expression on her face.

"What do you mean, political?" she asked.

She pushed herself off the wall and took a couple of steps towards him until their noses were almost touching. "You mean radicals, don't yer?" Her eyes were full of fire. "Oh my," she said, holding him at arms' length. "They're not Anarchists are they?"

"Eh, well…"

"Are you a radical?" she shot the question at him and pulled him close Her face was easy to read now; very interested, was the expression he saw.

"I'm not interested in politics, I'm just a piano player," he insisted, trying to lighten the mood.

"I am!" she declared, taking him completely by surprise, as behind her the river ran wild.

Five months they had been together, working side by side all week and spending every Sunday in each other's company. They had discussed at great length all the subjects that either of them had wanted to raise and not once had she shown any interest in politics, not once. It had been one of the things he had liked about her.

"Really?" he said, raising an eyebrow.

She nodded enthusiastically and he noticed that her cheeks had flushed deep red.

Foolishly, he couldn't resist showing off, "Would you like to meet some radicals?" he asked.

***

A few nights later just as he was heading home, she appeared at the stage door.

"Where are you goin' now?" she asked.

"Not to Vauxhall," he replied.

"Me neither!" she declared excitedly. "I'm not due home until late tonight, and I thought, well, if you were going to meet your radical friends I might just come along."

"Oh!" he said, meaning, "Oh, no."

Joff was too afraid to ask where she was supposed to be going.

So arm in arm they walked the Strand, heading east towards Whitechapel, towards the White Hart, towards their destinies.

The pub on that fateful evening was full to the rafters. Joff introduced her to a French Anarchist he was acquainted with, who tried unsuccessfully to seduce her before finally introducing her to a Belgian girl with whom she spent the rest of the evening in deep conversation.

* * *

As '68 turned into 1869 Aimee began to change. Subtly at first, a purple sash over her dress or an opinion unbecoming her position in life. By the summer of '69 she was, to all intents and purposes, firmly committed to women's suffrage. Opinions had hardened into argumentative rants that she threw about indiscriminately. Her new-found political conviction was not appreciated in Vauxhall and she had been evicted from her lodgings. Naturally she had moved in with Joff.

JANUARY 1871

Joff sat in the barber's chair with his eyes open and caught the swirl of a purple skirt in the mirror before him. He had just that split second of knowing what was about to come.

"There you are! What the bloody 'ell are you doin' in here?"

"Just gettin' a shave, dear. Mr. Hollingshead likes me to look smart for the public." He attempted to bounce a smile at her through the mirror.

"Bleedin' place, that's all you care about. You're pathetic an' you know it!"

Aimee turned on her heel, and slamming the door, stormed back across the mud towards the room in which they still lived.

"Ouch, she's a fiery one an' no mistake, eh!" the barber was outside the periphery of Joff's sight so he couldn't see the expression of pity the man wore.

"She's alright, Barney." The barber moved alongside him and Joff caught his eye for a split second in the mirror. "None of us is perfect, eh?" he added.

The barber paused and nodded at Joff, his scissors hovering over Joff's head.

"Yous in love!" he declared before focusing his attention entirely on his work. He carried on snipping furiously, not waiting for an answer, not wanting to discuss Aimee.

It was incredible how quickly her head had filled with all sorts of radical ideas.

Now, after four years, the sweet innocent he had fallen for had completely disappeared. In her place was an angry feminist. She blamed society for most things and him for completely ruining her life, her independence, her figure, everything. She had fallen pregnant almost immediately after they had moved in together and spent nine months lying in bed, soaking up the feminist manifesto.

After giving birth she returned almost immediately to the cause. She had grown more and more distant, both to him and to the baby, who had turned into an unruly and difficult infant.

Joff, however, had always wanted a wife, a son, a family, and a job at the piano. He finally had those things so he was determined to make the most of the situation. He bit his lip rather than argue and hoped things would take a turn for the better at some point in the future. It was fortunate he was still at the Gaiety but unfortunate he wasn't at home to help as much as Aimee would have liked. He was earning good money but she was always short, always giving it to those in more need.

When he did go home, day or night, Aimee would be surrounded by like-minded cronies and they would hold heated discussions into the early hours. They only ever met behind closed doors so they remained unobserved by the authorities, who had enough to keep them busy with the constant daily mayhem all around.

Meanwhile, Marx and his skillful rhetoric had grown from strength to strength. With the Association's help, workers were organising legally all across England.

* * *

On 17th January, 1872, the women's suffrage movement held a general meeting at the Langham Hotel in central London. Wealthy starlets from the East End rubbed shoulders with debutantes from the West End, and they discovered much common ground. Aimee was there with them.

The world seemed on the brink of momentous change. To women, to manual workers, to the vast majority of the population, it couldn't come quickly enough.

However, if the authorities were to be believed, danger lay beyond every horizon. Change, they warned, was not necessarily a good thing.

Tin and the Anarchists were scattered throughout Europe, unable to communicate without getting picked off as soon as they appeared in public. The revolutions in France, Poland, Italy, and Germany had all withered and died long ago. Always because there had been no plan for running large departments once the people seized power. They were good at being reactionaries but not so good at governing. They were used to running small operations, not international giants. All had resorted to watered-down versions of the systems already in place and nothing real was achieved. This, Tin had never tired of repeating, was why the system proposed by Marx could never work in reality.

However, Tin was no longer around to offer an opposing view and Marx was a quick learner and very cunning. He was beginning to be a real thorn in the sides of the established order.

Simultaneously, the women's suffrage movement was gathering momentum. Their policies attracted large numbers of formidable, energetic, middle-classed women with the time, the resources, and the inclination to really get amongst the old guard. Naturally the established few had not taken too well to this double-pronged attack on the 'natural order of things.'

Joff knew they were concerned because his friends were again being rounded up, this time radicals of both gender.

* * *

Around that time, Joff was sitting in the White Hart when a familiar sentiment caught his ear from further down the bar. An opinion he hadn't heard in public for some time. He listened and caught the speaker's next sentence very clearly.

"True progress lies in people making their own decisions, not relying on some corrupt corporation," the same voice declared.

A brave man was loudly uttering opinions Joff thought had been long abandoned. "There is nothing new in politics. Everything comes around again eventually," they said.

Even the old communal ways, it would seem. Joff was intrigued.

"We've thrown our lot in with Marx now," someone said, trying to shut the man up.

"Marx! Huh!" came the disrespectful reply.

"It's important that we stay united. There is strength in numbers," someone said firmly.

"You may not agree with the manifesto, stranger, but hold your council for the good of the majority. We are strongest when we stick together," someone else told him.

"Pah!" came the retort. "Wouldn't you rather keep the profit of your toil to improve your own lives? Why exchange one oppressor for another?"

It had been many years since Joff had heard the old opposing views. The drunken stranger's comments intrigued him. He moved along the bar, scanning the crowd as he went, seeking him out, this lone voice, this free thinker. He spotted him with ease. The man was sitting alone at a table that held eight. Joff sided up to him and slid into the seat opposite.

"'Oo are you?" he demanded.

Joff smiled, hoping to convey that he'd come in peace.

"Oh, I'm no-one. Just a man 'oo 'eard you speakin' an' thought I would come over an' introduce myself."

"Why?" he asked, taking a slug from his bottle.

Joff shrugged, "'Cos those things that you said…" He rubbed the stubble on his chin and looked at the other properly. "Well I don't often 'ear views like that no more."

Joff knew this old dog.

He was dressed in a heavy overcoat with the collar turned up. His hair was grey and thinning now and he was in dire need of a shave. He lifted his face to look at Joff and as the dim light caught his features he saw his old captain.

"Tin!" Joff declared. "Tin, how the devil are you?"

Joff wanted to give him a great big hug. Gather him to himself, feel his bones on his own bones. It had been so long he had assumed his old friend was dead. But no, here he was as large as life, right before his very eyes.

"Joe, is that you?" he squinted as he looked at Joff, who saw recognition wash across his face.

That was good enough for him. Joff lunged across the table and shook his shoulders for all he was worth.

"Yes, yes it's me." Joff held him at arms' length. He could hardly believe his eyes. His old friend was alive, he was here, right in front of him.

"Where 'ave you been all this time?" Joff asked, beaming at him.

Tin's eyes blazed briefly before fading back to some far away memory.

"Oh you know, 'ere and there." He cast his eyes down again but not before Joff saw a cloud of regret pass across his features.

Tin looked at Joff again. "An' you, what 'ave you been up to?" he asked, looking up at his old friend as though it was the most natural thing in the world to have him before him.

"Oh you know," Joff shrugged.

Joff could see he was just going through the motions etiquette demanded. There was no interest in his reply at all. He was shocked at how thin and old Tin now looked compared to the healthy sailor he had known before.

"Still playin' the ol' piano are yer?" This time he did seem interested in the answer.

"Yeah that's me," Joff admitted.

He smiled for the first time. "I always liked 'earing you play!" he said.

Joff smirked, "An' I'm settled down now. You remember Aimee?"

He frowned and nodded slightly.

"We got a boy," Joff said.

"A family man? You!" He smiled again, shaking his head in mock disbelief, then turned away to have a coughing fit before pointing at the younger man and wagging his finger, "You! A father!"

Joff shrugged in a 'you got me' kind of way and they hugged across the table and ordered drinks.

"So you threw your lot in with Marx then, did yer?" he accused a little later.

Joff smiled and said, "You know me, I ain't thrown my lot in wiv no-one. I'm just a piano player!"

He looked Joff drunkenly up and down.

"Yeah, my pal the piano player, that's right!" he took a great gulp of his drink.

"I work at the Gaiety theatre now!" Joff announced proudly.

"Ah, I know that one," he said, as Joff knew he would. "Nice place," he added, sounding genuinely impressed.

"Thanks," Joff beamed at him. That was exactly the response he had been expecting, everyone in London knew the Gaiety. It was impossible to miss from its imposing position on the Strand and Joff knew it impressed people that he was the piano man there.

"You in a union?" he asked.

Joff shrugged and looked downwards.

"They're recognised in law now you know!"

Joff shrugged again, "We ain't got a musician's union," he replied.

"Then start one, my boy, start one!" he slurred. "You owe it to them that's gone before!" he added, and Joff could see the memories were back with him in a flash.

"You alright?" Joff asked.

"So many good men sent to the gallows or off to the colonies." He spat a lump of black goo onto the floor. "We ain't never goin' to see them again, Joe."

"I thought I was never goin' to see you again." He tried to lighten the mood. "So that just goes to prove you never know 'oo will turn up."

"Well I'm back true enough," Tin agreed.

They clinked tankards again, drank, and talked.

Joff told Tin how he had married Aimee, told him how she had given birth three times but only their first, their son Jack, had survived. He told him how Jack was the bonniest, healthiest boy the world had ever seen. Joff didn't dwell on how the miscarriages and the suffrage had changed Aimee's whole outlook.

He told him about the marvellous Gaiety theatre and his job there, and Tin ribbed him a little about the chorus girls, and although his heart wasn't really in it, he feigned disappointment that he wasn't fooling around with any of them.

Finally they were drunk. Tin sat leaning on his elbow, nodding his head and pretending to listen, but wearing a far-away look and drifting off, both metaphorically and literally. Joff persevered, keeping the conversation going alone as long as he could, not really wanting the evening to end. Finally he admitted defeat.

Joff shook Tin awake for the second time.

"If you need somewhere to sleep you can always come back with me," he said.

"What, no, I'm not asleep!" he protested, sitting up straighter. "Tell me more."

So Joff plowed on with more tales until it got too late even for him. Again he shook Tin awake, a little more firmly. Injecting a small measure of impatience into his voice, he said, "Tin! Tin! You keep noddin' off. What's the matter with you? Why are you so tired?

"I'm sorry, Joe, it's great to see yer again, really it is. I'm just tired is all, it's nothin'. Let's meet tomorrow, I'll feel better then." He attempted a smile and his face looked so old it was shocking.

"Tomorrow then, in the morning. Here, eight o'clock?"

He nodded agreement.

"So which way are you walkin'?" Joff asked. Maybe they were heading the same way.

"Limehouse," he replied. "I got a little room just off the 'ighway!"

"Well I'm goin' the other way so I'll see you tomorrow."

Joff pushed the table out so he could go over to the other side and gave his friend one more hug. Even through the clothing and the heavy overcoat, he could feel Tin's ribs sticking in him, and the arm Tin clasped around him was no thicker than a young woman's would be.

"We'll 'ave some breakfast!" Joff said, holding him at arm's length.

"Yeah, that'll be nice!" he replied, the faintest hint of a smile playing across his lips.

His gaze shifted downwards briefly then he looked up and asked, "Do you think you can spare me a few coins 'til then?"

That caught Joff rather by surprise but he fished in his coat pocket and gave him the few coins he hadn't spent on drink.

"Here!" he said, "take it!"

* * *

Tin waited until his long lost friend had disappeared from view completely before he rose to his feet and shuffled off in the direction of the Docks, of Limehouse. He strode along the rubbish-strewn, uneven sidewalks, ignoring the commotion all around as he focused on not slipping over. He passed an open gulley hole from which sewage gurgled into the street, seeping onto the coat of a beggar who had passed out on the curb.

He walked around the beggar then after a few steps froze, gripping the coins in his pocket tightly as he sensed movement. He stood motionless, head bowed as four hooded figures cut hurriedly across his path. He let them pass. Then, using a wall for support he stepped gingerly over a broken wooden crate bridging the footpath. Once over the crate he cut left through an alley that skirted the edge of Cable Street, then looking first left then right he cut across the notoriously dangerous Ratcliff Highway.

Once across, once amongst the grimy, black buildings on the south side of the highway, he began to relax. He felt almost safe now. Quietly, he passed a sleeping family scattered either side of a narrow archway. Eyes in the shadows watched his progress, watched him pick his way through the dirt and filth, but no alarms were raised. The old man was well known in these streets.

At the end of the alley he tapped on an old wooden door, which was opened after a short wait by a woman. She wore a scarf wrapped around her head, as was the way of the Orientals. She had deep-sunken eyes and a waxy pallor to her skin. She spoke, however, in a thick London accent.

"You wanna come in, Dearie?"

Tin mumbled something and pushed past her to the interior of the house. It had been dark on the doorstep but inside visibility was in even shorter supply.

"You knows the way, Dearie," she said as she closed the door behind them.

Tin padded down the narrow hallway. Rats moved aside for him, reluctantly and unafraid. He ran his fingertips along the peeling, damp wallpaper for guidance. Halfway down the hall he pushed through a ragged curtain where a single bare light bulb high up in the ceiling offered at least some degree of light.

Where the light barely penetrated, it only showed that everything was coated in thick black soot.

Tin ignored the squalor; he had been here many times, seen it all before. He had been here when the sun was high in the sky, when light actually managed to permeate to ground level and the peeling wallpaper and the bugs that lived in it were impossible to ignore, and he had been here, like now, when it was hard to see where you were going. It made no difference to him; he padded along until he came to the kitchen at the end of the hall. A Chinese man bowed at the waist as he approached. He was the opium master and this was his domain.

"Ah, Mr. Tin, you are here again."

"Mr. Chang," he nodded a greeting in the Oriental manner.

Tin slumped down on a stained mattress beneath a shuttered window and watched the Chinaman as he lit a little paraffin stove and pulled out a package. He tipped a tiny amount of opium into the end of a long clay pipe and held it over the flame. On the mattress, Tin ignored the filth and the biting fleas. Soon he would be oblivious to it all. He reclined. The tingle of anticipation was dancing across his stomach as his body awaited the drug.

In the gloom about him other bodies were also stretched out on grubby mattresses. Some stirred as the sweet smell wafted through the room and caught in their nostrils. The opium paste began to vaporise, sending black smoke willowing down the kitchen where it disturbed then mingled with the tendrils of wispy smoke already hovering the length of the room. The Chinaman removed the pipe from the heat and offered it for Tin to inhale.

* * *

The following morning, Joff left in plenty of time to allow for the congestion on the streets. At the pub he ordered himself a nice, refreshing half and half and sat down to await Tin.

The time of their appointment came and went and he tried to stay patient. He knew how it could be trying to get around London sometimes.

He only had to come from Limehouse, though, Joff couldn't help thinking. *He could walk that in a few minutes surely. It wasn't as though he had to use the new underground trains to get here.*

Joff smiled, shaking his head at the thought of them.

The new underground system was supposed to have put an end to congestion but it had simply brought more and more people into the city. They could be found at Waterloo, Euston, Paddington, Kings Cross, and all the other new train stations. People from all over England were being ferried at great speed about the capital with no regard for fellow road users or pedestrians. The streets, already full of mules pulling carts, speedy little two-horse vehicles, bigger horse-drawn public carriages, could barely cope.

Things were getting so bad there was even talk of introducing a system of lights to control the flow on the main thoroughfares. Red for stop and green for go, apparently.

Joff knew congestion made people late for appointments these days, but still, the nagging voice in his head kept repeating, *'e only 'ad to come from Lime'ouse. It's 'ardly the other end of the Earth.*

Joff ordered another drink and waited at the same table they had occupied the night before. He sipped at his drink, watching the second hand and its slower friend the minute hand dragging themselves around the old wooden clock, until finally he was two hours late and Joff could not bear to sit still for another second.

Limehouse, he had said his room was, so Limehouse it would be. Joff hadn't been over that way for some time but it only consisted of a few streets. He knew it well enough to know that a skinny, white English man shouldn't be too hard to find amongst all those foreigners.

CHAPTER NINE

Joff had gone down to Limehouse where dark stares had tracked his progress from one end of that rat-infested den of iniquity to the other. His enquiries had met with not just blank expressions but with almost open hostility at times.

He went back the following day, and again the next. Finally, after a whole week, he found his old captain. He was face down in the corner of a filthy courtyard. He had been badly beaten and was barely able to walk.

"Come on, Tin," Joff had said. "Let's get you out o' here."

He had tried to object but Joff lifted him easily and supported his pathetic frame from Limehouse to Whitechapel, where he laid the captain out on the bed. Aimee had reluctantly forced some gruel between his lips and it seemed to give him just enough strength to sleep. Hours later he awoke, writhing and stretching. It looked as though he was in extreme pain throughout his whole body.

Joff sat with him while Aimee and Jack huddled together on the floor, the three of them spending a horrible day watching Tin and wondering what was wrong with him, what it meant.

Not a moment too soon Joff heard the church bells peel the hour of four and he went to his friend and wiped his sweat-soaked brow one final time. He leaned in close to his chattering lips and spoke, not sure if his words were getting through.

"I've gotta go to work now. Aimee will take care of you 'til I return."

It was impossible to know if he had heard. His brow was soaked again as soon as Joff wiped it dry. He was seriously ill but they had no idea what was wrong, and wondered if Tin would make it through to the following morning. Joff squeezed his hand and told him quietly, "You're goin' to be alright again, Tin."

Joff turned to where Aimee sat hunched in the corner of the room with the boy curled up unhappily on her lap.

"Look after 'im, Girl, won't you?"

She nodded but Joff could see she wasn't happy with the arrangement.

He went down the staircase carefully, across the courtyard, through the alley, and crossed Commercial Street, heading west. As he cut through Bishopsgate, his mind drifted. He couldn't help remembering his time on the boat with Tin, where he had first learned the true beliefs of the Anarchists.

He and the crew had declared with the confidence of religious zealots that all men mattered equally. That the brave new world would enable each to find his niche, the thing he excelled at. They would all become experts in something, no matter how trivial or unimportant their specialty subject might be. Human individuality would ensure all fields were catered to. Experts would be available when problems arose, cooperation needed for the common good. They believed that individuals came before nations. That there must be pleasure in functioning socially or what was the point?

In the future, they had said, local and personal initiative would be encouraged and the majority would most definitely not be responsible for creating wealth for the chosen few.

They used to call on numerous examples of small countries where property laws didn't exist, communities that had thrived until the purges. Now, as they had predicted, each nation wanted to be the world's strongest and was more than willing to block the progress, the growth, of all others. Cooperation was a dirty word nowadays.

They had always seen society without authority as the ultimate goal but had known this was a dangerous path to choose. Knew that airing such views made them targets, enemies of the State, of the Empire and the all-powerful landowners. But they had soldiered on nonetheless.

They persisted in their system because it benefitted all; it really was that simple. They believed from the depths of their hearts it was a better way.

They recalled how the Europeans had destroyed complex societies in Africa and South America in the name of commerce. Killed and enslaved the people, redrawn borders, and called the locals savages when they had tried to fight back. Nobody could say that life had improved for those people.

They had seen Native American tribes also denounced as bloodthirsty heathens, non-human, and eventually the masses had believed the lies.

Now the Native Americans were being wiped out and nobody cared because 'they are not like us.'

Cultures that had flourished for thousands of years had been systematically destroyed until capitalism was the only show in town.

Everywhere, you saw mass suffering, deep misery, and poverty on industrial scales. Deadly wars being waged right across the planet over property and mining rights. Battles being waged in every corner of the globe, and when the dust settled not one single negotiated outcome brought any obvious benefit to the indigenous people.

Nationalism was being actively encouraged as a means of diverting attention from any peaceful solutions to the suffering everywhere. Strong industrialised nations were bullying weaker, more peaceful societies. The European elite wanted to control the whole world and they were doing it in the name of 'freedom.' Tin had never ceased to question these methods, these beliefs, and Joff had always respected him for that.

Tin believed in self-sufficient communities where each adult had a place, a reason that made them feel useful. Where wise counsel was shared willingly with neighbouring communities, where 'openness,' 'transparency,' and 'for the good of all' were the key words in all transactions. Under such conditions, when a member of the human race anywhere had a problem that he could not solve, there would always be an expert somewhere able to assist. This reciprocity was actively discouraged these days; one had to think about profit, not people.

Tin and many others had acted, they had travelled all over Europe raising awareness and meeting like-minded people. It was a dangerous life, for which they were ridiculed and persecuted from Seville to Paris, from Lisbon to Berlin.

Communication is the key, they said.

They needed better communication for their plan to really be international. Equal principles had to apply everywhere, and when they did, they felt that only then would the system be fairer to all, would be globally acceptable. The authorities made communication between nations, between individuals, as difficult as possible. They didn't want citizens making friends in far-off places, making their own minds up about who they liked or didn't like. It was for the leaders to make decisions like that, for them to decide if anyone should talk to other nationalities or kill them in large numbers.

Tin and the rest all knew their activities might get them killed before their time and they had been correct on that score as well.

Bobby was taken from them way before his time.

Davie was gunned down in a Lancashire mill town for daring to inform workers of their rights. Benn and Tila were hung on the Newgate Cross for their radical beliefs. Noah was sent to the Australian colony, never to return, until now, only Tin and Joff remained of the old crew.

Joff had never been more than on the periphery, though, and Tin—well, he had disappeared on that fateful night, never to be seen again, until now.

Joff walked through the cobbled streets, dwelling on his friend's return, thinking how odd it would be if he were to come back into his life only to drop dead on him. Joff hoped that didn't happen. He felt it might be nice to have Tin back on the scene after all this time.

Meanwhile, in Mayfair, on the other side of London, Squire Bradshaw was sipping at a gin and tonic as the sun dropped gently below the yardarm. At his feet lay a hunting hound with a huge bone between its jaws. It was having trouble keeping hold of the giant bone and it brushed against the Squire's trousers, leaving a trail of dog saliva across the expensive fabric.

The Squire frowned slightly and looked down. Before he could speak, an immaculately dressed serving girl was at his side offering him the use of a beautifully crisp linen cloth.

"Don't give it to me, wipe it off, you stupid girl!" he declared.

The girl silently dropped to her knees and wiped at the saliva. The giant hound started to show an interest in the girl now that she was down at his level. He leaned his weight into her and she fell slightly against the Squire's legs. She dared not look at him but wiped and retreated as quickly as possible.

The Squire's glare followed her until she disappeared from sight.

Alongside the Squire sat another fine example of an English gentleman. He picked up a little bell that was sitting on the ornate iron circular table between them.

"Do you need me to call her back?"

Squire Bradshaw glanced over at his host, "Maybe tonight," he said, and they grinned at each other like naughty schoolboys.

"So you have to present to the house tomorrow?" asked the Squire.

"Don't worry, Bradshaw. We have men in place now in all areas of the civil service. Greedy, selfish men who will do as we ask so long as the price is right."

"I am worried," replied Squire Bradshaw. "These Communists will be the death of us."

His host smiled, "Don't worry, they are too late, everything is already in place. Capitalism will be adopted by every country in the world and we will sit at the head table, taking a small cut from all sides." He was smiling as he spoke.

The Squire looked into his eyes and saw confidence in abundance. Things had been quietly pushed through onto the statute books and now theft of property carried a heavier punishment than harm to a fellow human being. Industry was more important than pleasure and profits were now more important than people.

"I hope our cut won't be too small," the Squire whispered, sipping at his morning coffee.

"I don't think you need to worry about that," replied his host.

Squire Bradshaw returned his china cup to its saucer and asked in a more business-like tone, "Any news on my piano player?"

* * *

Back in the dirty hovel on the East side of town, Jack wriggled in his mother's lap.

Aimee gripped the lad tighter to her, digging her nails into his flesh so that she didn't have to raise her voice. The toddler flinched with the pain and stopped struggling. They both stared towards the man on their bed as he kicked and moaned and writhed and sweated. Sporadically, Jack would try and wriggle free when he thought his ma had relaxed her hold. Every time she was ready for him and he got a sharp pinch for his troubles. They watched as the patient wretched into the grime-encrusted bowl for the umpteenth time. Yet again, nothing came up, only this time he seemed to notice that they were there. He managed to prop himself up on one elbow and say something, but no recognisable words came forth. He beckoned them to come closer and Aimee pushed the boy forwards.

"See what 'e wants, Jack!" she hissed at the frightened infant.

Jack didn't want to get any closer to the scary old man. He wanted to cry, but he didn't want his mother's sharp talons digging into his skin again.

Tin beckoned the boy nearer and Jack edged unwillingly a few inches closer to the bed.

Then with a surprisingly swift movement for one so ill, Tin grabbed out and gripped the child by the neck. He pulled the boy unwillingly to within inches of his spittle-covered lips and hissed in his ear.

"I need my medicine, Boy! I need my medicine!"

Jack looked helplessly towards his ma. He hadn't particularly liked being imprisoned on her lap but this was far worse. The creepy old sailor was spitting in his ear and he smelled as though he hadn't seen a bath for months.

Jack started to wriggle. He wriggled so violently that he managed to extract himself from the grip. His mother made no attempt to cushion him as he fell backwards onto the floor. Aimee tutted, then looked up at the stranger on her bed.

She shrugged as though apologizing for the boy.

"My medicine?" Tin repeated.

"We've got no money for medicine," Aimee shot back.

Tin had lain back down but at this news he raised himself up on one elbow again. He tried to smile but the exertion of energy made him cough instead. She could see he wanted to say something and she waited until he was ready. Listened intently as he said, "I've got money."

Aimee smiled. He had her full attention now.

"'Ave you, Dear? In that case we'll soon 'ave you up an' about, then, won't we."

Tin had no choice but to trust her.

"Laudanum," he whispered, "I need laudanum."

Aimee stared at him, unsure whether to repeat that she had no money or whether to wait for him to remember. She waited.

Around his neck, Tin had a leather pouch on a lanyard. From it he fished out a couple of pennies. He tried to hand them to Aimee but dropped one on the filthy, damp bed and she scooped it up.

"Two pennies?" she said.

Tin nodded, "Yes... No," he suddenly changed his mind, fished back inside his shirt, and pulled out two more pennies. "Get four," his voice trailed off as he repeated, "Get four."

* * *

It was just another day in the life of a working musician. In the morning Joff had walked from Whitechapel to Islington to give a one-hour piano lesson to the lovely daughter of a nice Jewish family. Then he had walked down to the Strand for his usual four-hour show. Afterwards, he gave another hour's lesson for sixpence and then did the three-hour evening show.

The moon was high in the sky by the time he got home. He wearily climbed the stairs, exhausted and starving. He opened the door and was heartened to see that Tin was sitting up in bed, undoubtedly looking a million times better than he had been only that morning.

They smiled at each other as Joff swung the door further open. Behind it he saw Aimee slumped in the chair. He couldn't smell any dinner and couldn't see anything cooking, but there was calmness over the room that he hadn't experienced for some time.

"Hello, Dear." He approached Aimee and was thrilled at the winning smile she met him with.

He kissed her on the lips and she actually grabbed him round the waist, willed him to linger a moment longer. He couldn't remember when he last felt like a man getting home after a hard day's work to be greeted by his loving wife.

"Where's Jack?" he asked, addressing the top of her head.

"'E's 'ere," she replied as he felt her grip loosen on him.

Tin lay on the bed, and Joff could feel him watching.

"How you feelin' now?" he enquired.

He nodded, half smiling. "I'm good," he answered.

In the darkest shadows behind the door the boy had fallen asleep.

Laudanum was rife not just in the East End of the 1870's but in the whole of the country. It was well understood that it was a way of unwinding at the end of the day. A one ounce bottle of Laudanum containing ten percent opium was priced at a penny. Exactly the same amount as you would be expected to pay for a pint of beer in the local public house. Some people, mainly men, preferred the social effects of alcohol and the male-orientated environment to be found in their local pubs. Others, mainly women, did not have the option of going to the pub but still wanted something to help get them through the day.

For those who couldn't manage a trip outside, a door-to-door service was provided in even the darkest, most isolated, corners of London. All over the East End women could be seen in their drug-induced states, propping up the very same walls as men who couldn't handle their drink.

Aimee came and whispered in Joff's ear, "'E sent me out for laudanum an' it's perked 'im up no end."

Then she pulled a money pouch from her skirts and slapped it into the palm of her hand. It made the delightful chink of coin against coin. "An' he's given me some lodgin' money too." She smiled at him and he could see in her eyes that she was high, distant, contented.

"You're high!" he stated, smiling.

"Tomorrow I'll get one for you," she said, ignoring his comment.

Unexpectedly, she hugged him tight and he was ridiculously grateful for the contact. For once she was letting him in. He was relieved that the laudanum calmed her so.

Joff went out onto the busy street smiling, weary but glad at the peaceful atmosphere that had descended over their room. He stopped at a stall and bought some eels for his supper, then managed to climb the stairs and curl up gratefully on the floor, where he fell asleep.

The following night Aimee saved him a one-ounce bottle of laudanum. The three of them stayed in their room and dozed blissfully in and out of consciousness. Joff vaguely recalled Jack returning to disturb them at some point in the night but he was gone by the time Joff fully awoke.

Over the next week, Joff returned to his normal routine. Busy all day until after the final evening performance. Then he would return and the three of them would sit up till dawn. Aimee trying to convince them that women could run the world much better than men did, if only they would be allowed to participate. Tin telling her she was better off out of it.

Soon he was mobile again and he would head down to Limehouse and buy his own opium. The effects were more intense, he said, and the buzz lasted longer than the penny bottles of the watered-down version. He had lost his enthusiasm for politics. As long as there was a tonic to look forward to at the end of the day, nothing else mattered anymore.

He had been lodging with Joff and Aimee for a couple of weeks when Joff came home late from the theatre one night just in time to see his old captain heading out the door with his heavy coat on. He announced that he was feeling much fitter now, and besides, he said, his funds were running low and he had to go back to Limehouse to collect some cash that was owed to him.

"Maybe you want to come along an' keep me company," Tin had said.

"Money collectin'?" Joff raised a quizzical eyebrow. They both knew he was useless in such situations.

"It ain't like that!" he replied.

"Yeah I'll come," Joff nodded agreement.

As they walked out into the courtyard Joff heard the sound of Aimee's voice. She was leaning out of the window above. "Where's Jack?" she screeched down at him.

"Ain't seen 'im for days," he shouted back.

They were losing him and they both knew it, but what could they do? They grew up so fast around here, they had to.

"Wait for me!" Aimee shouted down.

Her words surprised him. He looked across to Tin. "That alright?" he asked.

He nodded and shrugged. "No bother," he said.

It was a clear night with just the slightest of breezes wafting through the alleys.

Joff walked slightly behind the others. Slowly it began to dawn on him how close they had become. He should have seen it, really, but how could he have? For weeks they had been home alone. Joff's thoughts began to run wild. He had slowed his pace while thinking about it, so he shook off his thoughts and upped his speed. He wanted to catch up with them so he could hear their conversation.

"It's a bit dirty, I got to say," he heard Tin tell her.

Joff hoped her reply might give him some idea as to what had been going on. It might shed some light on exactly what sort of relationship they had formed. He was disappointed Aimee did not launch into some long, explanatory reply, but instead, alerted by his footsteps, she turned to him and smiled. They parted slightly and allowed him to slot in between them.

"I was just sayin' to Aimee that I got to pick up some money from an ol' Chinaman an' it's pretty grubby down there." He turned to look at Joff before continuing, "Not dangerous, just dirty."

Joff looked around them. It wasn't exactly a healthy environment right here. How bad could it be?

"I'm sure we will be fine," he replied.

There had been more to their conversation, he was sure of it, but what could he do.

Tin stepped aside and looked up at Joff again, allowing him to go first as the path narrowed through a gap between two warehouses.

"Nearly there," Tin whispered as Joff passed.

Joff smiled and frowned together as he walked to the far end of the alley. He waited there for him.

"What did you say?" Joff asked.

Tin grinned like a mischievous boy, and his silence was deafening.

Joff stepped aside to let Tin take the lead again, shaking his head in mock despair as his friend passed. Tin winked and after a few more paces he stepped hard left and they followed him into a foul-smelling courtyard and huddled behind him as he knocked on a tatty old door.

Joff was curious, he had to admit, and one glance at Aimee confirmed she was more than curious—she was excited.

Looking back, Joff should have walked out of there right then. Walked out and insisted that she go with him. He should have left the old captain to fend for himself. He should have thought more about Aimee, about the boy, about their little family. Perhaps then things would have turned out differently.

But Joff was only a man and Aimee had wanted to stay, and his curiosity had gotten the better of him. He ignored the smell and the dilapidated surroundings. Instead, he focused on the friendly Chinese and the cheapness of their product, and when the old man enquired as to whether Aimee was to partake, she did so, without one word of protest from Joff.

CHAPTER TEN

A pile of feathers lay strewn across the courtyard, flapping in the wind, but most of them too sticky with mud to actually float away.

"What did you do that for, Jack?" Charley asked, although he already knew the answer.

"The fella said 'e wanted the cage but not the bird, you 'eard 'im yourself!" Jack shot back, excitement blazing in his eyes.

Charley shook his head, "Yeah but there weren't no need to...," he glanced again at the feathers and shook his head, realising he was wasting his breath.

"It don't matter," he continued. "Come on, let's go sell the bloody thing, I'm sick of carryin' it 'round anyhow."

Jack grinned; he kicked the tiny, wingless corpse hard against the wall and a burst of bright yellow feathers flew upwards. The boys ran off laughing. They dodged through the barrows and stalls of the market traders, skillfully avoiding the numerous hazardous objects that came at them in a steady procession.

They had a series of brief whistles or parts of words that they uttered as warnings to each other as they flew across the market.

Jack, as ever in the lead, let out a short, sharp hiss. 'The handle of that cart juts out at eye level' the hiss said.

"Hup!" and Charley veered left instantly and in full flight to avoid a moving wheel.

The wooden spoke of a mud-covered cart stuck out at ankle height under its dirty awning.

The fly rope of a canvas stall cut right across their path, practically invisible to the naked eye. All hazards were identified and negotiated at speed with the secret language they had developed.

The system worked so well because whilst Jack was looking out for obstacles, Charley was constantly scanning the sea of faces in the crowds. Searching out the well-dressed gentleman who had shown an interest in their hand-painted, delicately carved bird cage not more than ten minutes previously. He had mentioned that it might look rather nice in his parlour with a hart's tongue fern growing through its bars, but had been adamant that in its present state with its present occupier it was no use to him at all.

So Jack had ducked through the crowds to the nearest quiet spot and pulled the helpless, frightened little canary roughly from its perch. He had ripped each of its wings off with his bare hands and hurled the mortally injured animal slamming into a brick wall. The bird had hit the wall at quite some speed then bounced onto the cobbles. Jack had pounced with amazing speed and connected with the point of his hob-nailed boot. Feathers had flown off it in a blaze of yellow and from that moment it was unquestionably dead.

"One empty cage! We can sell it now, eh!" Jack had smirked.

Charley never ceased to be amazed at his friend's ability to suddenly break out into random acts of wanton violence, and when he did it was always accompanied by excitement blazing in his dark eyes.

There was no point asking his friend why he did it. He had asked many times and always the answer was the same: "I don't know, I just feel like it," followed by a shrug, like it was nothing.

The two boys found the well-dressed stranger in record time. They haggled and cajoled and convinced the man to part with far more than the cage was actually worth, and ran off laughing as soon as Charley had the coins in his hand.

Ahead of them, spread out on the barrier of the Ferris wheel, raised above the level of the rest of the crowd, three sharply dressed youths were watching the two seven-year-olds with the cage bobbing through their market crowds. They observed with great interest as the kids approached the dandy with the waxed moustache and they had been around long enough to tell, even at this distance, that a sale had just been made. Now the sellers, with the money in their hot little hands, were heading straight for them.

The middle youth looked about seventeen. He wore a peaked cap and an old fishing jumper over a once-white collarless shirt. His trousers were rolled up several times at the ankle and the buttons of a pair of braces could be seen holding the oversized trousers up before disappearing beneath his jumper. His feet were bare and caked in mud. He looked down where four more boys stood about at ground level, scanning the crowds and generally trying to appear tough.

They all paid attention as their leader spoke up.

"There's two kids comin' right towards us. They's carryin' for sure. Don, Terry, go that way, spread out to arm's length, go slow. Davie, Ron, go that way, same. Don't let the little bleeders slip through. Keep an eye on me; I'll point 'em out to yous." He frowned through three hundred and sixty degrees, including them all equally in his displeasure. "Now! Go!"

They moved into formation and went into work mode. Robbing children was the life blood of this firm. They were vastly experienced and each and every one knew what was expected of him.

Phillip, their leader, sat and watched things as they developed. He considered himself a master tactician with a critical eye for the subtle nuances that could rapidly transform into life-changing moments. The two kids were crowding together. That was good. It meant they were unaware they were being monitored. Phillip flicked his right hand discreetly and his hyper-alert troops caught the motion and altered tack accordingly, headed more to the right with tight, almost military-like precision.

Phillip was smirking, watching but making sure not to stare too intently. His boys had closed the gap to no more than six or seven feet now, and they were getting closer with each step. He caught the movement of Davie's arm and knew he was pulling a cosh out from under his jacket. Saw his shoulder raise slightly as they edged ever closer and then, right then, the two children made their move and Phillip realised he had been played, by a couple of kids.

The false smile never slipped from his face for a second, but beneath it he was seething. He had been too confident, too complacent, hadn't realised that they had been rumbled and the kids were acting out a plan of their own, an escape no less. Phillip watched them racing through the rows of carts and motioned furiously for his troops to speed up, to catch them before they were able to escape through the alley and out into the busy main road where there would be too many policemen to follow them.

"Poot!" Charley gasped.

Suddenly and without any rhyme or reason, Charley and Jack had scuttled right when they should have kept going straight ahead. Right under a cart and through a set of wheels, towards an alley and out to the high street.

Jack half turned, trying to catch sight of his pal.

"Oi you! Watch it!" a trader bellowed and Jack just dodged his dangling assortment of cured hams.

He ducked and weaved through them. For a brief moment he hesitated, lost the momentum. He allowed his concentration a split second's respite and one of the swinging hams caught him squarely in the temple. Instinctively he raised a hand to the stinging scrape. He glanced at his hand as he ran and saw a smear of blood. The blood, the hams, the chase—despite it all his legs kept carrying him forwards for the safety of the high street. Jack puffed out his cheeks and sprinted with his deepest reserves. He burst right across a main junction, swerved skillfully around a fast-moving horse and carriage, and finally began to slow down.

As he reached the far end of the alley the sharp, stinging pain in his temple had already turned into a dull aching thud. He was no longer running on instinct—reality was returning, he was thinking again.

Charley, he thought, *what about Charley?*

There were no echoing footsteps following him so he looked over his shoulder. No Charley. The large, imposing wall of the docks ran solidly on his right, and on his left he saw a maze of tenements that he was unfamiliar with, where he was not known. Up ahead he could see the crowds passing across the junction at the far end, see a wheel or a flash of cart here and there as the traffic rumbled noisily along the main road. He edged cautiously back towards the narrow alleys; he had to see what had happened to Charley.

Barely moments before when Jack had been fleeing, the route had seemed incredibly long. Now that he was creeping quietly back the other way, the market seemed to be coming at him far more quickly. With a few more cautious paces he would be back out in the open. When he reached the backs of the wagons he hesitated. He thought that the two wagons directly in front of him were lashed too tightly together. However, they hadn't done such a good job on the next one to his left. There was a gap between the wheels that he knew he could easily squeeze through. He eyed it and braced himself to move. He stepped around the blind corner and a cosh caught him right across the stomach. All the air rushed out of him and he slammed backwards against the grimy stonework. He registered more pain as his elbow connected with the wall. Then before he had a chance to fall forwards they were on him. Rough hands grabbing at his collar and lapels. Forcing him backwards, so they had a bigger target to rain their punches down on. They made him lurch forwards again and used the momentum to push him down into the dirt, where fists and coshes rained down across his little shoulders, back, buttocks, and legs.

"Check 'is pockets!" he heard somebody say.

Then he was rolled over and the back of his head connected with the floor as someone forced his arm behind his back.

Jack knew the odds were hopeless so he ceased his struggling and let them roll him and rob him. He accepted the extra unnecessary hits he took as a fair payment for the beatings he had dished out himself. He closed his eyes and pretended to be dead. As they beat him to within an inch of his life he imagined what it was like to really be dead. He made no attempt to cover his face or protect himself in any way. That was probably what saved his life.

Charley had not managed to go into a trance and accept the beating as 'his turn.' He had panicked, lashed out wildly, and like a pack of hungry dogs they had been ruthless. They had seen Charley pocket the cash, knew he was carrying, and laid into him every bit as enthusiastically as they had done to Jack. Then with Charley defeated, at their leader's suggestion they had lain in wait for Jack to return down the alley as Phillip knew he surely would.

Hours later when Jack had recovered enough strength to crawl around the corner, he found his best friend dead in a pile of rubbish. The market was closing up for the day, the wagons had moved, and the crowds were once again using the pavements. Hundreds of people were passing just inches from where a dead boy lay in a pile of old boxes. Not one stopped to see if they might be of assistance. Dead children were nothing new.

* * *

Aimee lay back on the filthy mattress as the opium pipe was held to her lips. She inhaled deeply and held the smoke in her lungs for as long as she could. Muscles were twitching throughout her whole body, from the tips of her toes to the top of her head, but especially her inner thighs. It felt as though an orgasm of massive intensity was coursing through her legs and she couldn't get enough of it. Greedily she sucked as the last embers glowed red then fizzed out of existence. A cloud of heavy white smoke, followed by the last wispy grey tendrils, passed through the glass pipe and into her mouth.

Joff watched her from the neighbouring mattress and could only smile. He could see the dragon had gotten hold of her, had seen the greedy sparkle in her eyes. Alarm bells were ringing extremely loudly, warning him that she was showing all the signs of someone who liked the taste just a little too much, that it was time to get her out of there.

Joff made no moves in that respect, though, just lay there watching, grinning like an imbecile. He did nothing because the feelings flowing through his bones were the best he had ever experienced. He was afraid that if he moved, even slightly, then the euphoria would vanish and he would never feel like that again. That was too terrible to contemplate, so he lay as still as he could with a ridiculous great grin spread across his face, and watched his lady as she was falling apart.

Behind her in the dim light something moved and Joff looked. He could just make out Tin. He was deep in conversation with their host, but his eyes kept catching the light. They were darting everywhere, and when he saw Joff looking at him he nodded.

What was he up to? There was far more to this than met the eye, and Joff could actually feel the muscles on his face gliding as his smile slipped into a frown. It was time to leave. He didn't really want to but he had to for Aimee's sake. Well for all their sakes—her, him, the boy.

He was only seven, after all. No matter how tough he acted he still needed his mother from time to time.

Joff somehow dragged himself into a sitting position and sat huddled over on the edge of the mattress, allowing his head to clear before he tried to stand upright.

"Come on Aimee!" he said, moving forwards and shaking her by the arm.

"Come on, it's time to go!"

Joff looked across at Tin, who was on his back again, beaming up at him.

"We're goin'," Joff told him. "You comin'?"

"Nah, I'm alright 'ere," he said as he waved at Joff dismissively, already trying to get the attention of the pipe boy.

Aimee had not moved at all in response to her husband's words. He turned to face her again.

"Aimee!" he said a little more loudly, and this time she turned to look at him.

"Come on," he repeated. "We're goin'."

Joff could see by her face that she would have preferred to stay exactly where she was. He grabbed her by the sleeve and shook her slightly, just to let her know that he was not in the mood. She frowned but gripped his outstretched arm and let him haul her to her feet. She didn't resist as he half dragged her out into the night air.

Normally she would have created a scene, but tonight she was so high, she didn't care.

Joff was supporting her with his arm around her narrow waist. She had both arms draped across his shoulders and was leaning against him as they walked, closer together than they had walked in years. He sensed she was trusting him to guide the way and he couldn't recall when that had last happened. Maybe things were turning a corner; he loved her again.

It must have rained whilst they were indoors because a wet sheen coated everything they passed, and these filthy streets, in his state of mind, looked beautiful and romantic under the moonlight. Aimee had a dreamy, far away, peaceful look on her face that he knew was the influence of the drug, but which he loved because it appeared as though all her problems had been lifted. The frowns had been wiped off her face and she looked so much younger, once more like the timid barmaid he had fallen in love with twenty years ago. He hugged her tight and she smiled up at him. She could feel it as well, one of those rare moments when they were still close after all the years they'd been together.

Almost too soon they were approaching the place where they lived. Joff let his feet slop through the mud so that she could stay on the drier part, and they both managed to smile when the gooey muck squelched up to his ankle.

"'ere we are," he said as their courtyard came into view.

"Yeah," she replied. "You go on, I won't be a mo'."

Joff headed for their door, still smiling. They may not have much but they still had each other and right now that was enough for him. He glanced back and saw Aimee was exactly as he had left her. She was standing in the middle of the road, staring back at him. They smiled at each other and he opened the door and went inside.

Aimee waited until he had gone into the building before she made her way unsteadily to the curb. She looked both ways before she slumped down and removed a little glass, one-ounce bottle of Laudanum from her pocket. She glanced around once more, checking for prying eyes, then she popped out the cork stopper and drained the fluid in a series of gulps.

She was already flying but she liked the effect. She liked it so much she wanted it to be stronger, more intense, and she wanted to make it last longer. She was getting her desire. Wave after wave of euphoria washed over her whole body. All her worries, the day-to-day, hand-to-mouth existence were completely forgotten. She had given up drinking some years before because it made her violent, but she had missed the booze, still struggled almost daily to stay off it. Well now she had found the perfect solution. This was the feeling she had been after all her life, she realised. God bless the day Tin had come back into their lives.

Aimee had one little bottle left in her pocket. She considered going inside and sharing it with Joff. They could have one more hit together and then perhaps in the privacy of their room he would enter her, a perfect end to a perfect day.

Instead, her inner demon took over. She decided she might as well finish it off and then go inside. She popped the cork, drank the liquid, and as it entered her blood stream her heart slowed down fractionally as it had been doing all evening. This, however, was the hit that sent her over the top.

Her vital organs relaxed slightly more. Her heart, her brain, both wanted to surrender completely to the glorious feeling of deep, deep relaxation. She lay down on the filthy pavement, still smiling.

* * *

Jack was badly injured. The walk from Limehouse to Whitechapel should have taken him fifteen minutes. Three hours after limping away from the alley, away from Charley, he was still not home. The moon was nearly full, casting long shadows that draped themselves across the slums. Despite the earlier rain, the stench of decay hung high in the air and rats scurried ahead of him constantly. Even at this hour, plenty of people watched him go. No one offered to help. They recognised his vulnerability and wanted no part of it. Slowly, one step at a time, he staggered and limped his way towards home.

He leaned against a wall and paused to catch his breath. The pain in his ribs was unbearable when he breathed deeply. He took four shallow gasps, and aiming for the opposite side of the street, he pushed off the wall, leaving a smear of blood as he did so. Little tell-tale smears of blood marked his slow progress all the way from the alley, each one slightly fainter than the last.

Finally he could see the courtyard. Four hours after leaving Charley he was in sight of home. It had been a long day and he wanted to lie down and sleep for a thousand years.

Ordinarily Jack would not have given the pile of rubbish on the steps of the tenement a second glance, but something about it caught his eye. Something was shining white in the moonlight and sticking out from the dark pile. It looked odd, out of place. The curiosity of the instinctive survivor, the eternal forager, meant he had no option but to investigate. No matter how tired he was, regardless of how much pain he was in, this might be something worth finding. He edged closer, his curiosity piqued. He was only four or five feet away before the shadows gave up their secret. It was an arm, a human arm pointing skywards. Jack was less interested now. The pockets of the dead were rarely worth emptying around here. Still, he stepped closer and crouched lower. He moved a newssheet that was covering the face, and a little empty Laudanum bottle rolled down and clinked onto the cobbles. Its movement meant his eye followed it briefly, for a split second, then he looked into the face of the dead person and his mother stared blankly back at him.

Jack rummaged frantically for her hand. It was still warm to his touch. Quickly he looked into her eyes and was convinced he watched as the light went out of them. He knew she was floating above him now, that she was leaving him, going to join the angels, and he was furious.

He was in excruciating pain every time he swallowed, but now he was swallowing hard; he couldn't stop himself. Then the swallows turned to great big sobs and his pain was somehow forgotten. Tears streamed down his face. Ma had been petty and vindictive, even downright cruel at times, and now she was floating off to heaven and she was taking the last pieces of love from his heart with her.

"Ma! Ma! Wake up, Ma!"

He sat there squeezing her hand, calling her name, and staring at her. He knew that nothing would ever be right again. First Charley and now Ma. He hadn't known he had loved them but he knew it now, now that they were gone.

* * *

Upstairs, Joff heard a noise coming from the street below. Aimee had been ages and he must have dozed off. He looked out through the window for her but four floors below in the dead of night he could see nothing. He considered going down for her but didn't want to ascend the rickety old staircase again. Whole sections of the banister had been taken for firewood recently and it was dangerous, especially in the dark, especially in his state. He looked again through the filthy glass as best he could, trying to see if there was any movement on the street below. But he could see nothing.

"Aimee!" he called, but no response was forthcoming.

Joff was frowning now, getting a little annoyed. If she was sulking because he had dragged her away from that drug den, well then, let her sulk. He was going to sleep.

* * *

Back in Limehouse, Tin was lying back with his eyes closed, having a beautiful dream. He was flying over a land where peace and harmony reigned supreme. People were looking skywards and waving at him with happiness on their faces. He felt that life should always be that way. Then he felt someone tugging at his arm. He tried to ignore it, tried to stay in the dream, but the tugging would not cease and the spell was broken.

"Tin! Tin!"

Someone was calling his name and they weren't about to stop. He had no option but to open his eyes, acknowledge their presence, and come back to Earth.

"What?" he hissed.

"It's me, Pearl, wake up!"

He groaned inwardly.

Pearl Wilson was the most perfectly proportioned female he had ever known. She had alabaster skin and the face of an angel. Dark curls cascaded down her back in a thick, shiny ponytail and her eyes were the deepest shade of green. She broke hearts everywhere she went.

However, she had no time for love, she was too busy being the most hard-core revolutionary Tin had ever heard tale of. She famously preached that the only crime was to hurt others, then cheerfully tortured bankers for the keys to their safes.

She maintained that the meaning of life was love, yet had a pathological hatred of men and their predictable ways.

"No social revolution can be accomplished by men," she said, "as all they ever want is to be the man on top, thus maintaining the status quo. Men," she said, "just want women for sex," and in her case it was usually true.

Tin opened his eyes and she had him.

"It's after midnight!" she stated accusatorily, and he could only close his eyes again.

There was no way she was letting him off that lightly, though.

"It's after midnight," she repeated. "I get a message from the Chinaman saying you will be with us in one hour an' you have this piano player with you."

With his eyes closed he didn't feel it coming but she grabbed him by the lapels and shook him with a surprising amount of strength.

"We waited. We delayed the meeting," then she raised her voice and continued, "FOR YOU! People were waiting, waiting in danger because you said you would come, an' what did you do?"

He knew it was a hypothetical question.

"You let us all down! That's what you did!" she spat out.

He knew she was working herself up into a fury. He had no option but to admit defeat, leave his drug-induced dreams for another time, and come clean.

"Alright, alright," he tried to placate her.

"Alright? Is that all you can say?" she hissed.

He shuffled up the mattress until his back was against the hard wall and he was more or less sitting straight. He didn't try to respond, just let her go on, but he was sitting up now and his eyes were open. She was beginning to slow down.

"We all knew that stuff 'ad you in its grip," she said, glaring at the empty pipe by his side. "An' now I've seen it wiv my own eyes!"

She grabbed him by the arm and said, "Come on, let's go!"

He shook her off and allowed a scowl to play across his face.

She took a step back and stood over him with her arms crossed, her face like thunder.

God, she's beautiful when she's angry, Tin thought.

"So where is 'e now then, this piano player?" she wanted to know.

"Gone 'ome," Tin answered, feeling his eyes start to droop again.

That was an end to the matter as far as he was concerned. Perhaps his dreams would still be waiting for him? Perhaps he should have another hit on the pipe?

It was not to be. No sooner had his eyes shut than she was tugging at his sleeve again.

"No you don't! Come on, you can show me where 'e lives!"

He had known Pearl long enough to know that he might as well get to his feet.

* * *

As they approached the court, it was obvious that something was amiss. Even for this neighborhood, there were too many shadowy figures leaning out of windows for the time of night. Craning their necks, all trying to get a decent look at the street below.

Clusters of people were scattered along the length of the road, talking in hushed tones, and Tin could hear enough snippets of conversation to realize that somebody had just died and been carted off to the mortuary.

Tin grabbed Pearl by the back of her coat and she was forced to stop.

"What?" she wanted to know.

"Maybe we should come back another time. Come back in the mornin', eh. What do you think?"

She stood with her hands on her hips and snorted with contempt at his cowardly suggestion.

"That's so typical of a man!" she began as she launched into a tirade against men in general and him in particular.

Tin stood there feeling chastised yet undeniably aroused as her breasts heaved and swelled in time to her rants.

"Listen to yourself; it's pathetic!" she declared.

She spat at his feet then launched into another scathing attack, lumping all men together as worthless and pathetic until her cheeks were glowing red with rage.

He stood with his head bowed until finally she demanded, "Where does 'e live? Take me to 'im!"

Tin led the way reluctantly through an unlocked, unpainted wooden door and slowly up the rickety stairs. As they approached the top floor he was surprised that a small number of people were gathered around the doorway to Joe's room, but he didn't really dwell on why that might be at such an ungodly hour. He knew Aimee often had her radical friends over to discuss politics. He checked behind him to make sure Pearl was still there, that she hadn't become ensnared on one of the vicious splinters or fallen through one of the many gaps in the banister. She was still there only three steps behind, scowling at him.

* * *

Joff sat on the bed numb with shock.

"Ma's dead," the boy had said, and then he had shot back down the staircase at a reckless speed, completely ignoring his calls for him to come back and explain. After a few minutes Joff realised he wasn't about to return and that he had better go and see for himself what Jack meant.

Ma was dead? That couldn't be right. His Aimee? He had only left her a short while ago.

He had gone downstairs, out into the night, and found her lying next to a pile of rubbish, facing the wall. He remembered screaming her name and remembered one of the neighbors leading him away, and now somehow he was back upstairs.

Joff was staring through the window when he heard his name being called and he slowly turned back to face the room and there was Tin.

"What's 'appened?" he asked.

"It's Aimee!" Joff told him.

There was no need to explain further; there must have been something in the expression on Joff's face. That and the crowd around the door at such an hour, perhaps. It was irrelevant, really. Tin rushed to him and they hugged. It gave Joff strength when he needed it most.

As they hugged he saw a woman come into view over his shoulder. She was extraordinary. Such beauty that she looked out of place there. He wasn't sure that she was real, and then their eyes locked. She stared at him and then, in a flash, she was gone.

CHAPTER ELEVEN

A week later Joff stood in respectful silence at the side of an irrelevant place which Aimee was to share with strangers for the rest of eternity.

She deserves more than this, he thought, staring into the municipal grave, as he wondered why there were no tears welling up in his eyes, only an angry knot in the pit of his stomach.

Tin was alongside him and he had to admit he had been a true friend this past week. Jack was supposed to have been with them but the boy had been nowhere to be seen this morning and in the end they'd left without him. Joff wasn't concerned that Jack was bottling it all in, not showing his emotions; that was generally a good thing growing up around there. No, Joff had told him about the funeral but if he didn't want to come he wasn't about to force the boy. Joff was sure that Jack had better things to do. He did at that age.

"Ashes to ashes, dust to dust. In sure and certain hope...," the minister's words interrupted his train of thought.

Joff jumped slightly as the man threw a handful of earth down onto the lid of the coffin, then he knelt, and, scooping up a handful, did the same. Tin followed suit and that was it, the official proceedings were over.

"Come on!" Tin had draped his arm over Joff's shoulders. "Fancy a drink?" he asked.

Joff nodded and allowed himself to be pulled away from the graveside. They walked slowly through the smattering of headstones. Most looked new and were well kept and they made him feel ashamed. He knew that he wouldn't get up there very often. Weeds would be allowed to grow around Aimee's grave, life would go on.

They sat in the nearest pub and Tin ordered, then sliding one glass along the bar to Joff and raising the other, he said, "To Aimee!"

Joff raised his glass and smiled for the first time that day.

"That's better," Tin said, noticing his friend's expression. "She wouldn't want you mopin' around now, would she?"

Joff shrugged, acknowledging the truth of his words.

"A pauper's grave, tho Tin." Joff looked at him sadly, shaking his head.

He touched Joff's arm briefly, "Yeah I know," he said in sympathy.

Tin raised his glass and drank without taking his eyes from Joff's face.

"So, what are you goin' to do now?" he asked after taking a hefty drink, and Joff shrugged without looking up.

Tin drank again and Joff could feel he was still looking at him.

"What are you goin' to do about the boy?" he said, putting his empty glass noisily down on the wooden bar.

This time Joff did look up although he said nothing in response, simply shrugged again, and his expression told his friend he was not really ready for such a train of thought.

"Come on," Tin declared, "drink up, let's get out of 'ere!"

Tin led Joff down Leman Street towards the river and then left into Cable Street. On their right side the dock wall loomed large, casting a long, dark shadow. A group of Irishmen had commandeered the pavement on one side. They were twisting long pieces of hemp together, making a ship's cable. It was work that had gone on here for so long they had named the street after the cable twisters. They took a break from their work and stood watching the two men approach with suspicion. Tin and Joff kept their heads down, refusing to meet their hostile stares. The newcomers were heavily outnumbered and the other fellows had a reputation for wanton violence, but today was not the day.

Once past the Irish, Tin angled himself away from the wall, which still dominated their right-hand side, and towards the dwellings on the left of the street. To Joff, the filthy hovels looked every bit as dangerous as the Irish rope weavers, but he followed regardless.

"'Ere we are," Tin said and led the way down a gap between two houses.

It was a narrow, dark passage that opened up into a square courtyard where unmarked doors ran off in all directions. Children were everywhere but they weren't playing, they sat and stared from the shadows with blank expressions. Tin ignored them and went straight up to a door halfway down the left-hand side. He didn't knock as Joff had expected, just held it open, motioning his friend to go in. Joff found himself in another shorter passage with another door at the end, and hesitated.

237

"Where are we goin'?" he asked.

"Go on!" Tin encouraged from behind.

Joff did as he was told. Tin had closed the outer door now and they were plunged almost into darkness. The passage was too narrow for them to squeeze through together, and Joff could feel Tin urging him forward by keeping tight behind him, Tin's breath on his neck.

"Go on," Tin said again, "down to the end!"

Joff did as his friend wanted, and when he got to the second door he opened it and pushed aside a filthy old curtain. He was in a cavernous old hall. There was a small stage straight ahead of him and a bar over to the right. The place was decorated with round wooden tables and chairs of a type that would be easy to pile away on top of each other. There were at least fifteen tables set up and room for the same number again. It was a large space, much larger than one would have expected to find tucked away in this labyrinth of closely packed buildings. Four or five people sat around each table, talking heatedly amongst themselves. The atmosphere here was much more heavily charged than you would find in a regular pub. Joff sensed tension, danger, excitement.

"Over there!" Tin had tapped Joff on the shoulder and now he motioned to the right with his eyes.

Joff headed in the direction Tin wanted and almost immediately spotted the beauty he had been with that night. She sat with two men and another girl. They were all looking his way.

There were two empty chairs at their table; obviously Tin and Joff were expected. Joff headed towards them and could tell by their looks of pity that they already knew where they had spent the morning.

Joff was pleasantly surprised when Pearl rose from her chair and went to meet him half way. She hardly knew him but she gave him a much appreciated hug.

"Death is never easy," she whispered in his ear. She held him at arm's length, studying his face, and repeated, "Never easy!"

Joff nodded solemnly, not sure what the correct response was to such a statement, but glad she wanted to express it nonetheless.

"I'm Pearl," she announced. "We didn't really get introduced before. How are you feelin'?" she asked.

He shrugged and said, "You know."

She made a face that reflected sympathy.

A seat was pulled out for him and he lowered himself into it, trying not to stare at Pearl.

"You are among friends now," said one of his new companions.

Joff looked across at the one who'd spoken. He was about thirty years old with the sharp jaw bone of a Slav or a Cossack and a thick mop of black hair hanging over his face. He was unshaven and dressed in the black overcoat of the revolutionary.

The other man was of similar appearance and dressed the same way, although he also had a peaked cap pulled down and covering half his face. The other girl with them looked about ten years younger and was probably a real beauty beneath the heavy man's overcoat and the frown lines etched into her forehead.

She reached across the table and took Joff's hand in hers.

"I'm Berit," she told him with great earnest, "and I feel as though we are friends already!"

He smiled at her to portray his thanks. Who were these people? They were strangers to him but friends of Tin's, clearly, and things felt very much the same as they had twenty-five years before. When Joff most needed it, Tin was there for him. He and his motley crew welcomed the new man among them without a moment's hesitation. Drinks were ordered and very soon he felt as though he belonged, he was amongst friends.

For a whole week since Aimee's sudden death, Joff hadn't been able to face going to work and Tin shocked by the tragedy, had taken the helm without a single word of complaint. He had sent word to the theatre, telling them he would be back after the funeral, paid the rent on their room, made sure the boy had something to eat, settled for Laudanum and most important of all, he had been there for Joff.

Pearl leaned forward, breaking Joff's train of thought, and said, "Tin tells us that you used to be active in the struggle."

He shrugged and replied, "I'm just a piano player."

"Yes, I understand," she said. "A working man, you had to consider the safety of your wife, your child."

He shrugged again. Obviously things were different now but he felt no need to say so.

"What about your boy?" Pearl broke the silence.

He looked at her not really understanding.

"What about 'im?" he asked.

"I would like to meet him," she said.

He shrugged.

Jack sat alone on the step of the decaying slum he called home and watched the other children of the court as they played a game of chase in the muddy yard before him.

"Wanna play, Jack?" shouted a grubby little boy of about six.

Jack just glared back, "Play!" he wanted to scream. "Play! They're burying my ma today and you think I want to play!"

He glared until the lad gave up and ran back to the others. Jack hoped—no, wished—he would trip and fall, hopefully hurting himself, hopefully drawing blood, but he made it safely back to his friends and Jack was angry about that as well. He used to think he could make things happen purely by willing them to, but he realised now that was just a foolish, childish fantasy. He knew better now; if he wanted that boy to fall he was going to have to push him.

He rose up from the step and went towards the cluster of children.

"'Oi Percy, 'oo's it?" he asked in as cheerful a tone of voice as he could manage.

"You are!" replied the same grubby six-year-old.

He had a lot to learn. Jack was on little Percy in two strides and he shoved him as hard as he could in the small of his back. The lad weighed next to nothing and had not expected the game to take such a serious turn. He went flying, landing heavily on the cobbles. Immediately blood could be seen on the palm of one hand and on both knees. The other children stopped playing and stood around, shocked. Even Percy on the floor wasn't crying as he should be. The sheer nastiness had been totally unexpected. They all watched dumbfounded as Jack stormed into the tenement without even a backwards glance for the well-being of his little victim.

* * *

They had been drinking so long it had turned dark and the conversation had long since turned to the struggle of the workers. Joff realised hours ago that he had been brought there to be judged. These were the people that Tin spent his time with. Immigrants, revolutionaries; he hadn't changed a bit. He had just gotten more deeply involved with more cautious people and had been waiting before introducing his friend.

Realising he was being examined, Joff had reiterated his belief that the authorities would never be beaten and the last time they had tried when he had been a much younger, fitter man, it had ended disastrously and nearly all their friends had ended up dead as a consequence.

Pearl had slammed her fist down on the table at that.

"But they couldn't kill the idea!" she had said, fire burning in her eyes, meaning it with every fibre of her being. "And when they passed bravely on they handed the baton to those left behind, to us!"

Her eyes blazed as she took them all in. Joff; Tin; his Latvian friends, Stefan and Goran.

Joff felt obliged to break the silence, to speak as the representative for the voice of reason.

"It's too dangerous," he said. "People get killed. Ain't that right, Tin?" he added.

He looked across to the skipper to add some logical perspective.

Tin glanced at him and Joff saw immediately that he could not rely on his old friend to offer caution. He sat back anyway to listen to his opinion.

"I have spent many of the last thirty years at sea and seen the world as it really is with my own two eyes. I have travelled the length of England, to Scotland, Ireland, France, Poland, Germany, and the situation has been exactly the same in all places." He was not raising his voice but every word came through loud and clear.

He continued, "I've seen the masses struggling to survive on a pittance. Being forced to produce goods that are then sold as far away from the place of origin as possible for the maximum profit. Farmers each year grow more than enough to feed themselves and their neighbours many times over. Yet they sit and watch as their fare is shipped to some distant market. The farmer now has no choice but to purchase what he needs to survive at vastly inflated prices. It is crazy, it is morally corrupt, and the people deserve better!" He slammed down his fist before continuing, "Better than being trapped by circumstances beyond their control, by the carefully designed system that attempts to trap us all in the end."

"It hasn't got you though, eh?" Joff attempted to lighten the heavy subject matter with a harmless little joke but this was clearly not a joking matter to them.

His comment was ignored.

"People are forced to survive on pathetic wages, barely enough to provide for their basic needs from one day to the next," said Pearl.

Joff glanced around the table and they all looked angry now.

Pearl glared across at him and said, "The system is broken, Joe, and we are going to re-build it."

They all nodded in solemn agreement.

He must have looked doubtful, because Pearl addressed him directly.

"Don't you want a better life for your son?" she said, and her beauty, combined with the drink, swung it for him.

Yes he did want a better life for his son, for all the children around there, but he was just a piano player, what could he do.

"Of course," he said, "but what difference can I make?"

"We can all make a difference," Pearl assured him.

"It will be just like the old days," Tin declared, "only now we are older, wiser, better prepared." He was positively beaming.

Joff didn't mention that the authorities could claim to be likewise and had unlimited resources to add to the equation.

It was best not to dwell on the negatives, best to just think about the positives, and there was no denying that something needed to be done before it was too late.

Since the revolutions throughout Europe twenty-five years earlier, governments of all hues had launched major offensives against any groups deemed a threat to their power.

Rules had been strengthened and free-thinking liberals across the continent were once again persecuted for their opinions. Many were rounded up and disappeared, never to be heard from again. Free thinking and solidarity were strongly portrayed as tools of the Devil. Religious conformity was being strongly recommended in their place.

Pearl was absolutely right, they had been lied to for years and it was time to fight back.

Joff and Tin were from the last generation of Europeans born truly free. They had grown up isolated from central government, grown up before the birth of the railways. As children they knew only self-sufficient families within self-sufficient communities. They experienced no state interference in their daily lives and they asked for no state hand outs. In their hearts they knew that people left to their own devices would get together and cooperate. They knew because they could remember. If anyone fell on hard times natural empathy surfaced, and they rallied around. They looked after the needy. They had no slums back then. They used to put people before profits.

In the last twenty years 'generosity' and 'cooperation' had been added to the list of dirty words. Mistrust of strangers, especially foreigners, had been actively encouraged and nowadays, beyond the walls of London, nobody spoke to anyone outside their immediate circle from one hamlet to the next.

Nowadays they were all in competition with each other. Other towns, villages, countries were not neighbours but rivals in the rush for customers. Everyone was suspicious of who might be getting more than they were getting themselves.

Naturally this mistrust resulted in huge armies being created. Not for violence but as protection, to protect the giant monopolies that they now all relied on in these suspicious times.

People weren't living; they were surviving at best, but only just. They had no time to be loving families any more, to be there as their children developed. They were being weighed down with the seismic task of just making it through to the next day.

As far as they could see they were making more profits than ever before but they weren't benefiting at all. Governments everywhere were spending all profits on weapons in order to go to war with each other and steal some other country's wealth.

Propaganda told them that armies were essential so nations could defend themselves. They all had to be on their guard, apparently. People everywhere were fed these lies so many times that in the end they actually believed them.

Then cleverly, subtly, authority had become combined with religion. Intimately entwined until the ultimate judgment of eternal damnation awaited any who dared to question authority or break authority's self-serving rules.

Now under the new electric lighting, men were working 14-hour days, very few had the opportunity or the finances to take a step back and see what was really going on in the world. They were being deliberately bogged down with trivia.

"So," Pearl hissed insistently, "those who do still see the truth have a responsibility, no a duty, to expose this rampant hypocrisy!"

She was looking about herself, sweeping them all into her statement.

"The state is using armies to protect their monopolies and the church is generating huge profits peddling dreams. Whilst simultaneously, both are creating deep misery amongst any who refuse to conform!" She had worked herself into a state of near rage.

"In Christian churches throughout Europe, nationalism and love for one's country long ago replaced 'love thy neighbor.' They deserve all they have comin' to them."

Complete agreement was all that greeted her words.

"You can remember the good old days, Joe, how it was, how it could be once more?"

He nodded.

"It is up to us to stem the tide. It may not be enough but we have to try." She scanned their faces and once again settled on Joff.

"Are you in, Joe?" she asked.

He didn't need time to consider. "I'm in," he said, smiling broadly.

He was back where he belonged. Back amongst people who saw things the way he saw them. He had tried to settle down and be a good citizen but it had meant turning a blind eye to injustice and suffering almost daily for too many years. The price was too high.

For the sake of Betsy and Aimee, for the sake of the boy, for the sakes of them all, he was in. Twenty years of knuckling under and he couldn't even afford to bury his own wife at the end of it. Then a week without work and but for the charity of Tin, he and the boy would be living on the street. No, it was time to take a stand before it was too late.

They beamed at each other across the table. As of this moment, with Pearl's unshakable commitment, the revolution was back on the agenda, and they all knew it.

A little later Stefan drained the last of his drink and rose to leave, and Goran followed suit. They hugged each of the others, and, turning up their collars, headed outside, where they blended into the crowds.

"So can you start tonight?" Pearl asked, leaning into Joff and grabbing hold of his hand.

"I'm there," he assured her.

"What about the boy?" she asked. "What's 'is name d'ya say?"

"Jack," he told her.

"Yes, Jack," she repeated. "What about Jack?"

"I should check on 'im," he conceded.

Joff turned to Tin, "I think I might 'ead back an' check on the boy."

"How about if we come wiv you?" he replied.

Joff looked at Tin, who was leaning forward earnestly, and then he looked at Pearl as she leaned back nonchalantly, and he shrugged.

"Yeah, if you like," he said.

CHAPTER TWELVE

Jack had spent the day at Liverpool Street railway terminus. He had robbed the pockets of countless passengers as they poured over the timetables or debated over which platform they needed to be on. Now he was returning home with the ill-gotten proceeds of his day's work. He wasn't expecting his pa to be in and he certainly wasn't expecting company. He was a little surprised to walk in on his pa, Tin the tramp, and now they had a woman with them. She smiled at the little boy standing frowning in the doorway.

"'Ello," she said, "I'm Pearl."

"Er, 'ello," Jack said and stared at the stranger sitting in his ma's usual place. He wasn't sure what to make of her.

"What's that you've got there?" she asked him, pointing to the jumble of silk hankies he had begun pulling out of his pocket before realising that he was not alone.

"Nothin'," he mumbled, trying to stuff the silks back out of view.

"Been out dippin', 'ave you lad?" Tin asked with a benevolent smile on his face.

Jack had been trying not to engage them.

"What you been up to boy?" Joff asked, swinging his feet onto the floor and stretching out.

Jack stood in the doorway staring at him.

"'E's been out robbin' silk 'ankies is what 'e's been doin'," Pearl spat out viciously.

She grabbed the hankies from his tiny fist and sent the boy spinning into the corner of the room.

"Is this 'ow you repay your poor dead mother? Is it?" She poked Jack in the chest and her finger jabbed painfully into his ribcage.

"Is this 'ow you repay your poor father?" She paused for breath and let the question hang in the room. "I think you need takin' in hand, my boy. The last thing your father needs is the police callin' round 'ere because o' you."

She turned to Tin then she turned to Joff and said in a voice that left no room for discussion, "I'll stay 'ere tonight. Keep an eye on 'im while you are out."

It was delivered as a fait accompli and Joff could have kissed her for her concern. Jack's mother had done all the raising of the boy. If the truth be told he wouldn't know where to start. Actually it was worse than that, he had already been thrust into the role and truly didn't know where to start. He was grateful for any help she was prepared to offer.

"Are you certain?" He couldn't believe his luck.

"Of course, you have important work to do," she said.

She was both beautiful and caring. It seemed too good to be true.

Tin spoke up from his position by the door. "That's taken care of then," he said. "Come on, let's go!"

"He'll be no trouble," Joff told her while putting on his jacket.

"Will ya?" he asked as he looked down at the boy who sat cross-legged on the floor staring at his feet. Jack didn't answer or even look up, so Joff left them to it and followed Tin down the rickety stairs and out into the court.

Outside Joff grabbed Tin by the arm and asked, "What's this all about? What's so special about me all of a sudden?"

He chuckled and pinched Joff's cheek. "Why the concern? What do you mean, why you? You know what's special about you!"

"Do I?" he replied.

"You're the piano man! Everybody knows you. The police see you walkin' out late; you've just finished a gig. They see you leading a wagon, you're movin' a piano! You got the perfect excuse to be out an' about at any hour of the day or night." He pinched Joff's cheek again. "For us it's not so easy."

"So I'm a messenger now, a glorified delivery boy, am I?" it came out sounding harsh but Joff was smiling.

"Yeah!" he said. "Yeah, you are."

It was dark and cold but the streets were alive with humanity. They cut across the traffic of Commercial Street and Joff followed Tin through alleys and side streets until they got to George Yard. They walked down the dark alley towards the narrow arch leading into Whitechapel High Street. Beneath the arch, Tin ducked into a side door and into the White Hart. It was busy as usual and they had to force their way through the throng of drinkers to the back of the bar. Some looked up to check them out, most didn't bother. Joff followed Tin's example and ignored them all.

At the very back of the long room Joff spotted Stefan and Goran sitting in the corner. As he and Tin made their way towards them, Goran switched seats, leaving the bench opposite them empty, and the newcomers quickly filled it.

Everyone shook hands across the wood and then, pleasantries over, they launched straight into business.

"'Ave you got 'em?" Tin asked quietly.

"Yeah, we got 'em," Stefan replied in his thick European accent. Smiling slightly, he added, "There is time for a drink first." He rose and went to the bar.

When Stefan returned from the bar, he said, "So, I hear about your wife. "I very sorry."

Joff shrugged and said, "Thanks." Stefan stared silently back at him.

"So where are we goin' tonight?" Joff asked.

Still they sat in silence and stared. Joff smiled and sat back, trying to appear nonchalant although his heart was racing. It felt great to be in the action. He needed to keep his mind busy and he needed to do something for Aimee. Tin coming back into his life was a godsend, and now here he was with a tray full of drinks. Beers and whiskeys all round.

Tin was smiling now but Joff knew inside he felt no different than he had all those years ago. Deep down, hidden inside, he was angry as hell because nothing had changed over the years.

"A beer and a whiskey! No half measures then," Joff said, trying to lighten the mood with a flippant remark.

"No," Goran interjected, "no to half measures!" He raised his glass in a toast, and looking Joff right in the eye, said, "Here's to going all the way!"

"Cheers!" Joff replied, and they drank the toast with false smiles all round and impatience burning deep in them all.

An hour later Joff stood at the busy junction of Aldgate, the city and the dock road, holding the reins to a pony and cart, trying to keep a look out in three directions simultaneously. He was hoping not to be left standing there too long and was very pleased to see Tin heading back towards him much more quickly than he had expected him to. Tin motioned for him to bring the cart and Joff followed him down the Minories, then left up an alley where the others were waiting with two large wooden crates. They loaded them up onto the cart and set off at an easy pace the short distance back to Whitechapel. This revolution would be financed by common burglary and now Joff was in it up to his neck.

CHAPTER THIRTEEN
1871-72

Pearl had been living with them for a month now. The new show was in full flow and Joff was glad of her help. He had two four-hour shifts afternoons and evenings, and on Monday, his day off, he was composing penny song sheets to be printed and sold to raise funds for the workers' cause. He was hardly ever home so it was only right that Pearl should take the mattress and the boy would take up most of the floor.

Tin had taken over the rent on a house in Soho's Wardour Street and Joff spent most nights there with him. Stefan and Goran had the room next to theirs, and a number of other foreign activists, mainly Italians and Poles, lived in the same building. They had a social club conveniently located next door and a warehouse opposite, large enough to contain its own printing press and hide a truck load of crates. All around them from Cleveland Street to Piccadilly Circus, secret Fenian societies, workers' groups, and trade organizations of the immigrants operated behind closed doors. Italian, Russian, and Polish dominated. Soho was an area where freedom was real, was in the very air they breathed. After the persecution in the countries and places most had left behind, they did not squander the opportunities London offered.

The group was printing leaflets and pamphlets in five different languages and distributing them in all the pubs around Soho, all the markets in the East End, and as far afield as Camden Town to the North and Brixton on the south side of the river.

Workers had the vote now and they were determined to make sure that men everywhere knew about the new rights they had been granted.

* * *

Back in Whitechapel Jack could not believe his pa had done this to him. He had thought that they would be seeing more of each other now that Ma was no longer with them. He had certainly not expected him to bring in a complete stranger and disappear for days at a time. It wouldn't be so bad—he was used to spending long periods away from his father, after all—but she was unbearable. Always preaching to him and stopping him from going outside.

* * *

Two weeks later in the first part of dawn the police raided the group's premises in Soho. They came streaming in, hundreds of them, and smashed everything they could lay their clubs on. They closed off the whole area from Great Windmill Street to Soho Square. Bursting into premises, smashing whatever lay within reach.

In the second part of the dawn, as the sun was starting to creep into the sky, they arrested all and sundry and carted them away. By mid-morning Joff and his friends were scattered in police cells right across London. Over the next few weeks, although they had broken no laws, they were each sentenced, one after the other.

The lucky ones got three months hard labour. Those who were considered to be the ringleaders, like Joff, got two years. It could have been worse, he supposed; they could have come charging in a day earlier, just after one of their robberies, then they could have caught them red-handed with stolen goods and charged them with armed robbery.

Joff walked from the dock down the steps to the cell below and considered himself not too hard done by. They could have been looking at fourteen years in the penal colonies.

In the first three months of 1871 they had managed to get thousands of pamphlets out into general circulation. The boy had Pearl to look out for him, so Joff entered prison not having to worry about him.

They already treated any custodial sentence as an excuse for a recruitment drive.

* * *

Tin, as was his forte, managed to escape the round-up, and he made it back to Pearl. She was sweeping dust off the front step when he came bursting into the courtyard in a highly agitated state.

"Pearl, Pearl. They got Joe!"

She glanced up to the open window. She didn't want the boy hearing such news.

"Sssh!" she hissed, silently beckoning him closer.

Once he was on the steps and they could not be overheard, she hissed at him, "What do you mean?"

"The police," Tin whispered, shaking his head in disbelief. "The police came an' the game's well an' truly up now."

"No!" she hissed at him. "You knew they would come. The game is not up, never say that! Go an' see who else slipped through their net." She locked her fiercely burning eyes on his. "Nothin' is over!" she declared with utmost conviction.

Pearl stood there watching him scurry away through the black alleyway. When he was gone she attacked the steps with renewed vigour, sweeping furiously, oblivious to the boy watching her from the top floor window.

With the chore completed she stomped back into the building and up the stairs.

She burst into the attic room where Jack was exactly where she had left him, sitting in the far corner where two bare walls met. In the gloom the grubby child in dark clothing was hard to spot against the backdrop of dark, peeling wallpaper, but her eyes searched him out as she came through the door. She expected him to be exactly where he should be, so even in the gloom she picked him out straight away. Satisfied that he had obeyed her command, she shut the door behind her.

Jack sat on the floor in his dark corner and quietly watched her as she moved around the room. He had never known a woman like her. She was the first person he had ever met who gave him orders and expected them to be obeyed. No, demanded that they be obeyed, immediately, her every whim.

Naturally he had ignored her at first. In his mind she meant nothing to him.

"Wash that filth off your hands before you sit down," she had said to him on their first time alone together.

He had ignored her and taken the seat at the window as he always did, and she had pounced across the room. She had slapped him an almighty open-hander right across his soft cheek. The slap had sent him sprawling off the window ledge and crashing hard against the floorboards. That sort of treatment he was used to; most adults he had dealings with felt it was only right that unruly, cheeky children should feel the back of a hand. What he was definitely not used to, though, what he had never witnessed before, was the way in which she had stood over him, raging with fury,

"You will listen to me," she had screamed, "and you will do as you are told and maybe you will not turn out to be a worthless piece of shit like every man that ever walked the Earth before you!"

Jack cowered before her bitter torrent of abuse.

"Understand?" she finally spat out.

Jack had nodded.

After that he found it was easier to head for his corner and keep out of harm's way no matter what mood she might appear to be in. She played different roles for different people but she undoubtedly ruled the roost.

Pearl stood now, staring at the boy, deciding how much or how little he would need to know.

"Your father has been arrested!" she announced as an opening gambit.

Jack watched dumbfounded as she walked to the window. *What does that mean? Arrested for what?* he wondered.

Pearl made a great show of looking outside, letting him digest the news before she turned to face him again.

"There are goin' to be some changes," she continued. "First, you are not to go outside unless I say you can. Second, you do not talk to anyone about anythin' you might see or 'ear in this room." She stared at him and continued, "Got it?"

Jack nodded and wondered what kind of a hell his life was about to become.

"Break either of those rules an' you are in deep trouble, understand?"

Jack nodded again.

So he sat in his corner as the hours passed into days. She accepted an endless stream of visitors who always joined her in ranting on about the people's rights and the government's wrongs. Slowly some of her rhetoric began to take root in his underdeveloped mind. He would listen as she ranted on about Paris, Manchester, and Berlin. Faraway places that seemed so appealing to him. He had no idea what any of it really meant, but he understood one point that always shone through clearly, over and over. Men were doing a terrible job of running things and women would do a whole lot better. Jack had never heard such radical views before.

Women running the world, that couldn't be possible, he thought. Surely that was a ridiculous concept, but he daren't say so out loud. So he sat in silence as the days crept along. Sometimes now he would go a whole week without uttering a single word to another human being. Just sit in the filth and listen to battle-hardened revolutionaries and activists from all over the world. Digest their tales of bloodshed and hardship, and watch and imagine.

One night as the adults sat drinking beer and talking passionately, Jack, who was listening intently, sat as quiet as a mouse, trying to comprehend even odd snippets of the adults' conversation.

"I warned you about becomin' too noticeable up there!" snapped Pearl.

"We thought..."

She cut off the reply, "You thought you was so damn superior that you became isolated from the people, an' the worst thing is, you didn't even realize it. Not so bloody clever after all, are ya!"

She spat out the window, "All lookin' the bleedin' same, acting the same. You was aloof towards the citizens, and," she paused to take a drink, shook her head and pursed her lips, "all livin' on top of each other in Soho. It was easy for the authorities to pick you out." She sneered at the four tough men before her, "Uniformity is always a mark of weakness."

She was chastising them, mocking them almost. Four grown men, hardened activists, violent revolutionaries, yet they took her criticism meekly, without a word. Jack watched and despised them their silence. She was absolutely right, he thought, they were weak. How could they let a woman talk to them like that? As far as he was concerned they ought to be ashamed of themselves. He knew he was no better. He took whatever she dished out without a word but he was a child, he had an excuse.

After a while Tin rose and mumbled something about a 'job' he had to do.

"What, right now?" Pearl demanded.

He nodded, already pushing open the door. "Yeah, see you tomorrow," he said, and he was gone.

"Weak!" screamed Pearl at the closed door, "he is weak." She scanned the room with its remaining occupants and cried out, "You are all so weak, it's pathetic!"

Somehow Jack knew she was referring to men, all men, everywhere, him included.

* * *

By the winter of 1872 the Anarchists and Communists had been forced out of Soho. However, a handful had managed to avoid the dragnet and as Christmas approached they began to re-emerge in the lawless streets of the East End.

Much further east than Whitechapel, they began popping up, home-grown and foreign, in the lawless drinking dens along the Limehouse causeway, well away from prying eyes. Pearl went down there every morning and brought home any she considered to be on the right path.

Jack sat in his corner with nothing to do all day but listen to the stories of Londoners, Northerners, and foreign nationals, and as the months passed more and more of their grievances made sense to him.

Pearl still refused to let him outside as she wasn't prepared to let him drift back into a life of petty crime and bring the law down on them all. Her form of parenting was to keep the boy where she could see him at all times, or when she went out, with someone who would follow her instructions to the letter. She was very big on the popular notion that children should be seen and not heard. She didn't concern herself too much with what might or might not be suitable for small ears. She had 'the cause' to consider, particularly the women's suffrage movement.

At the big arrest she had decided to stay put and look out for the boy until his father could return. That, she felt, could be expected of her and she did not give the matter much more consideration. Besides, it was useful having a base in the heart of the bourgeois capital.

"My mother had the right to vote way back in 1830!"

Pearl was screaming at a roomful of Russian Jews. They sat there fidgeting uncomfortably as this crazy woman ranted and her spittle rained down on them. This was not how they had envisaged it to be once they arrived in London, but they had been brought to her straight from the ship and now their interpreter, the fellow countryman they had followed here, had disappeared and they could only sit and await his return.

"If my ma could vote then so should I!" Pearl raged.

The Jews shifted and shuffled and avoided making eye contact with her. Jack hid in the shadows. He understood every word. So women had the vote before and now they wanted it back. That seemed reasonable to him and of course she was right to insist on using violence to get their will. What other way was there? None that Jack knew of.

* * *

Tin appeared from time to time and would occasionally sit on the floor next to Jack. They never indulged in much conversation but Jack took some comfort from the closeness of someone who knew his pa. Tin was different from the others. He tended not to stay drinking and talking into the night like the rest of them. He, it seemed, had better things to do with his time.

Jack always wondered where he went and wished he could go too. Instead he was forced to sit quietly in the shadows, listening, day after day, night after night.

Jack sat quietly with his legs tucked up under him, eating a sugar-coated mouse that the strange man in the room had just given him. He wasn't used to anyone paying him any attention and he listened as the man before him told his story.

He was from a place in northern Spain, far from the capital, Madrid. Beyond mountains so rugged, the railways couldn't reach them. His was an isolated community. He said the people there called themselves the Basque people and they operated a system that was the model all should be following. They lived peacefully with very little interference from Madrid. They cooperated with each other and now the people in the surrounding communities were crossing over to their system within a system.

As their numbers had grown so had their responsibilities, and they accepted each bigger project willingly. They adapted and accommodated everyone. There had been no bloody revolution, no coup or power grab. A small isolated community had simply continued to do things the old way and when others saw that it worked better than the current system, they joined the ranks.

Nobody had been trying to force events; they had relied on the force of events. Their system was and had always been a work in progress, a fluid entity, capable of tailoring ideas to suit the masses as situations evolved. It was an association of free and equal men, working well enough that they were soon running schools, factories, even a hospital.

"That, Jack, is the last example in the whole of Europe of the old community system that your father grew up with. Cornwall was that way before the railways allowed London to control everyone's lives."

Jack listened sullenly, missing his pa so badly; the longing manifested itself in a physical pain knotting up his empty stomach.

The Spaniard's story finished with the inevitable heavy-handed police raid, violent brawls and mass arrests.

Pearl listened and simmered.

Jack sucked his mouse and wished he was in that amazing place, with its mountains, eagles, goats, and wide-open spaces.

CHAPTER FOURTEEN
1875

"Remember brother, we stand for solidarity, we have strength, and can achieve great things through solidarity. We stand for reciprocity and cooperation. We can achieve great things if we stand as one!"

Joff shook hands with his cellmate and headed for the outside world. It seemed like everyone was a political genius these days. They all had the answers; he was sick of it. He hoped he could find a nice little pub that needed a piano player. He no longer had his job at the Gaiety but thought he could get odd gigs here and there in the upstairs shabeens that were apparently springing up and thriving all around the East End.

* * *

London, they said, was in the midst of a boom time, but as he passed St. Katharine Docks and walked up Leman Street towards Aldgate, he could tell that the good times had not penetrated far down there.

One sweeping glance was all he needed to inform him that these people were still living in dire poverty. He crossed Commercial Street and headed into Whitechapel and noticed there were far more varieties of people on the streets. Immigrants from all over the world had kept on coming whilst he'd been locked up.

"Twice as many people but half as many jobs," they said in prison and it looked true enough to him.

Church bells tolled ahead, reminding him of the prize awaiting the worthy.

A lifetime of misery in this world for a lifetime of joy in the next. That was the deal being offered.

In prison Joff had listened to the details of other religious beliefs and each had been as 'perfect' as the Christian one. He tended to side with Marx on the subject, somewhere between total belief and total disbelief; he had suspended all belief.

Joff supposed the only thing he really believed in was the power of music, and drink, perhaps.

He walked through the East End quietly, satisfied that things didn't look much different. He drifted aimlessly, or so he tried to tell himself, but he was kidding no one. Each step was taking him closer and closer to his old room. The closer he got the more the sense of dread, of the unknown, rose higher in his chest.

Jack and Pearl will be long gone, he told himself.

They may still be there, he retorted immediately.

He entered the courtyard and his eyes fell on the spot where Aimee had died. Instantly he cast them skywards, looking for the angel of his long-dead soulmate, and there was Pearl leaning through their old window.

She was still here. Inexplicably his heart soared and he raced for the staircase.

"I'm back," he called, charging through the door.

Pearl looked up from her chair by the window. "So you are," she acknowledged calmly as though Joff had just returned from the market. There was no emotion on her face, no smile, no evidence that she was pleased to see him. Joff didn't know what he'd expected. He probably deserved nothing, but something would have been nice.

"Where's Jack?" he asked. He, at least, would be pleased to see his old pa home.

She shrugged. "I tried keepin' him in but the boy is impossible!" She shrugged again, "Besides I have my own life, you know!"

Her involvement with the suffrage movement had meant she was no longer able to keep the boy on such a tight rein and he had been doing his own thing for six months now.

"Where's Tin?" he said next.

CHAPTER FIFTEEN
1885

London had really changed in the ten years since Joff had returned. At long last men could meet in public places and openly discuss politics. All politics, whatever they chose. People were free to form societies and associations and congregate with whoever they wanted. Getting the vote had changed everything.

Some friends had purchased a dilapidated, three-story property in the East End that they planned to open as a permanent meeting place. It was to be called the 'Berner Street Club,' and they held high hopes for the place.

As Joff climbed the stairs to the new club and looked around, he was filled with pride. The hall was capable of holding 150 people easily, and most important for him, it contained a piano. Joff was to be the resident pianist. The struggle had been long and hard but it had been worth it. Finally they had a place they could call their own and Joff had regular work. Things were really looking up. From there they intended to show the local people that the tide really was turning.

All over Europe the ruling classes were coming to the daunting realization that the workers were getting ready to turn ideas into actions. Berner Street was to be the group's London base and education was to be their aim. From the walls, Marx and Proudhon looked proudly down on the proletariat who were finally finding their voices. It should have been a time of celebration of how much they had achieved in the last forty years.

Joff looked again at the two portraits staring down at him. Marx with his Socialist ideas that half their members swore by, and next to him Proudhon, whose very different theories the other half of the members saw as the best way forward. The same old divisions were already showing. The Marxists were prepared to work with the bosses, to cooperate in some way. The others felt very strongly that the top-heavy wage system and the capitalist structures had to go in order for mankind to move forward as one.

Joff spent his time playing the songs they liked and acting as a peacemaker between the two camps. Diplomacy was a full-time job and not quite what he had expected.

He started spending the odd night sleeping over and soon moved into Berner Street completely. Jack had left home whilst he'd been away and Pearl didn't want him cluttering up what was effectively her place now.

In northern Spain, her friend was tried as one of the leading figures of the 'Black Hand Gang.' For the first time in history men were found guilty of 'collective responsibility.' They were hung by their necks until dead and the mountains of the Basque region fell under the jurisdiction of Madrid.

CHAPTER SIXTEEN
1886

Joff watched as a group of men hauled a large printing machine through the gates at the side of the club. They were all sweating and puffing heavily from the effort required. He would have helped but he had to be careful of his fingers. Instead, he stood and offered advice.

"Bit quicker, boys!" he called, smiling.

"Just go an' write some bloody songs, you!" came the abrupt reply.

Their very own printing press. Now they really could spread the word.

It was 1886 and they were going to take over the production of *The Worker's Friend*, a pamphlet that informed workers of their rights. Once they had the printing operation up and running, they could add their voices to the *Freedom* newspaper already being published in Whitechapel. They were fortunate indeed that their club was conveniently located right next to a yard and that Mr. Dutfield was willing to let them set up their press in his yard, for a fee.

Dutfield's yard was entered through the double gates that ran between their club at number 40 and number 42 next door. On the left-hand side after entering the gate were three stone cottages where some charming Jewish families lived. Past the cottages at the end was a taller building where men were employed in the manufacture of sacks that they sold to the market traders or the produce growers. On the right-hand side was the door into the club. Past the door were four windows running to the end of the building, and this housed the printing press. At the back of the yard sitting next to the sack makers was a smaller workshop where old man Dutfield made wheels for carts.

The yard was a busy, thriving place during the day. The children from the cottages played in the dirt as horse-drawn carts came and went through the middle of their games. Everybody was busy. The housewives from the cottages spent their time cleaning sawdust from their surfaces and from their children.

The men were printing pamphlets, making sacks or wheels, or preparing for the next crisis.

At night the yard was deserted.

After the meetings were over and all the members had drifted back home, Joff would curl up alone and revel in the silence. He would doze off wondering where his son was at that minute, and what he was doing with himself. Occasionally he would dream of returning to Cornwall and taking the boy with him. He opted instead to get roaring drunk and fall straight to sleep.

For the next twelve months the committee set to work improving existing associations and helping to set up new ones wherever workers were not being represented. They wanted to ensure these various clubs and associations scattered throughout the land had similar views to their own and therein lay the problem.

They were still undecided as to which was the view they, as the head association, represented. It was the same old story—should they nominate a representative of the people and try to get him elected to office, or should they refuse to have any involvement with a system that relied on misery for profit.

The debates would go on deep into the night while Joff sat playing, trying to lighten the mood.

* * *

Marx and his followers would commandeer the tables nearest the stage and insist, one after another, that, "We must vote, we must vote, we must vote!"

Then the French or the Italians would get up to offer the opposing view.

"No," they would disagree. "We must take to the streets, rise up, and overthrow those bourgeoisie dogs!"

"The people will not follow you!" the Marxists would be quick to point out.

"They will rise up! They are just waitin' for us to lead the way. You are all that is holdin' us back!"

Joff was glad to be excluded from such discussion. It seemed as though they were going around in circles, taking chunks out of each other, and if his experience was anything to go by, making themselves easier for the authorities to keep firmly in place when the time came.

But the club wasn't just about politics. They tried to be entertaining, tried to offer an alternative to the pubs, to drinking. Sometimes they would lay on grand meals or just refreshments and Joff would play while they danced. The massive chasm between the two camps was never far below the surface, though.

How could they insist all others must hold the same views, that all the associations must be connected, when they were not even singing from the same page?

Their greatest strength lay in collectivism but that, as ever, was proving elusive in the extreme.

Some associations wanted the revolution to come about via the ballot box. Their clubs believed in direct action and they were being accepted as members. Others wanted blood to run in the streets and they were being taken in as well. They all had common ground, of course. They all wanted a better deal for the working man, but they also had this huge difference of opinion that was always there, getting in the way.

Joff just played the piano and wondered why nobody spoke any more of the third way. What happened to just living in harmony, creating your own mini-system within the big system? Why couldn't they focus on doing their own thing? Then more and more would come to join them until the capitalist system would no longer be needed. It would wither and die without the need for a single shot to be fired.

Why couldn't they do that? Why couldn't they just start setting the right example for others to follow when they were ready? Trying to force people to come aboard had always proved to be a monumental task. It hadn't worked for forty years and that probably wasn't about to change now. People were, quite naturally, afraid of the unknown.

They would be much happier to be shown, to follow by example.

CHAPTER SEVENTEEN
1888

By 1888 the group had done a lot of good work. All the trades in the area were represented by their own chosen men, and all, from the dockworkers to the Jewish tailors, were happy to fall under the collective umbrella of the Working Men's Association, glad to be part of a bigger, more powerful union of men. As far as the workers themselves were concerned, Marx was slowly winning the war. They were not versed in the subtle differences so important in politics. They only heard what they wanted to hear, that the Socialists would, with their help, win the election and the country would be run for the benefit of the masses and not for the benefit of a chosen few.

The workers did not see that they were simply changing one master for another, but then they did not know Karl Marx as the Association knew him. How he seemed, to the group, just as interested in the power as he was in the philanthropy.

Yet Joff had to admit they had come a long way.

A little more than twenty years had passed since Disraeli had extended the right to vote to workers, making it impossible for the landowners to keep them down any longer.

Only forty years ago they were forbidden from gathering at all. Meetings back then had to be conducted in top secret. Now they had their own club, their own printing press, and they were on the streets daily, in large numbers, openly seeking out new members to strengthen their ranks.

Things were, over all, going much better than any of them could have dared to hope.

Then came the 29th of September 1888.

Joff was in the club that night. It was about eight o'clock in the evening when a lot of Jews and Poles came in and he had played some old militant songs that they always liked, that reminded them of home.

Around nine the other members began to filter into the room in dribs and drabs and by ten the hall was jumping. So Joff hit the keys harder, louder. Soon it would be time for his break. Sure enough, he was asked to stop right on cue. As he left his stool, William, the club secretary, took the stage to make a few announcements. Joff slipped out to grab a drink or two in the pub on the corner. He was out of the room almost before William had begun to speak.

Joff dashed through the rain and sidled up to Nelson's bar on the corner.

"Pint, please, Pattie!" he shouted to the landlord, who knew Joff, knew they didn't serve alcohol in the club, and that he was on a short break. He obligingly began to pour, ignoring the hordes of patrons clamouring for service ahead of him. It used to be the same in the public bar nearest the Gaiety, the staff would know the musicians by sight, most of them put a fair percentage of their wages into their till. They would always serve the musicians first so they wouldn't ever be late for the second half of a performance.

Joff found a space and stood alone, drinking quickly. Thirty minutes was just about enough time to get two pints and two whiskeys in him. At eleven o'clock he ordered his second round and positioned himself closer to the door. There were quite a few patrons coming and going, and Joff watched them as he drank. He saw a young girl who looked vaguely familiar out in the rain, but he was in the pub so often she was probably just one of the regulars. She stood arm in arm with a stocky little stranger. They walked towards Joff then hesitated, blocking the doorway, not wanting to get any wetter but equally unsure if there was enough room inside to accommodate them.

Then two burly men wanting to enter came up behind them and the decision was made for them. The crowd swallowed them up before Joff could decide where he knew her from, or if he even knew her at all. Still that was London in those days, so many strangers that you could spot a face in the crowd and never, ever set eyes on them again.

Joff drank up and made his way back to the club. As he walked down Berner Street he saw a woman being propositioned by the yard gate. There was nothing particularly unusual about that—this was the East End after all, sex was for sale. They both looked up as Joff came closer but he kept his head down and they quickly dismissed him. They moved closer together and lowered their voices conspiratorially, then the man said something that caused the woman to giggle, and arm in arm they strolled off down the street.

Joff spared them a quick glance as they moved away. With the Ripper on the prowl, you sort of looked at everyone a bit more closely these days. Well, most people did, but Joff wasn't expecting to get caught up in these terrible murders. He couldn't see that maniac coming around here. There was too much activity for the likes of him.

Once he returned to the club, he sat at his piano and as he began to hit the keys his mind drifted to the girl. Silently, he dedicated a song to her, whoever she might be. He launched into a Russian folk song of love and betrayal and the members danced for all they were worth. Their heavy boots clacked against the wooden boards whilst the portrait of Marx watched sternly over them.

* * *

By one o'clock in the morning the party was in full swing. Most of the Bolsheviks had gone and the usual tension went with them. Only Jews and Italians remained and their political opinions were so close as to be indistinguishable from each other. They didn't trust Marx but they loved belting out the old victory songs. Then, unusual for that time of night, Louis Diemschitz, the club steward, came running through the door and Joff watched curiously, his fingers dancing over the keys, as news Louis gave to his wife was passed around. Louis lived in the club so Joff knew him well, but he had never seen the man like this.

Whatever the commotion was, it was spreading. Isaac and Morris, two members, went outside with Louis and it was apparent that something was seriously wrong. Joff did what any musician worth his salt would do—he carried on playing.

Then Morris came running back in and a few more went out. By now everybody in the club was paying attention to the odd behaviour and the manager signalled at Joff to stop. He drew his playing to a big finale, which nobody seemed to even notice. He closed the lid and went outside to see what the attraction was, and there lying in the mud, her head touching the wall to the club, was the girl he had seen less than an hour ago. He stood in shock looking down at her. By the light of someone's candle he could see a pool of blood gathering on the cobbles beneath her and knew she was dead.

"It's the Ripper!" a voice muttered.

"Israel! Levi!" Go for help."

That maniac was hunting here? Joff had seen that poor girl in Nelson's only a few hours ago and now she was dead. He had got her, so close. A shiver ran up Joff's spine as he wondered if the man he had seen her with was the Ripper. Had he actually seen the killer? His blood ran cold. He needed a whisky.

Within a few minutes not just the club members were milling around. There were police men, doctors, and a growing number of interested bystanders.

"Get in there, yous lot! We will be in to talk to yous in a while," a policeman said while pushing members back towards the club as he barked out his orders. "Stay in there!"

"Capitalist dog!" someone said.

More and more police kept arriving. It seemed as though their orders were to make sure nobody left the area. Joff and all the others were herded back into the club like cattle.

"Another poor girl! This maniac is runnin' rings around you peelers. Are you even tryin' to stop 'im?"

"This monster, this Ripper, 'e is a product of the evil filth we 'ave to live in day after day," an Italian accent declared loudly.

"Evil surroundings are a breeding ground for evil intentions!"

Someone slammed a heavy fist down on the gate and more voices were raised in anger.

Not many years ago the conversation would have focused on what they could do to help those poor women forced through no fault of their own to walk such dangerous streets. Now it was almost taken for granted that they were here to stay and it was the club's job to point the finger of blame firmly at the ruling classes, almost as though they had trained this madman themselves and pointed him in the direction of the East End.

It was too absurd for Joff. The others wanted the Ripper's capture every bit as much as he and the group did, but with ol' Warren fighting for his political life there were cheap points to be scored. Joff wanted no part of it. There would be no more call for his playing that night. It was the first time for him that a gig had been cut short because of a murder. Clearly the show would not be going on. He was at a loose end before the final curtain had fallen; it was not a feeling he wished to grow accustomed to.

Joff went up to the nearest policeman and gave him his most charming smile.

"Evenin' officer, alright if I 'ead off to me next gig?"

The officer looked at him. A slight hint of confusion mixed in with a healthy dose of suspicion. "What?" he said.

Joff quickly explained that he was the piano player, so had a watertight alibi and had an important gig up west to be getting along to.

"Ask anyone," he pleaded. "They will all tell ya, I was playing the piano. So I couldn't 'ave 'ad nothin' to do with it, could I?"

Satisfied that Joff was in the clear, the officer allowed him to leave.

"William, I'm off," he mouthed the words to the club secretary, and motioned that he was leaving, moving his fingers in a walking motion, pretending to be feet, his arm held up high, like a child playing a silly game. William nodded in understanding. It was fair to say Joff would not be needed again this evening.

"It wouldn't 'appen in Mayfair an' you know it!" someone shouted.

Joff walked away from the yard in a daze. He headed up to Commercial Road and turned left towards the busy junction where Aldgate and Whitechapel meet. He stopped for a quick whiskey in a public house at the top of the Minories and wondered what he should do next. He couldn't decide but was certain that he needed some time alone.

Joff finished his drink and came back out. St. Botolph's church was directly before him at the end of the street. He crossed the road. It was quiet at this time of the morning and he wasn't taking his life in his hands as he normally would be by crossing here. He had the sudden bright idea to enter the church and seek divine guidance. He climbed the steps with the feeling in his stomach that God would know what he should do. At the top of the steps he tried to turn the heavy steel handle but it wouldn't shift. The church was closed. God, it seemed, was off duty.

Joff stood with his back against the church door, looking down the Minories. Lights were still on in many of the inns and lodging houses. About halfway down the street drunken men were spilling out into the road. He didn't want to go that way; they looked like potential trouble. He glanced left, back towards Whitechapel, but didn't want to go back that way either. He glanced right, knowing that way led to the city and most of it would be closed for business at this hour. There was a little square just beyond the main road. Mitre Square, it was. He could cut down the alley. It was so close he could see it from where he stood. Then he could gather his thoughts in the quiet of the square until the police moved him on. That seemed like a fair trade-off for a little peace and quiet.

He pushed himself off the big church door and descended the steps to the pavement and headed towards the alley. But before he had taken half a dozen steps his thoughts were rudely interrupted by the urgent, high-pitched note of a police whistle blowing frantically.

The officer wasn't looking for any assistance from Joff, that was for sure, so he ignored the whistle as best as he could and kept moving. He cut down the narrow passage leading into Mitre Square, and before him, in the shadows in the corner, he saw a gathering of about six people. At the same time a bobby hurried into the alley behind him, pushing him aside as he did so. One of his colleagues shot into the square via an opposite passage, and just then somebody shone a light on a bundle of rags lying at the feet of the crowd, and there Joff saw another blood-soaked woman. He stared in horror. She was lying on her back with her skirts up around her waist and her feet pointing towards him. A large pool of congealed blood was gathering on the pavement by her neck, and Joff watched as a doctor bent over her, attempting to ascertain there was nothing further that could be done for this poor unfortunate.

Rain splashed from the rooftops and ran in little streams down the cracks in the cobbles. Joff watched the woman's blood mingle with the water and flow into the square.

He had come looking for a little quiet and had stumbled into another horrific attack. This had also culminated in not just murder but murder most horrid. He scanned the faces of the watching crowd. At least four of them looked as though they would be capable of committing such a deed. Two of his suspects were even covered in blood. Although, to be fair to them, the blood was dried and they looked more like slaughtermen on the way home from work.

Shaking his head in disbelief, he scuttled away from the carnage. He decided to take his chances, and headed back East where Pearl would no doubt grudgingly let him in to rest his weary bones.

CHAPTER EIGHTEEN

The following morning Joff rose early. Pearl had let him in, as he'd known she surely would, but there had been a long lecture on the evils of men who turned up unexpectedly in the middle of the night when really he just needed a place to lay his head.

"You'll 'ave to go at first light tho'. I'm expectin' visitors an' they can't see you 'ere," she warned. The sort of visitors that disliked anyone not committed to the cause, he guessed.

"That's not a problem," he assured her.

It felt like he had just dozed off when she was shaking him and telling him to make himself scarce. He went down to the club while the sun still had not fully risen in the sky. After all, it was hardly his fault that the gig had been cut short. No, he had done his bit and expected to be paid for last night's work.

There were always people around at all times of the day or night, but this morning more than ever there were people all the way along Berner Street. The sightseers were out in force and they were working each other up nicely. Joff shook his head, smiling wistfully, as he heard an old housewife telling her equally elderly companion that she couldn't sleep at nights with the worry that she might be the next victim.

Joff spotted William on the corner and made his way through the crowd towards him. William looked up as Joff approached and nodded. There was no time for his usual long, drawn-out pleasantries this morning.

"It's terrible, terrible," he said, shaking his head at the terribleness of it all. "The police are all over the place. They are wantin' to speak to me again. They already spoke to me twice. It's terrible, I say."

Joff got the distinct impression that he wasn't referring to only the murder as being so terrible. No, he was more concerned about the extra police presence on Berner Street. How could they go about their normal business? he was implying. The police were, of course, delighted at having a good reason to sift through their headquarters.

Eventually, William realized Joff wasn't paying attention to his woes. He stopped in mid-flow, and facing Joff directly, said, "They want a list of all our members! Do you know why they want that list?" he asked.

Before Joff could hazard a guess, which might have been that it would help them to eliminate men from their enquiries, might even—dare he say it—help them catch this maniac, William was answering his own question.

"It's so they can identify members, that's why!" He stared angrily towards the policeman standing on duty at the gate, then looking back at Joff, he said, "Well they ain't gettin' it!" Then he spat into the gutter. "They ain't gettin' it off me an' that's for certain!"

He looked as though he was about to storm off into the crowds, so Joff spoke up before he disappeared.

"Yeah it's terrible, I totally agree. Only the thing is, I was lookin' to get paid for las' night. Can you sort me out?"

"What, now?" he asked, implying that murder negated the need for him to live up to his responsibilities. Suddenly it was even more to his advantage to feel something for that poor girl.

Joff nodded and held out his hand and continued, "Yes, that will be most helpful." He smiled for good measure.

William scowled back but he pulled his money belt from his pocket.

"'Ow much is it?" he asked.

"Six pence," Joff replied with his hand still out.

Shaking his head as though that was an exorbitant amount of money, he tipped six big pennies into the pianist's hand. As they fell, he said, "Tonight? You alright for tonight?"

Joff shook his head and stated, "I got the Hoxton Hall thing tonight! Remember I told ya' it's a big charity extravaganza." Joff puffed up his chest, expecting a compliment on landing such a prestigious chair.

"Oh!" he replied, "when shall we see you again then?"

Culture was lost on him, Joff decided. "Sunday, my night off, I'll play for yer Sunday!"

"Oh!" he said again as Joff walked away.

Joff strolled to the High Street to have some breakfast, feeling much better with the coins in his pocket. He couldn't go back to his place. Really, to all intents and purposes it was Pearl's place now, had been for years.

He knew why she had wanted him out in such a hurry. She and her friends were plotting. They had become less interested in changing the world and more interested in exacting revenge for the deaths and imprisonments of their friends. They were being dismissed as lunatics out to destroy everything that decent folk held sacred. This made them crazier, more scornful of the ineptitude of the masses. They were no longer individuals fighting the good struggle, they were purely anti-organization, in all its forms, and the revenge attacks were what kept them going.

Joff certainly couldn't stay at the club. It was a circus scene there with reporters and sightseers chasing each other from Berner Street to Mitre Square and back again.

* * *

Tin sat in a waterfront shack at Limehouse Basin and half listened to the conversation around him. He couldn't care less about this Ripper. All he was interested in was scoring some opium and then he would high-tail it back to his hole in the wall and quietly get wasted, not causing harm to anybody. Now that the authorities were clamping down on immoral, evil pastimes, the price of opium had suddenly doubled and the quality had dipped alarmingly. Tin's usual den had been raided, and now he was forced to wait around on street corners and do his dodgy deals in dark locations that were not really safe to be hanging around in.

The stench coming off the river was assaulting his nostrils. He dreaded to think what it was like for the mudlarks he could see down on the muddy foreshore. Young children sifting through the low tide, looking for something, anything that they could turn into cash for food. He would be gone as soon as he had made his connection; they would be here 'til last light and back again at first light tomorrow.

"'Ere 'e comes," whispered one of Tin's companions, and he looked up with acute interest. The mudlarks were forgotten now, their misery and suffering dismissed as Tin focused his attention on the stick-thin man stepping gingerly across the muddy road towards them.

"'E ain't carryin', 'e's too young!" Tin stated under his breath.

The Chinaman approached them until he was close enough that they could make out the mud splattered up to the knees of his black silk outfit.

"Follow me," he said, motioning with his hand that they should indeed follow him.

Tin and his four companions rose amidst a chorus of groans. They had been kept waiting all morning and now they would have to wait a little longer.

***

Early one morning, a few weeks later, Pearl was raided. It wasn't long before word of her arrest spread down to Berner Street, causing more arguments between the two factions.

"See all that violence! It turns the people against us, makes a mockery of the cause!" they would say.

"She lived there for years an' not a word to the authorities. As soon as she's 'anging round wiv them Fenians she's done for!"

"The people are useless! They do not know what is good for them!" came the retort.

"Viva la revolution!" the cry would go up.

There seemed to be very little time for dancing and playing music and talking about the old days any more. Young Turks had commandeered the club and they were drawing unwanted attention to the group. For three years the team had gotten the 'Worker's Friend' out on the streets, without ever a problem, and now! Now they seemed to have the police calling around every other week and this murder right on their doorstep.

Joff finished his glass of Russian Vodka and rose to his feet. His chair scraped across the floor unnoticed amidst the uproar. They were on the first floor and a young Italian was peeking around the shutter through the window that looked out over the street.

"They are still there!" he hissed. "Still there since five o'clock this evening an' it's what, one in the morning now! He huffed dramatically, "That's..." His eyebrows knotted as he tried to do the maths in his head. "That's seven hours!" he declared, wrongly. "I say we go out there now an' stick that bastard!"

The mumbles and the murmurs grew in volume as they agreed and disagreed, largely depending on their ages and the length of time they had endured the civil unrest erupting again right across mainland Europe.

Joff sat in silence and shook his head from side to side. *Jesus,* he thought, *the authorities don't have to do anything. This lot are going to tear themselves apart.*

"I'm leavin' now!" he said to no-one in particular and walked down the stairs as the sounds of their bickering grew thankfully quieter behind him.

Joff pulled his collar tighter around his neck as he stepped through the front door into Berner Street. Ironically, as is so often the case, they kept the side gates locked at night now. Now that it was too late for poor Liz Stride.

He crossed the road, ignoring the constable stationed outside the public house opposite, who would never know how his life was in danger of being snuffed out by a crazy young Italian who wanted to make a name for himself.

Joff walked towards Limehouse. He decided he would go and rest his head at the ruin Tin was now calling home.

* * *

Jack sat with his gang, counting their money. It had been a fruitful night and they were feeling pretty pleased with themselves. Robbery was the main way they knew to make enough money quickly enough to satisfy their passions for chorus girls and expensive carriages. They had watched the Chinaman lead the addicts to his carefully locked warehouse. It had been unnecessary to chase him down the path and cosh him over the head, but Jack had done so anyway. He was thinking about his reputation. Then it had been a simple matter to break in and steal the cash. It was money acquired from the sale of narcotics to those too weak to fend for themselves. Men like Tin.

Jack had looked up to Tin as a child and still looked to the old captain for the few happy childhood memories he was capable of turning his mind to. He had been momentarily shocked to see his old mentor amongst the addicts who had turned up to be robbed at precisely the wrong time. He had done the old seadog a favour. Patted him down under the guns of his gang in precisely the same way he had patted down all the other addicts, but he hadn't relieved Tin of the contents of his pockets in the same way he had the others. The old man had been smart enough to play the game and not reveal that they knew each other.

* * *

"Those young thugs..." The Chinaman shook his right fist at the night. In his left hand he held a blood-soaked patch of bandage. He was pressing it firmly against the gash across his forehead, holding his head at a crazy angle so the blood was running away to his side and not down his face or hitting his slippers. He was muttering loudly in Mandarin and it was pretty obvious he was cursing those young tearaways who had just made off with his cash. Tin kept quiet and stood with the others against the wall. It was a shame and all that, but they still wanted their high. They stood in silence, waiting for the Chinaman to calm down enough to tell them what he intended to do about the way things had turned out.

As the minutes dragged on it became obvious that the Chinaman's plan was simply to wait. Slowly the blood stopped flowing from his head wound and became more of a drip. They all watched it but nobody said anything or offered to help in any way.

Finally footsteps could be heard approaching, and of course they all looked up as six Chinese brandishing machetes came rushing into the courtyard and flew towards the small, pathetic group huddled on the floor, loudly declaring oaths that were threatening in any language.

Tin cowered under the whoosh of the steel blades flashing around. Finally, after what seemed far too long, he heard the injured man screaming multiple words at his fellows. In English one or two would probably suffice. Tin waited until he no longer heard the swords before he was in the mood to look up.

Two Oriental women had arrived behind the swordsmen and were tending to the wound. The six swordsmen gathered around as the old fellow told them what had happened.

Tin saw a wooden box passed across to the victim of the attack, then, as one, they fled back the way they had come, whooping and hollering and clearing the path of trouble before them as they went.

Tin watched the old man hide the box beneath his robes. The pass-over had been smooth, unobtrusive, but they had all caught it. Their dealer had been re-stocked, and an atmosphere of expectation hovered once more over the forlorn little group.

* * *

Joff was at the end of Leman Street just about to cross Cable Street and cut through the alleys to Tin's. It was quiet. Dark warehouses rose on all sides, blocking out any hopes of moonlight. There were rarely many people down here when the docks were closed, but you still had to be careful. The thieves and muggers knew where the desolate spots were just as well as anyone. As Joff crossed the road he heard a strange sound coming at him through the night. It put him in mind of ghosts or whirling dervishes—something terrible. It was coming at him from the opposite side of the square. He quickly changed direction, cutting down Well Street. It was probably nothing but there was no need to tempt fate in the wee small hours. He stayed alert but saw only rats and cats for the rest of his journey. He cut through the slums until he got to a gap where he knew he could cut quietly through to Tin's.

Their courtyard was deserted, so Joff made his way to the house, where he turned back on himself and carefully, using the handrail for guidance more than support, he made his way down to the basement where Tin lived. Down amongst the sewage and the rats, perhaps, but if you stayed on the boards out of the foul-smelling sludge, it wasn't too bad and at least it was free.

Joff stood at the broken hole that used to be the doorway and called softly into the darkness.

"Tin! You there?"

Shapes moved in the gloom but nobody answered. He would have to go further along the wooden planks that acted as roads down here. You had to look out for the upright beams as you walked; they came at you suddenly in the gloom, trying to knock you off the planks. Joff made his way carefully further under the house.

"Tin!" he called again.

On his fourth attempt he got lucky.

"Tin!"

"'Oo wants to know?" came his unmistakable voice.

Joff made his way carefully towards the direction of Tin's voice.

"It's me!" he called.

"Oo's 'me?'" he replied, and Joff followed the sound.

Joff saw him by the glow of a candle stump that threw the only light in the cavernous basement. He was slumped against the back wall, half propped up on a pile of rags, just visible through the smoke of a dozen pipes. As Joff got a few steps closer, Tin recognized him and sank back onto his rags.

Joff lowered himself gratefully onto the soft pile next to his friend and smiled.

"What you smilin' at?" he asked playfully.

"Just glad I found yer is all," came the reply as Joff scratched his arm. Then, addressing his words to the floor, he continued, "Will it be alright if I lay my 'ead 'ere tonight?"

He gestured around him.

"No problem, this hotel always has spare rooms." Tin looked up at Joff and asked, "Wanna pipe?"

Joff shook his head as he lowered himself into a more comfortable sleeping position before replying, "No thanks, I've got a gig tomorrow, can't get too wasted now, can I?" He smiled to show he wasn't judging anyone.

Joff closed his eyes and laid still. All around him he could hear the sounds of men coughing and scratching. It sounded like a hospital ward and in a way that's exactly what it was. These men were ill, each and every one of them. The majority either had addictions to opium or alcohol; all were malnourished and riddled with parasites. Most had psychological problems of varying degrees, and it was fair to say that they should probably all be under the supervision of medical professionals. Very few, if any, would actually experience such a thing, though. These were the unseen sick. They shuffled around on the periphery, neither asking for help nor being offered any until the day came when they would simply cease to function.

Joff forced his mind back to Gwithian beach down in Cornwall, where the air was clear, where the sky was blue, and where you could sit on the cliff tops and watch seals playing in the surf. Cornwall, where the sea was deep, deep blue and things moved at a slower pace. Mercifully, he managed to fall asleep.

* * *

The following day Joff had to be at the Hoxton Hall at seven in the evening for a four-hour gig. When he arrived, he thought the crowd seemed younger, more rowdy; perhaps he was beginning to feel his age.

He ended the show with a rousing rendition from the *Pirates of Penzance* and they all joined in the chorus,

"For I am a pirate king!" they sang. "A pirate king am I!"

* * *

Jack sat at a table in the back of the pub, listening to a bad luck tale and looking rather more bored than sympathetic.

Members of his gang occupied the remaining two tables in this section of the pub, and more of his cronies stood at the bar between him and the door. To all intents and purposes, this was his office and he was in the middle of business.

"The police just came burstin' in. We never stood a chance!" the worried man was explaining to Jack.

"An' they took Smally away?" Jack inquired.

The man nodded and looked down at his feet.

"An' they smashed up the gamin' tables?" Jack asked.

Again the man nodded, still refusing to catch the younger man's eye.

Jack was considering carefully what was being relayed to him. The members of his gang were in the business of supplying illegal gambling dens where patrons could be sure of a clean game and the opportunity to walk away with any winnings, knowing they would not be attacked the minute they hit the street. Jack and his boys got twenty percent of the pot and provided drinks and snacks. It was a situation that suited all parties, all except the authorities, who were not getting anything out of the arrangement.

"So go an' find another place that you can move to!" Jack told him.

This time the man did look up. He had been sure he was going to be out of a job at the very least, possibly even considered culpable, so this was good news indeed.

"Really?" he asked.

Jack stared back without smiling, without any humour in his expression. "Really!" he repeated. "Find a place an' tell the owners I will make sure they get theirs, alright?"

The man nodded enthusiastically, "Yeah, alright, Jack."

He made as if to leave but before he could, Jack added, "I want to be up an' runnin' again as soon as possible, alright?"

The man nodded and scurried away. He had a lot to be getting on with.

***

Joff made his way up Commercial Street towards Old Street just as the bells of Christ Church were striking the hour of six. The address he had been given at the end of Rivington Street was easy to find. He knocked on the door and waited. Suddenly a little flap was flung open at the height of his eyes and an unshaven, unsmiling man was staring at him.

"Oo are you?" he asked in a none-too-friendly manner.

"I'm the piano player," Joff replied.

The little hatch was slammed closed and inside Joff heard the sound of a bolt being slid free.

"Come in," the man said, looking suspiciously up and down the street as he held the door open for the visitor.

Joff stepped in and the door was shut hurriedly behind him. It occurred to him that this was unlike all the other working men's clubs he had played in. He looked into the room. There was an upright piano alongside a tiny dance floor at the end of the room and four tables covered in green baize. This was a gambling den, not, as he had been led to believe, a social club. What did he care? It was a gig and that was all that mattered.

He motioned towards the piano and raised his eyebrows.

"Was that my piano?" he was asking, and it was too stupid a question to actually put into words.

The doorman nodded.

Joff made his way to it and sat down to try out a few scales, check to see which notes were sticking or out of tune. He played up and down and the sound coming from it was surprisingly good for such a tatty-looking piece of kit. He attacked the keys with a little more gusto, just to see how the old girl would hold out. The notes rang sweetly all the way up the scale and all the way back down.

This will do nicely, he thought, and closing the lid made his way to the bar. There was always time for a drink before he started.

The barmaid stood smiling as he approached and he asked her for a whiskey.

"Comin' right up!" she declared sweetly before turning her back to get his drink.

He stood waiting and instinctively felt a pair of eyes burning into the left side of his face. He turned and there was a young blade smirking at him.

"Biggest smile I seen 'er give anyone all day!" he said cheerfully.

Joff smiled at him and nodded in thanks.

"I bet you get the girls everywhere you go?" he said, and Joff detected a hint of the Mediterranean lover in his tone.

"I used to do alright," turning to face him as he spoke. "Not as well as the Italians though!"

The young man smiled broadly, his chest puffed up with pride, and Joff knew he had guessed correctly.

* * *

Back in Berner Street the evening entertainment had already started. It was to be the same as every other night, a bitter, no-holds-barred quarrel to see which path would be the one.

There was a definite mood in the air that things were not quite as they should be. Some were putting it down to the recent spate of murders. Blaming this 'Jack the Ripper' for putting everyone on edge. William thought differently. He put it down to the recent string of arrests amongst the members. The authorities were taking men in for questioning with impunity and he was finding it a full-time job stopping some of the younger radicals from taking the law into their own hands.

The older members, men who had devoted many hours to establishing the club, who had built up working relationships with those representing authority in the East End, were seeing all their hard work undone by the impatience of youth, and to them it made no sense. They sat in their old, familiar corner and couldn't understand why these hotheads didn't grasp the folly of their ways.

The younger, newer members were mostly in London because they had been forced to flee war zones. They had witnessed, and in some cases participated in, horrific violence. It was all they knew, all they had been taught. They needed to unlearn their old ways but that took time and time was in increasingly short supply. Every new arrest made the chances of a confrontation, of the young bucks going it alone, disproportionately higher.

William knew full well that was exactly the sort of trigger the authorities were hoping for. They only needed the flimsiest of excuses and they would be down here like a ton of bricks. Laying waste to all the hard work that had been done in the name of the poor and needy. The police would go back to behaving like a private army looking after the vested interests of the privileged few, and the young Anarchists would be able to justify the stalemate as an excuse for even more direct action for which the authorities would, no doubt, clamp down even harder until the whole sorry scenario spiralled out of control completely, and unforeseen circumstances conspired to make absolutely certain there would be no winners in the long run.

William was proud of the International Working Men's Club that he had helped establish. He was dedicated to their cause of turning ideas into actions. Violence never seemed to solve much in his experience.

* * *

Joff slapped the keys of the tatty ol' girl and bellowed out the chorus of *Home Sweet Home*. A roomful of gamblers joined in at the tops of their voices and Joff knew he had them. They approved of the slight twist he had given the old favourite. They always appreciated it when you gave a song the personal touch. As long as you weren't trying to be too clever, as long as you only tweaked it. Gave them the hint of a maverick they all saw in themselves, someone not strictly wedded to the rules. It was a fine line between clever and coming across as too clever by half. Joff had successfully walked that line, again. He glanced up at the young Italian who had turned out to be the manager, who nodded and smiled towards Joff. That was a good sign; the man was happy with his performance.

As Joff played the old favourites, he watched the room. From time to time girls would come and dance in front of him. At one stage there were three of them dancing. That was all it took and the little dance floor was full. They were being paid to brighten up the room. Here to take the sting out of losing at the card tables, as the overwhelming majority of the punters were doing, as they always did.

The Italian watched it all from his stool at the corner of the bar. Tough-looking men would approach him at intervals and they would engage in serious conversation before heading purposefully back outside. They were obviously up to no good, so Joff stopped watching. He had played to men like him before and nosey piano players were not something they generally tolerated for very long.

* * *

Jack walked through the fog with his collar turned up, his cap pulled low, and his hands thrust deeply into his pockets. Alongside him, his second in command had a cocked pistol concealed beneath his coat. The gang had seven gambling dens in Shoreditch now, and four more in Whitechapel. The pair were doing the rounds, picking up their cut from each of the establishments. They had already lost the takings of one place due to the police raid and they were not about to take any chances with the cash they had collected.

Jack rapped firmly on the old wooden door while his comrade lurked in the shadows. The little window flew open and the giant on the inside recognized his boss in a flash. The hatch closed and the big door was unbolted and flung open as quickly as possible.

Jack strode in and headed straight for the bar with his colleague lagging slightly behind. Joff spotted him instantly, but, ever the professional, he didn't even miss a note. He just watched as Jack strolled across the room looking like he owned the place. Joff wasn't surprised when his son came to a halt alongside the Italian. He watched as the manager handed Jack an envelope and only once it was safely in his inside pocket did Jack scan the room. He spotted his father sitting at the piano. He looked at him with not exactly a smile but not exactly a scowl either. Joff nodded a greeting at him as his hands worked the ivory. In response, Jack drained his drink, whispered something to the Italian, pushed out his stool, and left. Joff watched him go and wondered where he had gone so terribly wrong with his own flesh and blood.

Four hours later and the room was nearly empty. As the last table rose to leave, the manager called Joff to him.

He headed over and took the stool next to his at the end of the bar.

The man smiled and said, "No' bad, No' bad!"

He missed the 't's of the end of the word 'not' in that endearing way some foreigners spoke English.

"Thanks," Joff mumbled, smiling back at him as the barmaid brought the pianist a whisky.

"The boss, 'e like you," he said, clasping Joff on the shoulder as he spoke. "'E says to offer you more nights." The manager looked at him more seriously before continuing. "You wan' more nights?" he asked.

"Does it come with a room?" Joff asked him.

"I 'ave a little room for you upstairs, sure, why no'."

"Then I'm very interested," he said.

The man gripped Joff's shoulder and beamed brightly. "Very good, piano man, very good!"

He released Joff and clicked his fingers at the barmaid, letting fly with a volley of Italian at her. She brought over a whiskey bottle and left it on the bar.

Joff poured himself a large one and by the time he had raised it to his lips the decision was made. He'd had enough of radicals and the way he always got dragged into their problems. Obviously he realized he would be, to all intents and purposes, working for Jack, but he had no problem with that. How much worse than the Anarchists can he be, he reasoned?

"Can I move in today?" Joff asked.

"Sure, piano man, no problem!" he replied. "Wha's your name? Wha' do we call you?"

"Joff," he replied. He'd had enough of being Joe. "It's a Cornish name," he added.

* * *

Joff kept meaning to go back to the Berner Street club to say his good byes, but something always seemed to get in the way. He was normally playing until the early hours of the morning so he generally didn't surface until after mid-day. The punters would get drinks in for him and he would accept them all and end up in credit. Each day it was as much as he could manage to drink all his credits before he was due on again and the whole merry-go-round would be back in full swing.

After a couple of weeks, his conscience got the better of him.

The next day he would make the effort, he would not be put off. He would go back to the club and say goodbye properly. It was the right and proper thing to do.

"I'm goin' to visit my ol' friends tomorrow," he announced.

"But is Saturday tomorro'," the manager shot back at him. "No' on a Saturday, is no' possible!"

He had a point. Saturday was their busiest night by far.

"Is no' possible!" he insisted.

"Not possible?" Joff repeated.

"Look," he said. "Is no' me, is the boss."

As far as Joff was aware, the manager still had no idea that Jack was his son, so the news came as a bit of a surprise.

"The boss?" he asked.

The man looked at him, weighing him up. They had only known each other for two weeks and he was clearly deciding how much of the truth Joff should hear. Still, he felt they were friends and so he waited for the manager to put his faith in him.

"Look, the boss, when he sees you playing that day, that first day…"

"Yeah," Joff replied.

"'E told me I should take you on, he heard you were very good, an' you are, very good." He was mumbling a bit now, getting side-tracked.

"What else did 'e say?" Joff asked.

"Said to make sure you kept away from people who was users."

"Well I ain't a user!" Joff tried to appear indignant but actually was rather touched. It was almost as though the boy was looking out for his old dad.

"So I go and visit my friends tomorrow," he began.

"No," he implored. "Is Saturday tomorro'. Go visit your friends on Sunday. Hey, hey, for me?"

"Alright." How could he refuse? "Sunday, I got the whole day off?"

"Sure," he said, "no problem."

Sunday was March the seventeenth, St. Patrick's Day. He could make a real day of it. Go to Berner Street and show his face, let them know he was still alive and why he had suddenly disappeared, then he could go over to the Hundred Marks Pub in Charlotte Street where the Irish Fenians would be sure to gather and celebrate their saint.

The thought of having a free day to look forward to cheered his mood immediately.

Saturday night was upon them in a flash and he played, even if he said so himself, like a man possessed. That night he forced down a few quick whiskeys and climbed the stairs to his bed, looking forward to his trip to the Berner Street club in the morning.

* * *

The club had not ceased to exist because Joe—or Joff, as he now preferred—suddenly disappeared. These men were more than used to someone vanishing. They, their families, and their friends had, in the main, fled to London to get away from military types dragging people from their beds in the middle of the night. So they carried on.

On the Saturday, when the missing piano man was intending to pay his surprise return, the members had organised a parade, a procession if you will.

Communists and Anarchists would be joining forces in the name of the greater good. Their aim was to draw attention to the terrible conditions of the workers sweating in the Jewish factories. The march was to leave Berner Street at half past mid-day and proceed to the Great Synagogue in Mitre Square, where the chief Rabbi would be presented with their petition. Among their demands was for the sweatshop machinists to work an eight-hour day.

Unfortunately, the rabbi had refused to admit them, so they had marched instead to the Mile End and held an impromptu meeting on waste ground there. Drink had flowed and both factions, once merry, set about goading each other, playfully at first. As they did so, the police officers sent to follow the march silently grew in number.

After the presentation and numerous speeches, a number of the members returned to the club in Berner Street and carried on drinking. By the time the sun had gone down, Marx and Proudhon were both being cheered and booed in equal measure. The young Turks were so drunk they began openly mocking Louis Diemschitz, one of their members. When he went inside to escape the torment, a boy was dared to tap annoyingly on the window. Suddenly Louis came flying out of the club in his shirt sleeves and whacked the cheeky urchin across the ear.

Within seconds, bottles were flying, fists were flying, police truncheons were landing indiscriminately, and the march rapidly deteriorated into a riot. A day that had promised so much ended up delivering nothing at all.

That night as Joff worked, all the punters were discussing the pitch battle in Berner Street. It was the talk of the tables, so he didn't bother going down there the following day.

That was the day the old guard finally began to lose control of the club they had worked so hard to establish and the younger Anarchists started to take over. Within a couple of years they had changed their name to the 'Knights of Labour' and thrown out the Socialists completely. Within another twelve months they were evicted from Berner Street for their anti-social, hard-partying ways.

* * *

A lot of money was changing hands in the shabeen where Joff worked. He was mainly there as a distraction from the tense, heavy atmosphere that prevailed without him and the dancing girls to soften the mood. Every mobster in the East End seemed to like to play there. He didn't mind that they could get a bit boisterous. He played the tunes they asked for and they were more than generous with their tips.

Joff felt comfortable, relaxed even. Sitting on his stool night after night until the sun came up, playing and drinking. With the girls providing his food, and a bed upstairs, he had very little reason to go anywhere.

They still hadn't caught the Ripper and there was another girl killed at the beginning of November, then another over in Poplar just a week before Christmas.

In the privacy of the club, Joff could drink and be merry, and forget the outside world.

* * *

As 1889 turned into summer, they still hadn't caught the Ripper, but there had been no murders for six months and Joff was beginning to think that he had left the area. It put the idea in his head that he could leave the area himself, if he had a mind to.

Then in mid-July another poor girl was found stabbed to death.

It was silly, but he kept thinking of the night of the double murder, how easy it was to get caught up in these things. It sounded dangerous out there. He was staying put until the police finally caught him.

A couple of months later he was sitting at the bar nursing a hangover.

"It's a beautiful day, Joe. You ain't staying in here again, are yer?"

With his head resting on the palm of one hand he turned slightly towards the speaker.

"Leave it out, will ya! My 'ead is bangin' I ain't goin' nowhere!" he said quietly.

The speaker winked at the barmaid and said, "It's September though, Joff. If you don't go out soon you'll 'ave missed the 'hole summer!"

Joff looked up at him.

"'Ave they caught the Ripper yet?" he asked.

"What?" the other man replied.

"Jack the Ripper, 'ave they caught 'im yet?"

He smiled slightly, shaking his head. "No, no", he said, "they ain't!"

"Knowin' my luck I'll stumble right across 'im. If I don't go nowhere I won't get involved."

The young man snorted, "You ain't gonna get involved again, you can't be that unlucky. Besides, I bet 'e's long gone. There ain't been one for months."

"I bet he kills again, soon!" Joff said.

The moment the words escaped his lips he knew it was a mistake. You should never say 'I bet' in there.

"Bet, do you? Alright what you got?" the man was a gambler, he couldn't help himself.

Joff tried to get out of it. Told him he had nothing, he wanted nothing, but the man insisted.

The bet was on.

If no other girl got killed before the end of the month he would win, and Joff would have to play at his sister's birthday.

If there was another death, then Joff would win and the other man would give him the fare back to Cornwall, so he could see out his days with the sea breeze blowing across his face. Sit in the sun where the air was cleaner, the food was fresher, and he could expect to put in a few more years than if he stayed in London with his current lifestyle.

Two days later another girl was found murdered in Pinchin Street, Whitechapel. He had won the bet.

* * *

"Yes, Squire, I'm afraid that's about the size of it."

Squire Bradshaw sat at his desk on the family estate with his arms folded across his chest.

"A gambling den, you say? Couldn't we get the police to raid it, flush them out?" he asked.

"We tried that, Sir, an' the police just laughed. Literally laughed in our faces. Said they didn't 'ave the manpower to raid every gambling den in the East End. Said they 'ad more important things to be gettin' on with."

"And they are hardened mobsters, you say, the one's protecting him?"

"They are, Sir. There are a lot of 'em, Sir, and they seem to 'ave a taste for violence. I think they might be a bit much to take on, Sir, without considerable manpower, Sir, an' well…"

He let the comment remain unfinished. He didn't have to add how that would cost a fortune and could easily be long, drawn-out, and very bloody.

"Perhaps this has gone on for too many years?" the Squire surprised him by saying.

"Oh, I quite agree, Sir!" He could barely contain his enthusiasm for this turn of events.

"Let him stay in that hell hole, then. As long as he never shows his face down here, he can live out whatever years God sees fit to grant him in the squalor of that slum."

The Squire looked at his servant and continued, "As long as he never shows his face in Cornwall again…," he paused before adding quietly, "it's over."

"Yes, Sir, very good, Sir." He left the room before his master changed his mind.

* * *

Mr. Brunel had indeed bridged the Tamar River with an engineering marvel that linked Cornwall to Plymouth and the rest of the country. Joff could climb aboard the steam-driven monster at Paddington Terminus and in just a few short hours it would deliver him safely to the platform at Bodmin Station, deep in the heart of his home county. He could travel further into the future quicker than ever before.

There were pictures as well, photographs, that froze a moment for ever. It was as though mankind had control over time itself.

What had been achieved in fifty years was truly incredible, but at what cost?

Undeniably the Capitalists had won the day. They had insisted so loudly that their form of governance was superior to all others that the people had been convinced. They had conceded that a few weak men might fall by the wayside under their system of rule, but insisted the numbers would be small, the price worth paying for the benefit of the vast majority.

The fifty years since those predictions were uttered had unfolded completely differently. Misery and envy were widespread. Slums had grown out of the big cities all over Europe. Places far worse than anything man had ever resided in before. Communication across borders was actively discouraged; discourse between like-minded people was impossible nearly everywhere, as suspicion was encouraged and neighbours considered rivals. How would the people ever hope to get organized now?

Joff sat in the carriage watching southern England flash by his window and figured it wasn't his problem. It was down to others to make things better. It was time to slow down, time to sit back and see out the rest of his days.

ABOUT THE AUTHOR

Ian's first full length professional novel *A Secret Step (Copperjob) was* published in 2013.
In 2014 he provided the opening chapter for the *Little Book of Jack the Ripper* (Historypress), as well as having numerous articles published on various aspects of the subject of London.

He has a keen interest in social history, particularly Jack the Ripper, the Kray twins and the slums of the East End. Ian is an active member of the Whitechapel Society, London.

Ian's style of using the old to make sense of the new, being praised by acclaimed authors Martin Fido and Bill Beadle, amongst others.

Ian's latest novel *The East End Beckons* (Linkville) is set in the era of Cornish smugglers and Oliver Twist. He has therefore been dividing his time between London Town and the South West of England.

Ian Parson has been a writer for many years winning competitions and working for magazines and newspapers in England and Spain before finally arriving at the Linkville Press Stable.

Made in the USA
Charleston, SC
09 July 2015